A
HIGHER
CALL

# HAROLD BELL WRIGHT

MICHAEL R. PHILLIPS, EDITOR

# A HIGHER CALL

## BETHANY HOUSE PUBLISHERS
MINNEAPOLIS, MINNESOTA 55438

Copyright © 1990
Michael Phillips
All Rights Reserved

Published by Bethany House Publishers
A Ministry of Bethany Fellowship, Inc.
6820 Auto Club Road, Minneapolis, Minnesota 55438

Printed in the United States of America

**Library of Congress Cataloging-in-Publication Data**

Wright, Harold Bell, 1872–1944.
    A higher call / Harold Bell Wright ; edited by Michael R. Phillips.
      p.   cm.
    Rev. ed. of: The calling of Dan Matthew. 1909.

    I. Phillips, Michael R. , 1946–
II. Wright, Harold Bell, 1872–1944. Calling of Dan Matthew.
III. Title.
PS3545.R45H5    1990
813'.4—dc20                            90–39126
ISBN 1–55661–136–6                      CIP

HAROLD BELL WRIGHT (1872–1944), the American novelist, was born to the farming life in upstate New York, working in the fields at an early age. As he grew he sought an education, which eventually led him into the ministry. Traveling to the Ozarks in the 1890s to recuperate from pneumonia, Wright began the work of a fill-in preacher in a little mountain log schoolhouse, remained there, and eventually was offered a regular pastorate. Over the next ten years he pastored churches in Missouri, Kansas, and California until declining health forced him once more back to his beloved Ozarks for a time of rest and seeking God.

After publishing his best-known book, *Shepherd of the Hills*, Harold Bell Wright went on to become one of America's top-selling inspirational authors. His nineteen books achieved estimated sales in excess of ten million copies.

Classic Fiction by Harold Bell Wright
Retold for today's reader by Michael Phillips

*A Higher Call*
*The Least of These My Brothers*
*The Shepherd of the Hills*

# CONTENTS

*The Pharisees do not eat unless they wash their hands ceremonially, observing the tradition of the elders, and when they come from the marketplace, they do not eat unless they purify themselves. And there are many other traditions which they observe, such as the washing of cups and pitchers and kettles.*

# INTRODUCTION

*The Calling of Dan Matthews*, first published in 1909, is technically a sequel to Harold Bell Wright's bestseller *The Shepherd of the Hills*. Its main character, Dan Matthews, is the son of Sammy Lane and Young Matt, and Dan was raised under the influence of the shepherd Dad Howitt, after whom he was named.

However, in a spiritual sense, the moving drama involving the young minister Dan Matthews, here retitled for the Bethany series *A Higher Call*, is much more a sequel to Wright's first book published by Bethany House as *The Least of These My Brothers*. By no means, as you will see, is this a mere work of fiction. Wright's heart burned with deep conviction to proclaim two truths which both these books illuminate: *the imperative reality of obeying* the life and teachings of Jesus, and the loathsome *unreality and hypocrisy* of much that goes on within the organized church.

Notwithstanding the seemingly stinging criticisms Wright levels at dead church structure and policy, this is *not* an attack upon the sacred institution whose head is Christ. Rather it is a hardhitting and penetrating call for revival, as Wright urges us to purge phariseeism from our midst—from our churches and from our *own* hearts. Wright loved the church dearly, being a clergyman himself, and was thus heartbroken to see what it had in many cases become. This book was part of his effort to call God's people to something deeper.

Wright's words to the Christians of his day were critical in the same way that Paul's were often critical in his effort to point out error, and build up into godliness. Paul's words to the Corinthians were certainly not soft. They were a people caught up in all kinds of immorality, and the church of Corinth was known by Paul to be immature in many areas. Not only was there a moral problem in the church, there were severe divisions and factions, each with its acknowledged head and all vying for power. Thus Paul wrote to Corinth to teach and help restore the church in its areas of weakness. And as always, Paul used strong language: "I appeal . . . that there be no divisions among you . . . I have been informed that there are quarrels among you . . . I cannot address you as spiritual, but as worldly—mere infants in Christ . . . you are still not yet ready for solid food, for there is still jealousy and quarreling among you . . . do not deceive yourselves . . . I am not writing this to shame you, but to warn you . . . some of you have become arrogant . . . and you are proud!"

It is scarcely an accident, then, to what fictional town Harold Bell Wright sends his young idealistic minister Dan Matthews. And there are many other parallels he draws and metaphors and images he uses as well. Most have either biblical or other hidden symbolism to help convey the author's point. As has been pointed out, this is far more than a mere novel, but I will leave you to discover the additional allegorical meanings on your own.

The underlying point is this: Wright attempted to draw a portrait of modern-day Corinthianism, from which Christ's church desperately needs to extract itself if it is to—in Paul's words to the Corinthians of *his* day—move on to the "solid food" of the Spirit.

If you haven't yet read *The Least of These My Brothers*, I'm certain you will find it a challenging companion volume to this one.

Michael Phillips

# CHAPTER ONE

# THE HOME OF THE ALLY

*"And because the town of this story is what it is, there came to dwell in it a spirit—a strange, mysterious power—playful, vicious, deadly; Something to be at once feared and courted; to be denied—yet confessed in the denial; a deadly enemy, a welcome friend, an all-powerful Ally."*

This story began in the Ozark Mountains, the beginnings of which have already been told. It follows the trail that is nobody knows how old. It is about what happened when someone from the Ozarks followed the trail from his home in the mountains to try to help his fellowmen live the Truth. Most of this story happened in Corinth, a middle-class town in a midwestern state.

There is nothing special about Corinth. The story might have happened just as well in any other place, for the only distinguishing feature about this town is its utter lack of any distinguishing feature whatsoever. In all the essential elements of its life, so far as this story goes, Corinth is exactly like every other village, town, or city in the land. This, indeed, is why the story happened in this particular place. It might as easily have happened in your town or city. Perhaps it has.

Years ago, when the railroad first climbed the backbone of the Ozarks, it found Corinth already located there. Even in the middle of the war between the states, this county seat was a place of no small importance, and many a good tale might be told of those exciting days when the woods were full of soldiers, and the village was raided first by one side, then the other. Indeed, many a good tale *is* told, for the old-timers of Corinth love to talk of the war days, and to point out in the old part of town the bullet-marked buildings and the scenes of many thrilling events.

But the sons and daughters of the passing generation, with their own sons and daughters, like better to look forward, and to talk of the great things that are coming—the proposed new factory, the talked-of mill which will bring jobs and money to the area, the dreamed-of electric line which is to be extended out from the city, or the arrival of the Businessman from Somewhere "back east" who will invest in land and vacant lots to build new homes and hotels and business enterprises.

The Doctor says that in the whole history of Corinth there are only two events worth remembering. The first was the coming of the railroad, the second was the death of the Doctor's good friend, the Statesman.

The railroad did not actually enter Corinth. It stopped at the front gate. But with Judge Strong's assistance, the fathers and mothers of Corinth recognized their golden opportunity and took the step which the eloquent Judge assured them would result in a "glorious future for all." If the train line would not come into the town, then they would extend the town to meet it. They would grow, he said, in the direction of the line, encompassing and surrounding it so that every train to come along would pass right through town, bringing with it people and wealth and progress.

So they left the beautiful, well-drained site chosen for the town's expansion by those who cleared the wilderness, and stretched themselves out instead along the mud flat on either side of the sacred right-of-way—that same mud flat being, incidentally, the property of the patriotic Judge. The sites for future buildings were neither so flat nor so dry and solid as those on the other side of town, but, said the Judge, progress and prosperity lay with the rail line.

Thus Corinth took the railroad literally to her heart. The depot, the switching and freight yards, the red brick section house, and the water tank all sit squarely in the very center of the town. Every train while stopping for water (and they all stop) blocks two of the three principal streets. And when, after waiting in the rain or snow until his patience is nearly exhausted, the humble man or woman of Corinth decides to go to the only remaining crossing, he always gets there just in time to meet a long freight train backing onto the siding. Nowhere in the whole place can one escape the screaming whistles, clanging bells, and crashing of drawbars. Day and night the rumble of the heavy trains jars and disturbs the peacefulness of the little town.

Though the railroad did more for Judge Strong, it did do something for Corinth as well. Not much, but something.

For a time the town grew rapidly. Fulfillment of all the Judge's prophecies of prosperity seemed immediate and certain. Then, as mysteriously as they had come, the boom days departed. All the mills and factories and stores and shops that were to be began to be established elsewhere. The sound of the builder's hammer was no longer heard. Loads of lumber and supplies no longer rumbled through town. The Doctor says that Judge Strong had come to believe too much in his own predictions, or at least, fearing that his prophecy might prove true without his getting his share of the wealth, refused to part with more land except at prices that would be justified only in a great metropolitan area.

Neighboring towns that were born when Corinth was middle-aged flourished and became cities of importance. The country all around grew rich and prosperous. And now every year more and heavier trains thunder past on their way to and from the great city by the distant river, stopping only to take on water. But in this swiftly moving stream of life, Corinth is caught in an eddy. Her small world has come to swing in a very small circle—it can scarcely be said to swing at all. The very children stop growing when they become men and women, and are content to dream the dreams their fathers' fathers dreamed, even as they live in the houses the fathers of their fathers built. Only the trees that line the streets have grown—grown and grown until overhead their great tops touch to shut out the sky with an arch of green, and their mighty trunks crowd contemptuously aside the old and broken sidewalks.

The old part of town is given over to weeds and decay. The few buildings that remain are fallen into ruin, except as they are patched up by their poor tenants. And on the hill, the old Academy, with its broken windows, crumbling walls, and fallen chimneys, stands as a pitiful witness of an honor and dignity that is gone. Neither inhabitants nor town has grown. Inside and out, upon buildings and inside hearts, are signs of stagnation.

Poor Corinth! Gone are the days of her true glory—the glory of her usefulness, while the days of her promised honor and power are not yet fulfilled.

And because the town of this story is what it is, there came to dwell in it a spirit—a strange, mysterious power—playful, vicious, deadly; a Something to be at once feared and courted; to be denied—yet confessed in the denial; a dreaded enemy, a welcome friend, an all-powerful Ally.

Weep not, therefore, for Corinth. Weep instead for her people, who think they stand so high within themselves. For they have joined forces with the Ally without realizing it. Weep for those of your own town and your own churches who are part of the Ally's army, yet know it not.

But for Corinth, the humiliation of her material and commercial failure is forgotten in her pride of the finer success of national recognition. That self-respect and pride of place, without which neither man nor town can look the world in the face, has been saved for Corinth by the Statesman, who gave it, if not riches, at least a name to be held in high esteem.

Born in Corinth, a graduate of the old Academy who went on to become town clerk, mayor, county clerk, state senator, then United States Congressman, the Statesman's zeal for advocating a much discussed political issue of his day won for him national notice, and for his town everlasting fame.

Unusual talents were combined in this man, with rare integrity of purpose and purity of life. He was a good man, a righteous man, desirous of helping both his neighbor and mankind. Politics to him meant a way whereby he might serve his fellows. However men differed as to the value of the measures for which he fought, no one ever doubted his belief in them nor questioned his reasons for fighting for them. It was not at all strange that such a man should have won the respect and friendship of the truly great leaders of the nation. But with all the honors that came to him, the Statesman's heart never turned from the little Ozark town, and it was here among those who knew him best that his influence for good was greatest, and that he was most loved and honored. Thus, all that the railroad failed to do for Corinth, the Statesman did in a larger and finer way.

After the Statesman died, it was the Old Town Corinth of the brick Academy days that inspired the erection of a monument to his memory. But it was the Corinth of the newer railroad days that made the cast-iron monument. And under the cast-iron, this newer Corinth placed a life-sized portrait figure of the dead statesman, with a quotation in small cast-iron letters from one of his famous speeches upon an issue of the day.

The Doctor argues in most vigorous language that the broken sidewalks, the uselessness of the railroad to the town, the presence and power of that Spirit, the Ally, and many other conditions in Corinth are all due to the influence of what he calls "that hideous, cast-iron monstrosity." By this it will be seen that the Doctor is something of a philosopher. Thus the town goes on immortalizing his dead friend by an equally dead monument, rather than living by the life principles which made the Statesman the man he was. "If he were here," the Doctor says, "he would be the first in line to tear down that statue! He'd want his life to stand for *life*, not death! He'd want to be remembered for how he treated people, not for some speech he made."

The monument stands on the corner where Holmes Street ends in Strong Avenue. The Doctor lives on the opposite corner with his wife Martha. It is a modest home, for they have no children and the Doctor is not rich. The house is white with old-fashioned green shutters, and over the porch climbs a mass of vines. The steps are worn very thin and the ends of the floorboards are rotted badly by the moisture of the growing vines. But the Doctor says he has no intention of pulling down such a fine old vine to put in new boards, and that the steps will outlast either he or Martha anyway. By this it will be seen that the Doctor is also something of a poet.

On the rear of the lot sits a woodshed and stable, and on the east, along the fence in front and down the Holmes Street side, grow the Doctor's roses—the admiration and envying despair of every flower-growing housewife in town.

A full fifty years of the Doctor's professional life have been spent in active practice in Corinth and in the country round about. He declares himself worn out now and good for nothing, except to meddle in the affairs of his neighbors, to cultivate his roses, and—when the days are bright—to go fishing. As for the rest, he sits in his chair on the porch and watches the world go by.

"Old Doctors and old dogs," he growls, "we are both equally useless, and yet how much—how much we could tell if only we dared speak!"

He is a large man, the Doctor—big and fat and old. He knows every soul in Corinth, particularly the children. Indeed, he helped most of them to come to Corinth. He is acquainted as well with every dog and cat, every horse and cow, knowing their every trick and habit, from the old brindle milker that unlatches his front gate to feed on the lawn, to the bull pup that pinches his legs when he calls on old Granny Brown. For miles around, every road, every lane, bypath, shortcut and trail is a familiar way to him. His practice, he declares, has practically ruined him financially, and come near to wrecking his temper. He can curse a man and cry over a baby. And he would go as far and work as hard for the illiterate and penniless backwoodsman in his cabin home, as for the president of the Bank of Corinth, or even Judge Strong himself.

No one ever thinks of the Doctor as loving anyone or anything, and that is because he is so big and rough on the outside. But everyone in trouble goes straight to him, and that is because he is so big and kind on the inside. It is a common saying that in cases of serious illness or bad accident a patient would rather "hear the Doctor cuss, than listen to the parson pray." There are other physicians in Corinth, but everyone understands immediately when his neighbor says, "Call the Doctor." No one ever calls him "Doc."

After all, who knows the people of a community so well as the physician who lives among them? To the world, the Doctor's patients were laborers, bankers, dressmakers, cleaning-women, farmers, teachers, preachers; to the Doctor they were men and women. Others knew their occupations, he knew their lives. The preachers knew what they professed, he knew what they practiced. Society saw them dressed up, he saw them in bed. The Doctor has spent more hours in the homes of his neighbors than he passed under his own roof, and there is not a skeleton closet in the whole town to which he does not have the key.

On Strong Avenue, across from the monument, is a tiny four-roomed cottage. At the time of this story it was badly in need of paint, and was not in the best of repair. But the place was neat and clean, with a big lilac bush just inside the gate, giving it an air of home-like privacy. And on the side directly opposite the Doctor's, there was a fair-sized, well-kept garden, giving the place also an air of honest thrift. Here the widow Mulhall lived with her crippled son Denny.

Denny was to have been educated for the priesthood, but the accident that left him such a hopeless cripple shattered that dream. And after the death of his father, who was killed while discharging his duties as the town marshall, there was no money left for Deborah Mulhall to buy even a book.

When there was anything for her to do, Deborah worked out by the day. In spite of his poor, misshapen body, Denny tended the garden, raising such vegetables as no one else in all of Corinth could raise. From early morning until late evening the lad dragged himself out among the growing things, and the only objects to mar the beauty of his garden were Denny himself, and the huge rock that seemed to grow out of the ground right in the very center of the little field.

"It is too bad that rock should be there," the neighbors would say as they occasionally stopped to look over the fence, or to order their vegetables from him for dinner. And Denny would answer with his knowing smile, "Oh, I don't know. It might be a bad thing if it should ever take to rolling around. But it lies quiet enough. And do you see, I've planted them vines around it to make it a bit soft-looking. And there's a nice little niche on the back side that does very well for a seat now and then when I have to rest."

Sometimes, when the Doctor looks at the monument—the cast-iron image of his old friend, in its cast-iron attitude, forever delivering that speech on an issue as dead today as an edict of one of the Pharaohs—he laughs, but sometimes, even as he laughs, he curses as well.

But when, in the days of the story, the Doctor would look across the street to where Denny, with his poor, twisted body, useless, swinging arm, and dragging leg, worked away so cheerily in his garden, then the old physician, philosopher, and poet declared that he felt like singing hymns of praise.

It all began with a fishing trip.

# CHAPTER TWO

# THE DOCTOR AND THE BOY

Martha says that everything with the Doctor begins and ends with fishing. Martha has a way of saying such things as that. In this case she is more than half right, for the Doctor does indeed so begin and end most things.

This story begins on the Doctor's first trip to the Ozarks.

Whenever there were grave cases to think out, knotty problems to solve, or weighty decisions to make, it was his habit to steal away to a shady nook by the side of some quiet, familiar stream. And he confidently asserts that he owes his professional success, and his reputation for sound, thoughtful judgment on all important matters, to this practice more than to anything else.

"It is your impulsive, erratic, thoughtless fellow," he will argue when in the mood, "who goes smashing and banging about the fields and woods with dogs and gun. Your true thinker slips quietly away with rod and line, and while his hook is down in the deep, still waters, or his fly is dancing over the foaming rapids and swiftly swirling eddies, his mind searches the true depths of the matter, and every possible angle of the question at hand passes before him."

For years the Doctor had heard much of the fishing to be had in the more unsettled parts of the Ozarks, but with his growing practice he could find leisure time for no more than an occasional visit to nearby streams. But about the time Martha began telling him that he was too old to stay out all day on the wet bank of a river, and his assistant Dr. Harry had come to relieve him of the heavier and more burdensome part of his practice, a railroad pushed its way across the mountain wilderness. The first season after the line was finished, the Doctor decided to go and cast his hook in new waters.

Ever since that fateful trip, throughout all the years that came after, those days so full of mystic beauty lived in the old man's memory as the brightest days of his life. For it was there he met the boy—there in the Ozark hills, with their great ridges, clothed from base to crest with trees all quivering and nodding in the summer breeze, with their quiet valleys, their cool hollows and lovely glades, and their deep and solemn woods.

And the streams! Those Ozark streams! The Doctor questioned whether there could flow anywhere else on God's earth such clear and sparkling waters as run through that land of dreams.

The Doctor left the train at a little station where the railroad crosses White River, and two days later he was fishing near the mouth of Fall Creek. It was late in the afternoon. The boy was passing by on his way home from a point farther up the stream. Not more than twelve, but tall and strong for his age, he came along the rough path at the foot of the bluff with the easy movement and grace of a young deer.

He paused a moment when he saw the Doctor, as a creature of the forest would pause at first sight of a human being. Then he came forward again, his manner and bearing showing frank interest in this newcomer to his home region, and his clear, sunny face flushing a bit at the presence of a stranger.

"Hello," said the Doctor, with gruff kindness, "any luck?"

The boy's quick smile showed the most perfect set of teeth the physician had ever seen, and his young voice was tuned to the music of the woods, as he answered, "I have caught no fish, sir."

By these words and the light in his brown eyes, the philosopher knew him instantly for a true fisherman. With wonder he noted that the lad's speech was not the rude dialect of the backwoods, while he marveled at the depth of wisdom in one so young. How incidental, after all, is the catching of fish, to one who fishes with true understanding. The boy's answer was both an explanation and a question. It explained that he did not go fishing for fish alone; and it asked of the stranger a declaration of his standing—why did he go fishing? What did he mean by fisherman's luck?

The Doctor deliberated over his reply, while slowly drawing in his line to examine the bait. Meanwhile, the boy stood quietly by, regarding him with a wide, questioning look. The man realized that much depended upon his next word.

Then the lad's youth betrayed him into eagerness. "Have you been farther up the river," he asked, "just around the bend, where the giant cottonwoods are, and the bluffs with the pines above, and the willows along the shore? Oh, but it's fine there! Much better than this."

He had given the stranger his chance. If the Doctor was to be admitted into this boy's world, he must now prove his right to citizenship. Looking straight into the boy's brown eyes, the older fisherman asked, "A better place to catch fish?"

He laughed aloud—a clear, clean, boyish laugh of understanding. And then, throwing himself to the ground with the easy air of one entirely at home, he answered, "Not necessarily that, though sometimes it can be good that way too. But just a better place to fish." So it was settled, each understanding the other.

An hour later, when the shadow of the mountain came over the water, the boy sprang to his feet with an exclamation. "It's time for me to go. Mother likes me home for supper, and I can just make it."

But the Doctor hated to see him go. "Where do you live?" he asked. "Is it far?"

"Oh no, only about six miles. But the trail is rough until you strike the top of Wolf Ridge."

"You can't walk six miles before dark."

"My horse is only a little way up the creek," he answered, "or at least he should be."

Putting his fingers to his lips, he blew a shrill whistle, which echoed and re-echoed from shore to shore along the river, and was answered by a loud but faint neigh from somewhere in the ravine through which Fall Creek reaches the larger stream. Again the boy whistled, and in another two or three minutes a black pony came trotting out of the brush, the bridle hanging from the saddle horn.

"Tramp and I can make it alright," he said, "can't we, old fellow?" he added, patting the glossy neck, as the little horse rubbed a soft muzzle against his young master's shoulder.

While his companion was making ready for his ride, the Doctor selected four of the largest of his catch—beautiful black bass. "Here," he said when the lad was mounted, "take these along."

He accepted them graciously without hesitation, and by this the Doctor knew that their friendship was firmly established. "Thank you!" said the boy. "Mother is so fond of bass, and so are father and all of us. This is plenty for a good meal." Then with another smile, he added, "Mother likes to fish too. She taught me."

The Doctor looked at him wistfully as he gathered up the reins. "Look here," he said as the boy began to pull the horse away, "how about if you come back tomorrow? We'll have a great time. What do you say?"

The boy lowered his hand. "I would like to," he answered slowly. Then, after thinking seriously for a moment or two, he went on, "I think I can meet you here day after tomorrow. I am quite sure Father and Mother will be glad for me to come when I tell them about you."

Was ever an aging old fisherman and doctor so flattered with such a simple statement? It was not so much the words themselves, as the boy's gracious manner, and the meaning he unconsciously put into his voice.

He had turned his pony's head when the old man shouted after him once more. "Hold on! Wait just a moment! You have not told me your name. I am Dr. Oldham from Corinth. I am staying at the Thompson's down the river."

"My name is Daniel Howitt Matthews," he answered. "My home is the old Matthews place on the ridge above Mutton Hollow."

Then he rode away up the winding Fall Creek trail.

The Doctor spent all the next day near the same spot where he had met the boy, afraid that the lad might perhaps come again and not find him. He even went a mile or so up the little creek, half-expecting to meet his young friend, all the time wondering within himself why he could not break the spell the lad had cast over him.

"Who was he?" he asked himself over and over. He had told the Doctor his name, but that did not completely satisfy. Nor, indeed, did the question itself ask what the old man really wished to know. There was something different, something compelling in the lad's character, in his very countenance, that could not be explained by the mere attachment of a name.

The words persistently shaped and reshaped themselves—Who is he? . . . *What* is he? On the surface, the physician's brain made answer clearly enough—He was a boy, a backwoods boy, with unusual beauty and strength of body, an uncommon sensitivity of mind, perhaps unusual in these parts, and unusual anywhere in one so young. Yet with all this, was he not, after all, still just a boy?

But that something that sits in judgment upon the findings of our brain, and in lofty disregard of what we consider our rational selves, accepts or rejects our most profound analysis and conclusions, refused this answer. It was too superficial. It was not an answer which addressed the calm on the boy's face, nor the deep penetration of his peaceful eyes. And it in no way explained the strange power that the lad had exerted over the Doctor.

"What has come over me?" he said to himself, "that I should be so captivated by a lad I scarcely know! I am a hard old man, calloused by years of professional contact with mankind. I have brought too many hundreds of children into this world, and have carried too many of them through the measles, whooping cough, chicken pox, and the like to be so moved by a mere boy!"

The Thompsons could have told him about the lad and his people. But the Doctor instinctively shrank from asking them. He felt that he did not want to be told about the boy—that in truth no one could tell him about the boy, because he already knew the lad as well as he knew himself. Indeed, the feeling that he already knew the boy was what troubled the Doctor most of all. It was the feeling that he had always lived with him, but that he had never before met him face to face. He felt as a blind man might feel, if after living all his life in closest intimacy with someone, he were suddenly to receive his sight, and for the first time, actually look upon his companion's face.

In the years that have passed since that day, the Doctor gradually came to realize that the lad was to him, not so much a mystery as a revelation—the revelation of an unspoken ideal, of a truth that he had always known but never fully confessed even to himself, a truth about his own person and character that lay at last too deeply buried beneath the accumulated rubbish of his life for him to have perceived before meeting him. In the boy he met this hidden, secret, unacknowledged part of himself, that part of his being he knew to be the truest, most precious, and most sacred part, a part of himself he had, like most people, always persistently ignored, even while conscious that he could no more escape it than he could escape his own life. In short, young Daniel Matthews became to the Doctor that which the old man felt he ought to have been himself, that which he might have been, but never allowed himself to be.

# CHAPTER THREE

# SAMMY AND YOUNG MATT

It was still early in the forenoon of the following day when the Doctor heard a cheery hail, and the boy came riding out of the brush of the little ravine to meet his friend, who was waiting on the riverbank. As the lad sprang lightly to the ground, and with quick fingers took some things from the saddle, loosed the girths, and removed the pony's bridle, the physician watched him with a slight feeling of—was it envy or regret?

"You are early," he said.

The boy laughed. "I would have come earlier if I could." Then, dismissing the little horse, he turned eagerly and asked, "Have you been there yet—to that place up the river?"

"Indeed I have not," said the Doctor. "I have been waiting for you to show me."

The boy was delighted at this, and very soon was leading the way along the foot of the bluff to his favorite fishing ground.

It would be entirely too much to attempt the telling of that day, how they lay on the ground beneath the giant-limbed cottonwoods and listened to the waters flowing gently past, how they talked of the wild woodland life around them—of flower and tree, moss and vine, and the creatures that nested and denned and lived therein—how they caught a good catch of bass and perch, how the Doctor pulled off his boots and waded in the water like another boy while the hills echoed with their laughter, and how, when they had their lunch on a great rock, an eagle watched hungrily from his perch on a dead pine high up on the top of the bluff.

When the day was late and the shadow of the mountain was come once more down into the valley of the stream, and in answer to the boy's whistle the black pony had trotted from the brush to be made ready for the evening ride, the Doctor again watched his young companion wistfully.

When he was ready and mounting the pony, the boy said, "Father and Mother asked me to tell you, sir, that they—that we would be glad to have you come to see us before you leave the hills."

Then, seeing the surprise and hesitation on the Doctor's face, he continued, "You see, I told them all about you, and they would like to meet you too. Won't you come for a visit? I'm sure you would like my father and mother, and we would be so glad to have you. I'll ride over after you tomorrow if you'll come."

Would he *go*! Why the Doctor was so taken with this unusual boy that he would have gone to China or Africa if the boy had asked him!

That visit to the Matthews' place was the beginning of a friendship that was never broken. Every year thereafter the Doctor went to see them for several weeks, and always with increasing delight. Among the many households that he was privileged to know in his professional career, this home in the Ozarks stood like a beautiful temple in a world of shacks and hovels. But it was not until the philosopher had heard from Mrs. Matthews the story of Dad Howitt that he understood the reason. In the characters of Young Matt and Sammy, in their home life and in their children, the physician found the teaching of the old Shepherd of the Hills bearing its legitimate fruit. Most clearly did he find it in young Dan— the firstborn of this true mating of a man and woman who had never been touched by those forces in our civilization which so dwarf and cripple the race, but who had been taught to find in their natural environment those things that alone have the power to truly refine and glorify life.

Understanding this, the Doctor understood Dan. The boy was well born. He was natural. He was what a man-child ought to be. He did not carry the handicap that most of us stagger under so early in the race. And because of these things, to the keen old physician and student of life, the boy was a revelation of that best part of himself—that best part of the race. And with the years, this feeling of the Doctor's toward the boy continued to grow as their friendship and fellowship deepened.

It was always Dan who met the Doctor at the little wilderness railway station, and who said the last goodbye when the visit was over. Always they could be seen together, roaming about the hills, on fishing trips to the river, exploring the country for new delights, or revisiting their familiar haunts. Dan seemed, in his quiet way, to claim his old friend by right of discovery, and others laughingly yielded, giving the Doctor—as Young Matt, Dan's father, put it—"a third interest in the boy."

And so, with the companionship of the yearly visits and frequent letters in the intervening months, the Doctor watched the development of his young friend, and dreamed of the part that Dan would play in life when he became a man. And often as he watched the boy, there was on the face of the old physician a look of half-envy, half-regret.

In addition to his training at the little country school, Dan's mother was his constant teacher, passing on to her son, as only a mother could, the truths she had received from her old master, the Shepherd. But when the time came for more advanced intellectual training, the choice of a college was left to their friend.

The Doctor hesitated to offer his advice. He shrank from sending the lad out into the world. He could not bear the thought of that splendid nature coming in touch with the lower elements of life as he knew it.

But Sammy answered, "Why, Doctor, what is the boy for?" And Young Matt, looking away over toward Garber where an express train thundered over the trestles and around the curves, said in his slow way, "The brush all about is cleared, Doctor. The wilderness is going fast. The boy must live in his own age and do his own work."

Then as they spoke further about the changes coming to their homeland, their friend urged them to develop or sell the mine in the cave on Dewey Bald, and go with the boy when his time to leave came. But they both shook their heads emphatically, saying, "No, Doctor, we belong to the hills."

When the boy finally left his mountain home for a school in the distant city, he had grown to be a man to fill the heart of any mother with pride. With his father's powerful frame and closeknit muscles, and the healthy life of the woods and hills leaping in his veins, his splendid body and physical strength were refined and dominated by the mind and spirit of his mother. His shaggy, red-brown hair was like his father's, but his eyes were his mother's eyes, with that same trick of expression, that wide questioning gaze that seemed to demand every vital truth in whatever came under his consideration. He also had his mother's quick way of grasping another's thoughts almost before he or she was fully conscious of them himself, with that same saving sense of humor that made Sammy Lane the life and sunshine of the countryside.

"Big Dan," the people of the hills had come to call this son of Sammy and Young Matt, and "Big Dan" they called him in the school. For in the young life of the schools, as in the country, there is a spirit that names men with names that fit.

Secretly the Doctor hoped that Dan would choose the medical profession so dear to him. What an ideal physician he would make, with that clear, powerful, well-balanced nature, and above all, the love for his race and his passion to serve mankind that was the dominant note in his character. The boy would be the kind of physician that the old Doctor had hoped to be. So he planned and dreamed for Dan as he had planned and dreamed for himself, thinking to see the dreams that he had failed to live realized in the boy.

It was a severe shock to the Doctor when a letter came from Dan, telling him that he had decided upon another profession than what the Doctor had hoped. For the first time the boy had disappointed him.

Seizing his fishing tackle, the old man fled to the nearest stream.

And there, gazing into the deep, still waters into which he had cast his hook, he gradually calmed and came to understand everything Dan had said in his letter. It was that same dominant note in the boy's life, that inborn passion to serve, that fixed principle in his character that his life must be of the greatest possible worth to the world, that had led him to make his choice. With that instinct born in him, coming from the influence of the old Shepherd upon Young Matt his father and Sammy his mother, the boy could no more escape it than he could change the color of his brown eyes.

"But what does he know about it?" the Doctor argued within himself. Then he paused, reflecting upon his own words as he watched the bobbing up and down of his cork in the water from a nibbling fish.

"He'll find out the truth, of course," he thought. "He's that kind. And when he finds it—that's when he'll need me. He'll need me mighty bad!"

The cork went under and the Doctor felt a strong tug on his line. He jerked back, and knew he had a big one.

"Yes, sir," he said to himself as he reeled against what felt like a fifteen-inch bass, "he'll need me all right!" He was thinking clearly again, and saw what he should have seen before. "When that time comes, he'll need me to stand by him!"

# CHAPTER FOUR

# A Great Day in Corinth

Corinth was in the midst of a street fair. The neighboring city, several times larger and a true metropolis, had held a street fair that year; therefore Corinth felt she must have one too.

All that the big city does Corinth imitates. Thereby, with a beautiful rural simplicity, she thinks of herself as up-to-date and metropolitan, just as those who take their styles from the Eastern cities feel themselves well-dressed. The very Corinthian clerks and grocery boys, lounging behind their counters and in the doorways, the lawyer's understudy with his feet on the windowsill, the mechanic's apprentice, the high-school youths—all imitated their city kind, trying to act more important than they were, talking smartly about the country "rubes" who came to town; never dreaming that they themselves, when they "go to the city," were just as much a mark for the similar wit of their city brothers who considered them country bumpkins. So Corinth was in the midst of a street fair.

On every vacant lot near the center of town sat makeshift pens and stalls and cages, in which grunted, squealed, neighed, bellowed, bleated, cackled, and crowed exhibits from the neighboring farms. In the town hall or opera house (it was both) there were long tables with almost everything that grows on a farm, or is canned, baked, preserved, pickled, or stitched by farmers' wives. Upon either side of the main street stood booths containing the exhibits of the local merchants—farm machinery, buggies, wagons, harnesses, and the like being most conspicuous. The chief distinction between the town and country exhibits was that the farmer displayed his goods to be looked at, the merchant his to be sold. It was the merchants who promoted the fair.

In a vacant storeroom the Strong Memorial Church was holding its annual bazaar to coincide with the fair. On different corners other churches were serving chicken dinners or ice cream, and were in various other ways actively engaged for the conversion of the erring farmer's cash to the coffers of the village sanctuaries. In this way the promoters of the fair were encouraged by the churches. From every window, door, arch, pole, post, corner, gable, peak, or cupola—fluttered, streamed, and waved decorations—banners mostly, bearing advertisements of the enterprising merchants and of the equally enterprising churches.

In the afternoons baseball games were held between town and country teams, races, horseback riding, a greased pig to catch, a greased pole to climb, and other entertainments too exciting to think about, too attractive to be resisted.

From the far backwoods districts, from the hills, from the creek bottoms and the river, the people came to crowd about the pens, stalls, and tables to admire their own and their neighbors' products and possessions that they had seen many times before in their neighbors' homes and fields. They visited on the street corners. They tramped up and down past the booths. They yelled themselves hoarse at the games and entertainments, and in the intoxication of their pleasures bought ice cream, chicken dinners and various other things of the churches, and many goods from the merchants who promoted the fair.

But it was not because of the fair only that this particular day was one of distinction for Corinth. Whether by coincidence or design, this was also a red-letter day for the leaders and members of the Memorial Church. For after several years of faithful service, their aging minister had retired some months back, and this was the day of the arrival of his replacement, a young man about whom the reports to reach the Church were enthusiastic.

The Doctor was up that day at least a full hour before his regular time. At breakfast Martha looked him over suspiciously, and when he folded his napkin after eating only half his customary meal, she remarked dryly, "It's still three hours yet till train time."

Without replying, the Doctor rose from the table and walked out onto the porch.

Already the country people, dressed in their holiday garb, bright-faced, eager for the coming day, were on their way into town for the fair. Catching sight of the physician, many of them hailed him gaily as they passed, shouting good-natured remarks in addition to their greetings, and laughing loudly at his friendly replies.

It may be, the Doctor said to himself, that the good Lord had made days as fine at that day, but he could not remember one. His roses so filled the air with fragrance, the grass in the front yard was so fresh and clean, the flowers along the walk so bright and dainty, and the great maples that made a green arch of the street, so cool and mysterious in their leafy depths, that his old heart fairly ached with the beauty of it. With the sights and smells combining in his heart with the sense of expectation that was rising within him, the Doctor was all poet that day!

It had worked out just as he had hoped. At first Martha was suspicious when he broached the subject, as she often was when her husband offered suggestions touching certain matters. But the wise old philosopher knew just what strings to pull, and so it had all come out right, as he would have said. Sammy had written him expressing her gladness over how things had worked out.

There on his vine-covered porch that morning, the old man's thoughts went back to that day when the boy first came to him on the river bank, and to all the bright days of Dan's boyhood and youth that he had passed with the lad in the hills. "His life—" he said, talking to himself—"His life is like this day, fresh and clean and—"

He stopped, and looked across the street to the monument that stood a cold, lifeless mask in a world of living joy and beauty. Then from the monument he turned to Denny's garden. "And," he finished at length, "full of possibilities."

"What are you muttering about now?" said Martha, who had followed him out after finishing her breakfast.

"I was wishing," said the Doctor, "that I—that it would be always morning, and that there was no such thing as afternoon and evening and night."

His wife replied sweetly, "For a man of your age, you do say the most idiotic things! Won't you ever get old enough to think seriously?"

"But what could be more serious, my dear? If it were morning, I would always be beginning my life work, and never giving it up. I would be always looking forward to the success of my dreams, and never back to the failures of my poor attempts."

"You haven't failed in everything, John," protested Martha in softer tones.

"If it were morning," the philosopher continued with a smile, "I would be always making love to the best and prettiest girl in the state."

Martha tossed her head and the ghost of an old blush crept into her wrinkled cheeks. "There's no fool like an old fool," she quoted with a spark of her girlhood fire.

"But a young fool gets so much more out of his foolishness," the man retorted. "Talk of the responsibilities of age! They are nothing compared to the responsibilities of youth. There's Dan now—"

He looked again toward the monument.

"My goodness, yes!" exclaimed Martha. "And I've got a week's work to do before I even begin to get dinner. You go and kill me three of those young roosters—three, mind you."

"He will only be here for dinner, my dear."

"Don't you mind that. The dinner's my business. I've cooked for preachers before. I hope to the Lord he'll start you to thinking of your eternal future instead of mooning about the past." She bustled away.

When the Doctor had killed the three roosters, he took his hat and stick and started downtown, though it was still a good hour before train time. As he opened the front gate, Denny called out a cheery greeting from his garden across the street, and the old man went over for a word with the crippled boy.

"It's mighty fine you're looking this morning, Doctor," said Denny, pausing in his work and seating himself on the big rock. "Is it the ten-forty he's coming on?"

The Doctor tried to appear unconcerned. He looked at his watch with elaborately assumed carelessness as he answered: "I believe it's ten-forty. And how are you feeling this morning, Denny?"

The lad lifted his helpless left arm across his lap. "Oh, I'm fine, thank you kindly, Doctor. Mother's fine too, and my garden's doing pretty good for me." He glanced about. "The early things are all gone, of course, but the others are doing well. We'll get along. I told Mother just this morning that the Blessed Virgin hasn't forgotten us yet. I'll bet them potatoes grew an inch some nights this summer. And look what a day it is for the fair."

The Doctor looked at his watch again, and Denny continued. "Everyone's so pleased at the preacher's coming. Seems like folks haven't talked of much else for a month, except for the fair, of course. Things in this town will liven up now, sure. I can feel that something's about to happen."

"I expect you two will be great friends, Denny."

The poor little fellow nearly twisted himself off the rock. "Oh, Doctor, really? Why I—the minister'll have no time for the likes of me. And is he really going to live at Mrs. Morgan's there?" He nodded his head toward the house next to his garden.

"That's his room," the Doctor answered, pointing to the corner window. "He'll be right handy to us both."

Denny gazed at the window for a solemn moment. "That is grand, isn't it?" he said at length. "It has such a fine view of the monument!"

"Yes," the Doctor interrupted, "the monument and your garden."

He turned abruptly and continued on his way, lest he should foolishly try to explain to the bewildered and embarrassed Denny what he meant.

It seemed to the Doctor that nearly everyone he met on the well-filled street that morning had a smile for him, while many stopped to exchange a word or two on the coming of his friend. When he reached the depot the agent hailed him. "Good morning, Doctor," he said. "Looking for your preacher?"

"*My* preacher!" exclaimed the Doctor in return. "Why is it that everyone in this town thinks he's *my* preacher?"

The old physician turned his back and walked off down the platform. At the other end stood a group of women, active members of the Memorial Ladies' Aid who had left their posts of duty at the bazaar to have a first look at the new pastor. The old Elder of the church, Nathan Jordan, with his daughter Charity, was just walking up as well.

"Good morning, good morning, Doctor," said Jordan, grasping his friend's hand as if he had not seen him for years. "Well, I see we're all here."

He turned proudly about as the group of women came forward with an air of importance, the Doctor thought, as though the occasion required their presence. "Reckon our boy'll be here all right," Nathan continued.

"*Our* boy!" thought the Doctor angrily to himself. "He's not even here yet, and they are already thinking how they can mold him to *their* designs!"

The ladies all looked sweetly interested. One of them put her arm lovingly about Charity. "So nice of you to come, dear."

The Doctor could distinctly feel the subtle, invisible presence of the Ally. It was well that someone just then saw the smoke from the coming train two or three miles away, around the curve beyond the pumping station.

The porter from the hotel opposite the depot came bumping across the rails, with the cases belonging to two traveling men in his little cart. The local expressman rattled up with a trunk in his shaky old wagon. And the sweet-faced daughter of the division track superintendent hurried out of the red section house with a bundle of big envelopes in her hand. As the train approached the platform, it was crowded with all kinds of people, carrying a great variety of bundles, baskets, and handbags, and asking all manner of questions, on their way to and from all sorts of places.

Swiftly the long train with clanging bell and snorting engine came toward the depot. As it slowed, the conductor swung easily down onto the platform, watch in hand, and walked quickly to the office. Next porters and other trainmen tumbled off, and with a long hiss of escaping white steam and a steady puff-puff, the train came to a screeching stop.

Amid the bustle and confusion of crowding passengers getting on and off, tearful goodbyes and joyful greetings, banging trunks, rattling trucks, and hissing steam, with painfully thumping heart the Doctor watched, scanning every face.

Then he saw him, his handsome head towering above the pushing, jostling crowd. With his back to them all, Dan pushed his way to an open window of the car he had just left, where a woman's face turned to him in earnest conversation. For the moment the tall young man seemed completely unaware of all the people and activity about him.

"There he is," said the Doctor, "that tall fellow by the window there." At his words, the physician heard several doubtful comments. He glanced around and saw the women staring eagerly. The Elder's countenance was stern and frowning.

"Seems mighty interested in that woman there in the train," said one of the ladies suggestively.

"You can't deny she's a pretty one," added another, while the Elder continued to watch the proceedings with dubious expression.

The Doctor listened in disbelief. The words which came to his lips were, "Why you pack of fools, that's—" But he caught himself before making an outburst, the expression on his face gradually turning to a grin, and he held his peace and said nothing.

The conductor, watch again in hand, shouted, the porters stepped aboard, the bell rang, the engineer, with his long oil can, swung up to his cab, and slowly the heavy train inched forward again and began to gather headway. As it went, Dan walked along the platform beside the open window, still talking to the woman inside, until he could no longer keep pace with the moving car. Then with a final wave of his hand, he stood looking after the train, seemingly unconscious of everything but that one who was being carried so quickly beyond his sight.

He was still standing at the edge of the platform staring into the distance toward the receding train when his old friend approached and grasped his arm from behind. He turned with a start.

"Doctor!" he exclaimed, his face exploding into a sunny grin.

What a handsome fellow he was, with his father's great body, powerful limbs, and shaggy red-brown hair, and his mother's eyes and mouth, and her spirit ruling within him, making you feel that he was clean through and through. It was no wonder people on the platform stood around looking at him. The Doctor felt again that old mysterious spell, that feeling that the boy was a revelation to him of something he had always known, the living embodiment of a truth never acknowledged. His heart swelled with pride as he turned to lead Dan up and introduce him to Elder Jordan and his company.

The church ladies, old in experience with preachers, seemed strangely embarrassed. This one was somehow so different from those they had known before, but their eyes were full of admiration. Charity's voice shook a little as she bade him welcome. Nathaniel Jordan's manner was that of a judge. Dan himself was as calm and self-possessed as if he and the Doctor were alone on the bank of some river, far from church and church people. But the Doctor thought that the boy flinched a little when he introduced him as Reverend Matthews. Perhaps, though, it was merely the Doctor's fancy. The old man felt too, even as he presented Dan to his people, that there had come between him and the boy a something that was never there before, and it troubled him not a little. But perhaps this too was but a fancy.

When the introductions were over, and the company was leaving the depot, the Doctor, still thinking about what was troubling him, managed to steer Dan into a collision with a young woman who was standing nearby. She was carrying a small suitcase, having evidently arrived on the same train that brought the minister. It was no joke for anyone into whom Big Dan bumped, and a momentary look of indignation flashed on the girl's face. But it vanished quickly in a smile as the big fellow stood, hat in hand, offering the most abject apology for what he called *his* rudeness.

The Doctor noted in the girl a fine face, a strong graceful figure, and an air of wholesomeness and health that was most refreshing. But he thought that Dan took more time than was necessary for his apology.

When she had assured him several times that it was nothing, she asked, "Can you please tell me the way to Dr. Abbott's office?"

Why that was his very own office! the Doctor thought to himself—but Dr. Harry's *and* his now. He looked the young woman over curiously, while Dan was saying, "I'm sorry, but I cannot. I am a stranger here, but my friend—"

The older man interrupted with the necessary directions, and the information that Dr. Abbott was out of town and would not be back until four o'clock.

"Will you then direct me to a hotel?" she asked.

The Doctor pointed across the track. Then he got Dan away.

The church ladies, with Charity and her father, were already on their way back to the place where the bazaar was doing business. Half way down the block the Doctor and Dan were checked by a crowd. There seemed to be some excitement ahead. But in the pause, Dan turned to look back toward the young woman who had arrived in Corinth on the same train that had brought him. She was coming slowly down the street toward them.

Again the thought flashed through the Doctor's mind that the boy had taken more time than was necessary for his apology.

# CHAPTER FIVE

# WHO ARE THEY?

Jud Hardy, who lived at Windy Cove on the river some eighteen miles back up in the hills from Corinth, had been looking forward to Fair time for months.

Not that Jud had either things to exhibit or money to buy things exhibited. For while Jud professed to own and ostensibly to cultivate a forty-acre parcel near the river, he gained his living mostly by occasional "spells of work" on the farms of his neighbors. In lieu of products of his hand or fields for exhibition at the annual fair, Jud invariably made an exhibition of himself, never failing thus to contribute his full share to the "other amusements" announced on the circulars and in the Daily Corinthian newspaper as "too numerous to mention."

The citizens of the Windy Cove country have a saying that when Jud is sober and in a good humor and has money, he is a fairly good fellow, if he is not crossed in any way. The meat of which saying is the well-known fact that Jud is never in a good humor when he is not sober, that he is never sober when he has money, and that with the exception of three or four kindred spirits, whose admiration for the bad man is equalled only by their fear of him, no one has ever been able to devise a way to avoid crossing him when he is in his normal condition.

With three of the kindred spirits, Jud arrived in Corinth that day with the earliest of the visitors, and they proceeded at once to warm up after their long ride. By ten o'clock they were well warmed. Just as the ten-forty train was slowing up at the depot, Jud began his exhibition.

Because the mail was about to arrive, a large crowd was gathered in front of the post office. Stationing himself near the door, the man from Windy Cove blocked the way for everyone who wanted to pass either in or out of the building. For the women and young girls he stepped aside with elaborate, drunken politeness, and maudlin, complimentary remarks. For the men who brushed him he had a scowling curse and a muttered threat. Meanwhile, his friends watched nearby in tipsy admiration, saying among themselves that "there was bound to be somethin' doin', for Jud was sure a-huntin' trouble."

Finally the town marshall approached. He was a little man with a big star on his breast, carrying a walking stick in his hand. Politely he asked Jud to move on.

Jud saw the opportunity to give a most convincing exhibition of his might and bravery. He returned the marshall's request with a few opening remarks—mostly profane—and then with a sudden blow of his fist, lay the representative of the law onto the floor, while he rushed into the street laughing loudly.

The passing crowd stopped instantly, scattering about from every side to make room for the drunken river man to pass. And between the wall of humanity on either side of the street strolled Jud Hardy, roaring his opinion and defiance of everyone in general, and the citizens of Corinth in particular, enjoying to the full having the street all to himself.

There were several men in the crowd who were not afraid of Jud. But there was that inevitable hesitation, while each man was muttering to his neighbor that the thing ought to be stopped, everyone waiting to see if someone else was going to be the first to stop it.

Jud made his triumphant way nearly the length of the block, leading his small parade. But at the corner, where the crowd was not so dense, he saw a figure starting across the street in front of him.

"Hey there," he roared, "get back there where you belong! What the devil do you mean, walkin' out in front of me? Don't you see the procession's a comin', and this street is mine!"

The crippled Denny had left his garden to go to the butcher's for some meat for dinner, and had just rounded the corner and started across the street. He did not realize Jud's shouts were meant for him, and, forced to give all his attention to his own halting steps, he did not grasp the situation but continued his dragging way across the path of the drunken and enraged bully. Seeing the lad ignore his loud commands, the ruffian strode heavily forward with menacing fists waving, shouting foul curses upon the head of the helpless Irish boy.

The crowd gasped. Several men started forward, but before they could force their way through the press of the crowd, the people saw a large well-dressed stranger spring from the sidewalk and run toward the two figures in the middle of the street. But Dan had not arrived upon the scene soon enough. Almost as he left the pavement the blow fell, and Denny lay still—a crumpled heap in the dirt.

Flushed with this second triumph, Jud turned to face the approaching stranger.

"Come on, you pink-eyed dude! I've got plenty for you too! Come and git your medicine, you—"

Dan was approaching—so quickly that Jud's curses had not left his lips when the big fellow reached him. With one clean, swinging blow the man from Windy Cove was lifted off the ground to fall several feet away from his senseless victim.

An excited yell rose up from the crowd. But Jud, lean, loose-jointed and hard of sinew, had the physical toughness of his kind. The effect of the alcohol seemingly disappeared for a moment. Almost instantly he was on his feet again, with murder in his eye, while his hand reached toward the holster on his hip with a familiar movement.

Seeing him go for his gun, a wild scramble erupted in the

crowd as those closest by sought cover.

"Look out! Look out!" cried several of the onlookers.

But the mountain-bred minister needed no warning. With a leap, cat-like in its quickness, Dan was again upon the other. There was a short struggle, the sharp report of gunfire, a wrenching twist, a smashing blow, and Jud lay in the street once more, this time senseless. His weapon lay beside him in the dust. The bullet had gone wide above the crowd.

The spectators cheered, yelling their approval. But even while they applauded, the people began asking one another, "Who is the man? . . . Have you ever seen him? . . . Where did he come from?"

Several men rushed in. Seeing the bully safe in as many hands as could lay hold of him to keep him down, Dan turned to see the young woman whom he had met at the depot kneeling in the street a few yards away over the unconscious form of Denny. With her handkerchief she was wiping the blood and dirt from the boy's forehead. Dan had only a second or two to notice the calmness of her face and manner when the crowd closed in about them.

In another moment the Doctor pushed his way through the throng, and at the sight of the familiar figure, the people obeyed his energetic orders and drew aside. A carriage was brought and Dan lifted the unconscious lad in his arms. The Doctor spoke shortly to the young woman. "You come too," he said. And with the Doctor, the two strangers in Corinth took Denny to his home.

In the excitement no one thought of introductions, while the people seeing their Denny's defender driving in the carriage with a young woman, also a stranger, changed their question to, "Who are *they*?"

When Denny had regained consciousness, and everything possible for his comfort and for the assistance of his distracted mother had been done, the physician assured them that the lad would be as good as ever in a day or two. Then the two men left and crossed the street to the Doctor's little white house.

"Well," exclaimed Martha when Dan had been presented and they had told her briefly of the incident on the street, "I'm mighty glad I cooked them three roosters."

Dan laughed his big, hearty laugh. "I'm glad too," he said. "Your husband used to drive me wild out in the woods with tales of your cooking. We always hoped he would bring you with him on some of his trips," continued Dan. "We all wanted to meet you."

"Maybe I will go some day," Martha replied. But then her manner underwent a change, as if she had suddenly remembered something. "You'll excuse me now while I put the dinner on," she said stiffly. "Just make yourself at home. Preachers always do in this house, even if the Doctor don't belong." She hurried away, and Dan looked at his host with his mother's questioning eyes. The Doctor knew what it was. Dan had felt it even in the house of his dearest friend. It was the preacher Martha had welcomed, welcomed him professionally because he was a preacher, not because he was her husband's friend. And the Doctor felt again that something had come between him and the lad.

"Martha doesn't care much for fishing," he said gently.

They walked out onto the porch, and the old man pointed out to Dan the room that would be his across the way—where it looked out upon the garden and the monument.

"Several of your congregation wanted to have you in their homes," he explained. "But I felt—I thought you might like to be—well, it was near me, you see, and handy to the church." He pointed to the building up the street.

"Yes," Dan answered. "You are quite right. It was very kind of you." Then looking at the monument he asked whose it was.

The Doctor hesitated. Dan faced him waiting for an answer.

"That—oh, that's our famous Statesman. You will need time to fully appreciate that work of art, and what it means to Corinth. It will grow on you. It's been growing on me for several years."

The young man was about to ask another question regarding the monument when he paused. The girl who had helped the boy in the street was just now coming out of Denny's little cottage. As she walked away under the great trees that lined the sidewalk, the two men stood watching her. Dan's question about the monument was forgotten.

"I wonder who she is," he said in a low voice.

The meeting at the train depot came back to the Doctor's mind, and he chuckled to himself just as Martha called them to dinner.

And for the rest of the day, on the street corners, at the ladies' bazaar, in the stores and the church booths and in the town's homes, people talked of nothing but the exhibition of the man from Windy Cove, while everyone asked each other, "Who are those two young people?"

# CHAPTER SIX

# DR. HARRY AND MISS FARWELL

After dinner was over and they had visited awhile, the Doctor took Dan over and introduced him to his landlady. Then, making some trivial excuse about business, he left the boy in his room. The fact is that the Doctor wished to be alone. If he could have done it decently, he would have gone off somewhere with his fishing tackle. As he could not go fishing, he did the next best thing. He went to his office.

The streets were not so crowded now, for the people were at the ball game, and the Doctor made his way downtown without interruption. As he went, he tried to think out what it was that had come between him and the boy whom he had known so intimately for so many years. Stopping at the post office, he found a letter in his box addressed to "Rev. Daniel H. Matthews." In his abstraction he was about to hand the letter in at the window with the explanation that he knew no such person, when a voice beside him said, "Is Brother Matthews fully rested from his tiresome journey, Doctor?"

The Doctor's abstraction vanished instantly. He jammed the letter into his pocket and faced the speaker with some annoyance.

"Yes," he answered sarcastically, "I think Brother Matthews is fully rested. As he is a grown man of unusual strength, and in perfect health of body at least, and the tiresome journey was a trip of only four hours in a comfortable railway coach, I think I may say that he is fully recovered." Then the Doctor slipped away without further discussion.

But in that brief conversation he had discovered what it was that had come between the boy and himself: the *man* Dan Matthews was no longer the Doctor's boy, his friend, the lad from the river.

He was now "Reverend" or "Brother"—the *preacher*. All that morning it had been making itself felt, that something that sets preachers apart. No one, not even the Doctor's own wife, could keep from treating them differently than other men, as if they were somehow weak and in constant need of handling by tender gloves and soft-spoken words. The Doctor wondered how his young hill-bred giant would stand being coddled and petted and loved by the wives and mothers of men who, for their daily bread, met the world bare handed, and whose hardships were accepted by them and by these same mothers and wives as a matter of course. But preachers—no, they could not be treated like other men! They must not soil their dainty hands! One must speak softly and gently in their presence! *Rubbish!* thought the Doctor to himself.

By this time he had reached his office, and the sight of the familiar old rooms that had been the scene of so many revelations of real tragedies and genuine hardships, known only to the sufferer and to him professionally, forced him to continue his thoughts.

There was Dr. Harry, for instance. Who ever petted and coddled *him*? Who ever thought of setting him apart? Who ever asked if *he* were rested from his tiresome journey—journeys not made in comfortable railway coaches, but in his buggy over all kinds of roads, at all times of day or night, in all sorts of weather, during winter and summer, in rain and sleet and snow? Whoever "Reverended" or "Brothered" him? No, he was only a man, a physician! It was his business to work hard and kill himself trying to keep other people alive!

Then the Doctor's thoughts drifted to Dr. Harry's coming to Corinth. He had initially been the Doctor's assistant, then his partner. And now that the Doctor had retired, he was his successor. Of a fine old Southern family, his people had lost everything in the war when Harry was only a lad. His father was killed in battle and the mother died a year later, leaving the boy alone in the world. Thrown upon his own resources for the necessities of life, he had managed somehow to live and to educate himself, besides working his way through college and medical school, choosing his profession for the sheer love of it. He came to Dr. Oldham directly from school, when the Doctor was beginning to feel the burden of his large practice too heavily. And it was while he was the old physician's assistant that the people learned to call him Dr. Harry. And Dr. Harry he had remained to that very day.

*How that young man has worked!* thought the Doctor.

Dr. Harry's profession and his church activities (for he is a member, a deacon now, in the Memorial Church) occupied every working minute of his life, and many hours besides that should have been given to sleep.

As the months passed after his coming, Dr. Oldham placed more and more responsibilities upon him. And at the end of the second year took him into full partnership. It was about this time that Dr. Harry bought the old Wilson Carter place, and brought from his boyhood home two former slaves of his father to help keep house for him, Old Uncle George and his wife Mam Liz.

Every year the younger man took more and more of the load from his partner's shoulders, until at length the older physician retired from active practice.

And since that time there never has been a word but of confidence and friendship between them. The only difference still is this: that Harry will go to prayer meeting when the Doctor says he should go to bed instead, and that Harry will not go fishing.

The young man has remained the same courteous, kindly gentleman, intent only upon his profession, keeping abreast of new things pertaining to his work, but ever considerate of the old Doctor's whims and fancies. Even after Dr. Oldham had stepped down, Dr. Harry insisted that he leave his old desk in its place so that he could come in whenever he chose. And Dr. Harry still talked over his cases with him.

The Doctor was sitting in his dilapidated office chair thinking over all these things when he heard his brother physician's step on the stairs. Harry came in, dusty and worn, from a long ride in the country on an all-night case. His tired face lit up when he saw his friend and mentor, Dr. Oldham.

"Hello, Doctor!" he said. "Glad to see you!" As he spoke, he dropped his case, slipped out of his coat, and moved toward the sink to bury his face in cold water. "Well, has he come?" he went on. "How is he?"

"He's all right," the Doctor muttered, his mind slipping back into the channel that had started him off thinking of his fellow physician. "Got in on the ten-forty. But you look tuckered out! Why the devil don't you get some rest, Harry?"

Standing in the doorway rubbing his face, neck, and chest with a coarse towel, the young man laughed. "Rest!" he exclaimed. "What would I do with a vacation? I'll be all right, just as soon as I sit down to one of Mam Liz's dinners."

"Where've you been?"

"It was that baby of Jensen's. Poor little chap. I thought two or three times during the night that he wasn't going to make it. But I guess he'll pull through now."

Dr. Oldham knew the Jensen's well. Eighteen miles from Corinth over the worst roads in the country.

"It'll be more years than there are miles between here and Jensen's before you get a cent out of that case," he growled hoarsely. "You're a fool to make the trip. Why don't you let 'em be doctored by that old bushwhacker at Salem? He's only three miles away."

Harry pulled on his coat and dropped into his chair with a grin. "What'll you give me to collect some of *your* old accounts, Doctor? The Jensens say that the reason they have me is because you have always been their physician. So why did *you* ride all the way out there to tend them?"

Then the Doctor, in characteristic language, proceeded to express his opinion of the whole backwoods Jensen tribe, while Harry calmly glanced through some letters on his desk.

"Look here, Doctor," he exclaimed, wheeling around in his chair and interrupting the old man's eloquent discourse. "Here's a letter from Dr. Miles—says he's sending me a nurse. Just what we need!"

He tossed the letter to the other. "There'll be the deuce to pay at Judge Strong's when she arrives," he went on. He took in a deep breath. "Well," he said, "I guess I better trot on home and get something to eat and forty winks. A Jensen breakfast, as you remember, isn't the most staying thing for a civilized stomach, and I need to be fit when I call at the Strong mansion. I wonder when she'll arrive."

"She's here already," said the old Doctor.

When Dr. Harry cast him an inquiring glance, he went on to tell him about the meeting at the train depot and the fight on the street. "But go on and get your nap," he finished. "I'll look after her when she comes."

Harry had just put on his hat when there came a knock on the door leading into the little waiting room. He hung his hat back in the closet, and dropped into his chair again with a comical expression of resignation on his face. But his voice was cheerful as he said, "Come in."

The door opened, and the young lady of the depot entered.

The old physician took a good look at her this time. He saw a girl of fine, strong form and good height, with clear skin, showing perfect health, large gray eyes serious enough, but with a laugh behind all their seriousness—brown hair, firm rounded chin, and a generous sensitive mouth. Particularly he noticed her hands—beautifully modeled, useful hands they were, made for real service. Altogether she gave him the impression of being very much alive, and very much a woman.

"Is this Dr. Abbott?" she asked, looking at Harry who had risen from his chair. When she spoke the old man again noted her voice. It was low and clear.

"I am Dr. Abbott," replied Harry.

"I am Hope Farwell," she answered. "Dr. Miles asked me to come. You wanted a nurse for a special case, I believe."

"Yes," exclaimed Harry. "We have his letter right here. We were just speaking of you, Miss Farwell. This is Dr. Oldham. Perhaps Dr. Miles told you of him."

She turned with a smile. "Yes, indeed, Dr. Miles told me. But I believe we have met before, Doctor."

The girl broke into a merry laugh when the old man answered gruffly. "I should think we had. I was just telling Harry there when you came in."

"How soon can you be ready to go on this case, Nurse?" asked the younger physician.

She looked at him with a faint expression of surprise. "Why, I'm ready to go now, Doctor," she answered.

"You'll do no such thing," broke in the old Doctor. "This is a hard case. You'll be up most of the night. You're tired out from your trip, and Dr. Harry here is beat himself from being out in the hills all last night."

"Why, Doctor," said the young woman, "it is my business to be ready at any time. Being up nights is part of my profession. Surely you know that. Besides, the trip on the train was a really good rest, the first good rest I've had for a long time."

The Doctor sat back down into the chair, out of which he had half risen, and sighed. "I know . . . of course," he said at length, in a softer tone. "I was thinking of something else. You must pardon me, Miss Farwell. Harry there will explain to you that I am subject to these little attacks now and then."

"Oh, I know that already," she returned smiling. "Dr. Miles told me all about you!" There was something in her laughing gray eyes that made the rough old man wonder just what it was his friend Miles had told her.

"All right, get back to business you two," he growled. "I won't interrupt again! Tell her about the case, Harry."

The young woman's face was serious in a moment, and she gave the physician the most careful attention as he explained the case for which he had written Dr. Miles to send a trained nurse of certain qualifications.

The Judge Strong of Corinth at this time was the only son of the old Judge who first moved to Corinth years ago. He is a large man physically, as large as the Doctor. But where the Doctor is fat, the Judge is lean. He inherited not only his father's title of Judge (a purely honorary one) but also his father's property, his position as an Elder in the church, and his general disposition— together with his taste and skill in collecting mortgages and ac- quiring real estate and wealth in general.

The old Judge had but the one child. The present Judge, though just passing middle age, has no children at all. Seemingly there is no room in his heart for more than his church and his properties. His mind is thus wholly occupied with titles to heaven and to earth. He lives with Sapphira, his wife, in a big house on Strong Avenue, beyond the Strong Memorial Church (named in honor of his father), with never so much as a pet dog or cat to roughen the well-kept lawn or romp in the garden.

The patient whom Miss Farwell had come to nurse was Sap- phira's sister, a widow with neither child nor home. The Judge had been forced by his fear of public sentiment to give her shelter, against his own better judgment, and he had been compelled by Dr. Oldham and Dr. Harry to employ a nurse. The case would not be a pleasant one, they told her, and Miss Farwell would need all that abundant stock of tact and patience which Dr. Miles had declared she possessed.

Dr. Harry explained everything to her, and when he had fin- ished, her matter-of-fact reply caught Harry off guard. "What are your instructions, Doctor?"

It caught the old Doctor off guard too. Not even so much as a comment on the disagreeable position she knew she would oc- cupy in the Strong household, for Harry had not slighted the hard facts about the Judge. She understood clearly what she was going into.

A light came into the young physician's eyes that his old friend liked to see. "I guess Miles knew what he was talking about in this letter," said the old Doctor. The young woman's face flushed warmly at his words and look.

Then in his professional tones, Dr. Harry instructed her more fully as to the patient's condition—a nervous trouble greatly aggravated by the Judge's disposition and temper.

"Well, what do you think, Miss Farwell?" said Harry when he finished.

She smiled. "When do I go, Doctor?"

Harry stepped to the telephone and called the Strong mansion. "The nurse from Chicago is here, Judge," he said. "Came this morning. We'd like her to come over today. Can you send your man to the depot for her trunk?"

By the look on his face the old Doctor knew what Harry was getting. The younger physician's jaw was set and his eyes were blazing, but his voice was calm and easy.

"But Judge, you remember the agreement," he said at length. "Dr. Oldham is here now if you wish to speak to him."

There was another pause, then Harry spoke again. "We shall hold you to the exact letter of your bargain, Judge. I am very sorry, but—Very well, sir. I will be at your home with the young lady in a few minutes. Please have a room ready. And by the way, Judge, I must tell you again that my patient, your sister-in-law, is in a serious condition. I warn you that we will hold you responsible if anything happens to interfere with our arrangements for her treatment. Goodbye."

He turned to the nurse with a wry face. "I don't envy you, Miss Farwell." He then made another call to arrange to have the young woman's trunk taken to the house. When the man had called for the claim checks, Harry said, "Now, Nurse, my buggy is here, and if you are ready I guess we had better follow your trunk pretty closely."

From the window the old Doctor watched them get into the buggy and drive off down the street. Mechanically he opened the letter from Dr. Miles, which he still held in his hand. "An ideal nurse, who has taken up the work for love of it—have known the family for years—thoroughbreds—just the kind to send a Kentuckian like you—I warn you, look out—I want her back again."

The Doctor chuckled when he remembered Harry's look as he talked to the young woman. "If ever a man needed a wife," he thought, "Harry does. And who knows what might happen!"

Then the Doctor went home to Dan. He found him next door in Denny's garden, with Denny enthroned on the big rock—listening to his fun. Inside the house his mother Deborah looked on, hardly able to believe that "it was the parson sure enough" out there talking with her crippled son—Denny, who was to have been a priest himself one day, but who would never now be good for much of anything.

CHAPTER SEVEN

# THE CALLING OF DAN MATTHEWS

Dan, with the Doctor and Mrs. Oldham, were to take supper that evening at Elder Jordan's. Martha went over early in the afternoon, leaving the two men to follow.

As they were passing the monument, Dan stopped. "Did you know him?" he asked curiously after he had read the inscription.

The Doctor answered briefly: "I was there when he was born and was his family physician all his life, and I was with him when he died."

Something in the Doctor's voice made Dan look at him intently for a moment. "Was he a good man?" he asked in a low tone.

"One of the best I ever knew—too good for this town. Why, just look at that ridiculous thing. They say it expressed their appreciation of him—and it does too," he finished grimly, "though not in the way they intended."

"But," said Dan in a puzzled way, turning once more to the monument, "this inscription—" he read again the sentence from the Statesman's speech on the forgotten issue of his passing day.

The Doctor said nothing.

Then gazing up at the cast-iron figure posed stiffly with outstretched arm in the attitude of a public speaker, Dan asked, "Is that like him?"

"Like him! It's like nothing but the people who conceived it!" growled the Doctor indignantly. "If my friend there were still living today, he would not always be talking about issues that have no meaning to this present day. He would be giving himself to the problems that trouble us *now*. This thing—"

He rapped the monument with his stick until it gave forth a dull, hollow sound. "This thing is not a memorial to the life and character of my friend. It memorializes the dead issue to which he gave himself at one brief passing moment of his life, and which, had he lived, he would have forgotten, as the changing times brought new issues to be met as he met this old one. He was too great, too brave, to merely stand still and let the world go by. He was always on the firing line. But this thing—"

He rapped the hollow iron shaft again contemptuously, and the hollow sound seemed to add emphasis to his words: "This is a dead monument to a dead issue. Instead of speaking of his life, it cries aloud in hideous emphasis that he is dead."

They stood silently for a moment, then Dan said quietly, "After all, Doctor, they meant well."

"And that," retorted the old man grimly, "is what we doctors say when we see our mistakes go by in the hearse." He paused, then added, "You will come to know them in time, my young friend. Then you will see that oftentimes they seem to mean well, when it is something else altogether that they really mean."

They continued on up the street until they reached the church. Here Dan stopped again. He read the inscription cut large in stone over the door. "The Strong Memorial Church." Again Dan turned to his friend with an inquiring look.

"Judge Strong . . . the old Judge," explained the Doctor. "That's his picture in the big stained-glass window there."

Again they moved on, and at length arrived at the Jordan home. Nathaniel Jordan was one of the best-intentioned of men. Surely, if in the hereafter a man receives credit for always doing what his conscience dictates, Elder Nathan Jordan will. He was one of those characters who give up living ten years before they die. Nathan stayed on for the church's good, for the church was his very life.

Miss Charity, Elder Jordan's only child, was born, raised, and educated to be nothing but a parson's wife. That was all her mother and father cared for her to be. At three she had taken a prize in Sunday school for memorizing certain verses, at seven she was baptized, and could tell the reason why, at twelve she played the organ for a meeting of the Christian Endeavor group. At fourteen she was teaching a class, leading prayer meeting, attending conventions, was president of the local Young People's Union, and pointed with pride to the fact that she was on more committees than any other single individual in the Memorial Church. The walls of her room were literally covered with badges, medals, tokens, prizes, and emblems, with the picture of every conspicuous church worker and leader of her denomination. Between times the girl studied the early history of her church, read the religious papers, and in various other ways prepared herself for her life work as a religious woman.

Poor Charity! She was so cursed with what she considered a holy ambition, that to her men were not men, they simply *were* or were *not* preachers.

When Dan and the Doctor reached the Jordan home they found this daughter of the church at the front gate watching for them, a look of eager hope and expectancy on her face. The Elder himself, with his wife and Mrs. Oldham, were on the front porch.

Martha could scarcely wait for the usual greeting and the introduction of Dan to Mrs. Jordan before she started on her husband. "It's a pity you couldn't bring Brother Matthews here sooner," she said. "Supper is all ready now. You'd think you had an important case to have been so long in coming."

"We did have an important case, my dear," the Doctor replied, "and it was Dan who caused our delay."

"That's it, lay it on somebody else like you always do. What in the world could poor Brother Matthews be doing to keep him from a good meal?"

"He was studying—let me see, what was it, Dan? Art, Political Economy—or Theology?"

Dan smiled. "I think it might have been the theory and practice of medicine," he returned. At which they both laughed and the others joined in, though for his life the Doctor couldn't see why.

"Well," said the Elder when he had finished his shrill cackle, "we better go in and discuss supper awhile. That's always a pretty satisfactory subject at least."

When the meal was finished some time later, they all went out onto the front porch again, where it soon became evident that Nathaniel did not propose to waste more time in light and frivolous conversation. By his familiar and ponderous, "Ahem—ahem!" even Dan understood that he was anxious to get down to the real business of the evening—which in this case amounted to a serious questioning of the young minister to determine his character, qualifications, and general suitableness according to the Elder's own standards. To himself he would have said that he was determined to do his full duty as one of the Church's two Elders, or—as he would have phrased it—"to keep that which was committed unto him."

"Ahem—ahem!" The Elder cleared his throat again. A hush fell upon the little company, the women turned their chairs expectantly, and the Doctor slipped over to the end of the porch to enjoy his evening cigar. The Elder had the floor.

With another and still louder "Ahem!" he began. "I am sorry that Brother Strong is not here this evening. Judge Strong, that is, Brother Matthews—he is our other Elder, you understand. I expected him, but evidently he has been detained."

Thinking of Dr. Harry and the nurse, the Doctor chuckled, and Nathan turned a look of solemn inquiry in his direction.

"Ahem—" articulated the Elder again, "you did not come to Corinth directly from your home, I understand, Brother Matthews?"

The Doctor could see Dan's face by the light from the open window. He fancied it wore a look of amused understanding.

"No," answered the young minister. "I spent yesterday in the city."

"Ahem—ahem," coughed the Elder. "Found an acquaintance

on the train on your way here, did you? We noticed you talking to a young woman at the window of your car after you got out."

Dan paused a moment before answering, and the Doctor could feel the interest of the company. Then he answered dryly, "Yes. I may say though that she is something more than a mere acquaintance."

There were smothered exclamations from the women. "Ah, hah," voiced the Elder, thinking he had uncovered some scandal.

The Doctor grinned to himself in the dark. *The young scamp!* he said to himself. *He's baiting the old fool!*

"Ahem! She had a pretty face, we noticed. Are you—that is, have you known her long?"

"Several years, sir."

"And you—that is, your—ah, your relationship with her is—"

"The lady you saw is my mother," said Dan at last. "I went with her to the city day before yesterday, where she wished to do some shopping, and then I accompanied her on her way home as far as Corinth."

"Why, Doctor," cried one of the women, "you never told us it was his mother!"

"You never asked me," chuckled the Doctor.

The two older women rose and drifted into the house. Charity settled herself in an attitude of rapt attention, and the program was continued.

"Ahem," went on Nathaniel, doing his best to subdue the feeling of righteous indignation attempting to surface at looking foolish in the eyes of his guests. "You may not be aware of it, Brother Matthews, but I know a great deal about your family."

"Indeed," exclaimed Dan.

"Yes, sir. You see I have some mining interests in that district where you are from, quite profitable interests I may say. Judge Strong and I together have quite extensive interests. Two or three years ago we made a good many trips to your part of the country, where we heard a great deal of your people. Your mother seems to be a remarkable woman of considerable influence. Too bad she is not a regular member of the church. Our preachers often tell us, and I believe it is true, that people who do so much good out of the church really injure the cause more than anything else."

Dan made no answer to this, but as the Doctor saw his face in the light it wore a mingled expression of astonishment and doubt.

The Elder proceeded. "They used to tell us some great stories about your father too. Big man, isn't he?"

"Yes, sir, fairly good size."

"I remember some of his fights we used to hear about. And there was another member of the family they mentioned a good deal. Dad—Dad—"

"Howitt," said Dan softly.

"That's it, Dad Howitt. A kind of shepherd, wasn't he?"

"A *kind* of shepherd—I think you could say that."

"Discovered the big mine on your father's place. One of your father's fights was about the old man, wasn't it?"

"That's right."

"Ahem—ahem—I judge you take after your father. I don't know just what to think about your whipping that Hardy fellow this morning. Someone had to do something of course, but— ahem, for a minister it was rather unusual. I don't know how the people will take it."

"I'm afraid that I forgot that I was a minister," said Dan uneasily. "I hope you do not think that I did wrong, sir."

"Ahem—ahem, I can't say that it was wrong exactly, but as I said, we don't know how the people will take it. But there's one thing sure," and the Elder's shrill cackle rang out, "it will bring a big crowd to hear you preach! But, well, that's off the subject. Ahem—Brother Matthews, why haven't your people opened that big mine in Dewey Bald?"

"I expect it would be better for me to let my father or mother explain that to you, sir," answered Dan calmly.

"Yes, yes, but it's rather strange, rather unusual you know, to find a young man of your strength and opportunities for wealth entering the ministry. If you would develop that mine, the money from it could educate a great many preachers if it were given to the seminaries."

"Father and Mother have always taught us children that in the battle of life one cannot hire a substitute, that whatever work one volunteers to make his own he must look upon as his ministry to the race. I believe that the church is an institution divinely given to serve the world, and that, more than anything else, it helps men to the highest possible life. I volunteered for the work I have undertaken, because naturally I wish my life to count for the greatest possible good, and because I feel I can serve men better in the church than in any other way."

*Now there is something for Nathan to chew on!* thought the Doctor to himself. As he spoke, the lad's face made his old friend's nerves tingle. His was a new conception of the ministry, new to the Doctor at least. Forgetting his cigar for the moment, he eagerly awaited the Elder's reply.

"Ahem—ahem, you feel then that you have no special Divine call to the work?"

"I have always been taught at home, sir, that every man is divinely called to his work, if that work is for the good of all men. His faithfulness or unfaithfulness to the call is revealed in the *motives* that prompt him to choose his field." He paused a moment and then added slowly—and no one who heard him could doubt his deep conviction—"Yes sir, I feel that I *am* divinely called to preach the Gospel."

"Ahem—ahem, I trust, Brother Matthews, that you are not taken up with these new fads and fancies that are turning the minds of the people from the true worship of God."

"It is my desire, sir, to lead people to the *true* worship of God, which is nothing more, nothing less than obedience *to* God."

The Doctor lit his cigar again.

"I am glad to hear that—" said the Elder, "very glad. I feared from the way you spoke that you might be going astray. There is a great work for you here in Corinth—a great work. Our old brother who preceded you was a good man, sound in the faith in every way, but he didn't seem to take to it somehow. The fact is— ahem—many of our congregation have left to join the other churches."

For another hour or more, Elder Jordan, for the new minister's supposed benefit, discussed in detail the religious history of Corinth, with the past, present, and future of Memorial Church coming in for its full share in the tale, while Charity, drinking in every word of the oft-heard discussion, grew ever more entranced with the possibilities of the new pastor's ministry, and while the Doctor sat alone at the farther end of the porch with his cigar.

The Elder finished at last with: "Well, well, Brother Matthews, you are young, strong, unmarried, and with your reputation as a college man and an athlete, you ought to do great things for Memorial Church. We are counting on you to build up the numbers of our congregation wonderfully. And let me say too, that we are one of the oldest and best known congregations of our denomination in the state. We have had some great preachers here. You can make a reputation that will put you to the top of your—ah, your calling."

Dan was just saying, "I hope I will please you, sir," when the women appeared in the doorway. Martha had her bonnet on.

"Come, come, Nathan," said Mrs. Jordan, "you mustn't keep poor Brother Matthews up another minute. He must be nearly worn out with his long journey and all the excitement."

The Doctor thought again of the girl who had made the same journey in the car behind Dan, and who had also shared the excitement. He wondered how the nurse was enjoying her evening and when she would get to bed.

"Yes, yes, you're so right!" exclaimed the Doctor rising to his feet. "We're all such brutes to treat the poor boy so!"

# CHAPTER EIGHT

# DEBORAH AND THE DOCTOR

Nathaniel Jordan's prediction proved true.

In the two days between Dan's arrival and his first Sunday in Corinth, the Ally was actively engaged in making known the identity of the big stranger, who had so deftly punished the man from Windy Cove. Much talk there was too about the young woman who had gone to Denny's assistance, and her name and profession were fully known to everyone by the time Sunday came.

The new minister of the Memorial Church was the sensation of the day. On Sunday morning the building could scarcely hold the crowd, and many of the rival churches were almost deserted. With the people who had attended the fair, the Ally journeyed far into the country. And the roads being good with the promise of a moon to drive home by, the country folk for miles around came to worship God, and incidentally to see the preacher who had fought and vanquished the celebrated Jud Hardy. There were many in attendance that day who had not been inside a church for years. The Ally went also, but then the Ally is a regular attendant at all the services of every church on every Sunday.

Judge Strong, with an expression of pious satisfaction on his hard face, occupied his own particular corner of his favorite pew.

From another vantage point Elder Jordan watched for signs of false doctrine from the young man's lips. Except when her fingers were busy at the organ, Charity never took her adoring eyes from the preacher's face. At the last moment before the beginning of the sermon, Dr. Harry slipped into the seat beside the Doctor in the last row.

Facing this crowd that even in the small town of Corinth represented every class and kind, Dan felt all the various motives that were in the hearts of those staring at him from the congregation: the low curiosity, the craving for sensation, the admiration in some, the suspicion, the true welcome, the antagonism, the spiritual dependence. And the young man from the mountains, who had entered the ministry from the truest motives and with the highest ideals, shrank back and was for a moment afraid.

Dan was, to this church and people, a different breed than they had ever associated with the pulpit before, literally a messenger from another world. It was hardly to be wondered at that many of them thought, *How out of place this big fellow looks in the pulpit.* Many of them felt dimly too, that which the Doctor had always felt, that this man was somehow a revelation of something that might have been, and that ought to be. But no one tried to search out the reason why.

The theme of the new minister's sermon was, "The Faith of the Fathers," and it must have been a good one, because Martha said the next day that it was the finest thing she had ever heard, and she had it figured out somehow that the members of the neighboring churches who happened to be there got some straight gospel for once in their lives. Elder Jordan assured the Doctor in a confidential whisper that it was a splendid effort. And though the Doctor knew Dan was a splendid young man, and though he could tell he had moved the crowd, as far as he could see the sermon wasn't much more than might have been taken from the barrel of any one of the preachers that had served Memorial Church since its beginning, although Dan had certainly added interest and strength to his words by his earnestness and personality.

In the evening, the Doctor slipped away from church as soon as the service was over, leaving Dan with those who always stay until the janitor begins turning out the lights. Martha could walk home with some of the other women, for the Doctor wished to be alone.

Crossing the street to avoid the crowd, he walked slowly along under the big trees, trying to accustom himself to the thought of the boy dressed in the conventional minister's garb, delivering what he had to confess were little more than time-worn conventionalities in a manner equally conventional. He had hoped his young friend would not be swallowed by the church and its ways and methods and religious traditions. But now here he was preaching in the way all preachers preached, using the same mannerisms, the same orthodox jargon. It was by this strange thinking the old man imagined it was almost as if he had seen Dan behind the grated doors of a prison cell.

Very slowly he went along, unmindful of anything but the thoughts that troubled him. At last he came to the Widow Mulhall's little cottage, where Denny and his mother were sitting on the porch. Across the street in front of his own home, Martha and her friends were engaged in an animated conversation.

The Doctor paused.

"Come in, come in, Doctor," called out Mrs. Mulhall's cheery voice. "It's a fine evenin' and only beginnin'. I was just tellin' Denny 'tis a shame folks have to waste such nights in sleep. Come right in, I'll fetch another chair—take the big rocker there, Doctor, that's right."

The Doctor did as she indicated, and took a seat. He asked how Denny was.

"Oh, the boy is all right again just as you said. Why the minister had him out in the garden that same afternoon. 'Twas the blessing of God, though, that his Reverence was there to keep that devil from beatin' the poor lad to death. I hope you'll not be forgettin' the way to our gate now, Doctor, that you'll be crossin' the street so often to the house beyond the garden there to visit your friend."

In the widow's voice there was a hint of her Irish ancestry, as, in her kind blue eyes, buxom figure, and cordial manner, there was more than a hint of her warmhearted, whole-souled nature.

"I'll try to make sure I walk equally both ways," laughed the Doctor. "And how do you like your new neighbor, Deborah?"

"It's a fine big man he is, Doctor, danged fine man inside an' out. Denny and me are almighty proud, havin' him so close. He's right sociable too, not at all like a priest. It's every blessed day since he's been here he's comin' over to Denny in the garden, and helpin' him with the things, talkin' away all the time. 'Tis the very exercise I need,' says he. 'And it's real kind of you to let me work in the garden a bit now and then,' says he. But anyone can see it's just the big heart of him, wishin' to help the boy. But it's queer notioned he is for a preacher."

"Didn't I see you and Denny at church this evening?" asked the Doctor.

"You did that, sir. You see, not having a Catholic church of our own within reach of our legs, an' wantin' real bad to hear a bit of a prayer and a sermon-like, Denny an' me slips into the protestant meetings now and then. After all, there's no real harm in it now, do you think, Doctor?"

"Harm to you and Denny, or to the church?" the Doctor asked.

"Aw, go on now, Doctor, you're always havin' your joke," she laughed. "Harm to neither or both or all! But I guess that while Denny and me are sayin' our prayers in our little cabin on this side of the street, and you are sayin' yours in your fine house across the way, 'tis the same blessed Father of us all gets to hear them both. I don't imagine God had much to do with layin' out the streets of Corinth anyhow. I've heard how 'twas the old Judge Strong did that."

"And what did you think of Mr. Matthews' sermon?"

"It's ashamed I am to say it Doctor, but I never heard him."

"Never heard him? But I thought you were there."

"An' we was, sir, so we was. An' Denny here can tell you the whole thing. But for myself I never heard a blessed word, after the singin' and the preacher stood up."

"Why, what was the matter?"

"The preacher himself."

"The preacher?"

"Yes, sir. Upon my soul, Doctor, I couldn't hear what he was sayin' for lookin' at the man himself. With him standin' up there so big an' strong an'—an' clean-like through an' through, an' the look on his face! It set me to thinkin' of all that I used to dream for—for my Denny here. You mind what a fine lookin' man my poor Jack was, sir, and how Denny here, from a baby, was the very image of him. I always knowed he was goin' to grow up another Jack for strength an' looks. And you know yourself how our hearts was set on havin' him be a priest, him havin' such a turn that way, bein' crazy on books and studyin' and the like—an' now—now here we are. My man gone, an' my boy just able to drag his poor broken body around, an' not able to do nothin' but dig in the dirt. No, sir, I couldn't hear the sermon for lookin' at the preacher an' thinkin'."

Denny moved his twisted body uneasily. "Let's don't be spoilin' the fine night for the Doctor with our troubles, Mother," he said.

"You're right, Denny. Indeed we will not! Don't you think Denny's garden's been doin' fine this summer, Doctor?"

"Fine," agreed the Doctor heartily. "But then it always does well. There's a lot of us would like to know how he does it."

Denny gave a pleased laugh.

"You're just flattering me, Doctor," he said. "But they've all been doing especially well this year, I think."

"I tell you what it is, Doctor," said the mother. "The boy naturally just loves them things into growin'. If folks would take as good care of their children as Denny does for his cabbage an' other vegetables, it would be a blessin' to the world."

"Those things out there seem just like people to me, Doctor," put in Denny. "I tell Mother it ain't so bad after all, not bein' a priest. The minister was sayin' yesterday that the people needed more than their souls looked after. If I can't be tellin' people how to live, I can be growin' good things to keep them alive, and maybe that's not so bad as it might be."

"I don't know what we'd be doin' at all, if it weren't for that garden," added Deborah, "with clothes an' wood an' groceries to buy, to say nothin' of the interest on the place that's always comin' due. We—"

"Shhh," said Denny in a low tone as a light flashed up in the corner window of the house on the other side of the garden. "There's the minister come home."

Reverently they watched the light and the moving shadow in the room. The moon, through the branches of the trees along the street, threw waving patches of soft light over the dark green of the little lawn. Martha's friends had moved on, and Martha herself had gone in. The street seemed deserted and very still.

Leaning forward in her chair Deborah spoke in a whisper. "We can always tell when he's in of nights, an' when he goes to bed. You see it's almost like we was livin' in the same house with him. An' it's a great comfort to us too, with him such a good man, an' our havin' him so near. Poor boy, I'll warrant he's tired tonight. But it must be a grand thing to be doin' such holy work, an' livin' with God Almighty like, with nothin' to think of all the time but the Blessed Jesus an' the Holy Mother, an' all the people so respectful, an' lookin' up to you. Sure is a grand thing, Doctor, to be a priest, savin' your presence, sir, for I know how you've little use for churches, though the lady your wife does enough for two."

The Doctor rose to go, for he saw that it was late.

As he stood on the steps to say his good-night, Denny interrupted, pointing toward a woman who was crossing to the other side of the street. She walked slowly, and, reaching the sidewalk in front of the Doctor's house, hesitated in a troubled and undecided way. Approaching the gate, she paused, then drew back and moved on slowly up the street. Her movements and manner gave the impression that she was in trouble, perhaps in pain.

"There's something wrong there," said the Doctor. "Can you see who it is, Denny?"

"Yes, sir," he answered.

Then his mother broke in. "It's that poor girl—of—of Jim Conner's, sir."

The Doctor made no reply, but rather felt a little nervous with the situation. For it was Jim Conner who had killed Deborah's husband.

"Poor thing," murmured Mrs. Mulhall. "For the love of God, look at that now, Doctor!"

The girl had reached the corner and had fallen in a crouching heap against the foot of the monument.

The widow was already starting for the street, but Denny caught her by the arm. "No, mother," he said, "you mustn't! You know she's scared to death of you. Let the Doctor go."

The physician was already on his way as fast as his old legs would take him.

# CHAPTER NINE

# THE WORK OF THE ALLY

Every place has its own Grace Conner. She is a type common to every village, town, and city in the land, the saddest of all sad creatures—a good girl with a bad reputation.

Her reputation Grace owed first to her father's sinful ways and misdeeds, for which she could in no way be blamed. But secondly she owed it to the all-powerful Ally, without whom the making of any reputation, good or bad, is impossible.

Doctor Oldham knew the girl well. She had been at their house frequently as a youngster when she had been a member of Martha's Sunday school class. Later she had herself become a member of the church and a Sunday school teacher and active worker and participant in many church functions.

But then came her father's crime against Jack Mulhall, followed by his arrest and conviction. Shortly thereafter the mother died, and, with her father in jail, Grace was left to shift for herself. Since that time she had kept herself alive by working here and there, in the canning factory and restaurants, and wherever she could. But no one would now, because she was associated with her father, a murderer, give her a permanent place in a home.

Imitating their elders, the young people in the church shunned her. It was not considered good policy to permit her to continue teaching in the Sunday school, and she was relieved of her duties. No mother wanted her child to associate with a criminal's daughter. Other activities and committees of which she had been a faithful part now took to being rescheduled without her awareness, and when her face did appear within the hallowed walls, it was to be greeted with vacant stares where before had been cordiality. It was clear enough to Grace that her presence was no longer desired. Naturally she drifted away from the regular services in time as well, and soon it was publicly announced that her name had been dropped from the roll of membership. After that she never came.

It did not take long for the girl to begin to be "talked about," for the Ally makes sure that tongues in places like the Strong Memorial Church are constantly about his work. And thus before many more months were out, the girl had such a name and reputation—most of it having little or nothing to do with her real character—that no self-respecting man or woman dared be caught giving her so much as a nod when they met her on the street.

The people always spoke of her as "that Grace Conner."

Hurt so often, and hurt deepest by the most religious in the town, Grace grew to fear everyone. She tried to avoid people on the street, or if she did meet them, she passed with downcast eyes, not daring to attempt to greet them. She was barely able to earn enough bread to keep life within her poor body, her clothing grew shabby, and her form thin and worn. These very evidences of her goodness of character worked to accomplish her ruin. But she remained pure through it all.

She was cowering at the foot of the monument, her face buried in her hands, when the Doctor touched her on the shoulder. She started and turned up to him the saddest face the old physician had ever seen.

"What's the matter, my girl?" he said as kindly as he could.

She shook her head and buried her face in her hands again. "Please go away and let me alone," she said.

"Come, come," said the Doctor, laying his hand on her shoulder again. "This won't do. You must tell me what's wrong. You can't stay out here on the street at this time of night."

At his tone she raised her head again. "This time of the night!" she laughed pitifully. "What difference does it make to anyone whether I am on the street or not?"

"It makes a big difference to you, my girl," the Doctor answered. "You should be at home and in bed."

"Home! In bed!" She laughed out again, but it was an empty, hollow sound, with no laughter in it.

"Stand up and tell me what's the matter," said the physician sharply, for he saw he must be firm or she would soon be over the line where he could help her no more.

She rose to her feet with his help.

"Are you sick?" he asked.

"No, sir."

"Well, what have you been doing?"

"Nothing, Doctor. I—I was just walking around."

"Why don't you go back to the hotel? You are still working there, aren't you?"

She wrung her hands and looked about, but answered nothing.

"See here, Grace," said the physician, "you know me, surely— old Doctor Oldham. Can't you tell me what's wrong?"

Still she said nothing.

"Come, let me take you to the hotel," he urged. "It's only a few blocks."

"No—no," she cried out. "I can't go there! I don't live there anymore."

"Well, where do you live now?" he asked.

"In Old Town."

"But why did you leave your place at the hotel?"

"A—a man there said some things about me, and then the proprietor told me that I must go, because some of the people were talking about me, and I was giving the hotel a bad name."

"That's pure rubbish!" said the Doctor angrily.

"Oh, Doctor, I'm not a bad girl. I haven't ever been! But they're driving me to it. That or—or—" she hesitated.

The Doctor knew what she said was true. What could he say to comfort her?

"It's the same everywhere I try to work," she continued in a hopeless tone. "At the canning factory the other girls said their folks wouldn't let them work there if I didn't go. I haven't been able to earn a cent since I left the Hotel. I don't know what to do!" She broke down crying.

"Why didn't you come to me?" the Doctor asked. "You knew you could come to me. Didn't I ask you to?"

"I—I was afraid. I'm afraid of everybody." She shivered and looked over her shoulder.

"Come with me," he said. "You must have something to eat."

He started to lead her across the street toward Mrs. Mulhall, whom he could see at the gate watching them. But the girl hung back.

"No, no," she panted in her excitement. "Not there. I dare not go there! That woman hates me, don't you know."

The Doctor hesitated. "Well, come to my house then," he said.

The girl followed him as far as the gate, then stopped again, as if just recalling something.

"Oh no, Doctor," she said, "I can't go with you—Mrs. Oldham—she's in the church—and those folks—"

*The girl was right*, the Doctor thought to himself. He was never so ashamed in all his life. He thought for a moment, then said with decision: "Look here, Grace, you sit down on the porch for a few minutes. Martha is in bed and fast asleep long ago. Don't you worry about a thing."

He stole away as quietly as possible, and in a little while returned with a basket full of what provisions he could find in the pantry. He chuckled to himself as he thought of Martha when she discovered the theft in the morning, yet muttered half aloud his frustration at the thing that made it necessary for him to steal from his own pantry for the girl whom he would gladly have taken into his own home if only he could.

He made her eat some of the cold chicken and bread and drink a glass of milk. When she was feeling better, he walked with her down the street a little way to be sure she was all right.

"I can't thank you enough, Doctor," she said. "You have saved me from I don't know what."

"Go on home now, Grace," he said, "and mind you look carefully in the bottom of that basket."

He had put a little bill there, the only money he had in the house. "This will help you until times are better, and promise me that if you run against it again, you'll come to me or go to Dr. Harry at the office and tell him that you want me."

She nodded. He watched her down the street, then went home, stopping for a word of explanation to Deborah and Denny, who were waiting at the gate.

The light was still burning in Dan's window when the Doctor again entered his own yard. He thought for a moment of dropping in on the minister for just a short visit, but then remembered that "the boy would be tired after his great effort defending the faith of Memorial Church." With the sarcastic phrase still running through his mind, the Doctor took a walk down the block and then back to his house instead.

He told himself he was an old fool to be prowling about so late at night, and that he would hear about it from Martha tomorrow. Then, as he climbed into bed, he chuckled again, thinking of the empty kitchen pantry and the missing basket.

The light in Dan's room went out a little while later.

A few persons were still out in Corinth, but not many. Some belated souls, going home for the night. A man and a woman, walking close together talking in low tones, strolled slowly by in the shadow of the big trees. The quick step of a horse and the sound of buggy-wheels could be heard a street or two away, coming swiftly nearer and nearer, then they passed and died away in the stillness. It was Dr. Harry answering a call.

In Judge Strong's big brown house down the street, a nurse in her uniform of blue and white, by the dim light of a night-lamp, leaned over her patient with a glass of water.

In Old Town a young woman in shabby dress, with a basket on her arm, hurried—trembling and seemingly afraid—across the lonely, grass-grown square.

Under the quiet stars in the soft moonlight, the cast-iron monument stood—grim and cold and sinister. In the peace and quiet of the night, Denny's garden wrought its mystery. And in the little room that looked out upon the monument and the garden, Dan Matthews—all unknowing of the subtle currents which rippled under the surface of this town and his church—slept.

And over all brooded the spirit that lives in Corinth, and all such communities, and gains its sustenance from the self-righteous traditions of its elders—the Ally—that dread, mysterious thing that never sleeps.

# CHAPTER TEN

# THE EDGE OF THE BATTLEFIELD

Dan was trying to prepare his evening sermon for the third Sunday of what his old friend the Doctor called his Corinthian ministry.

The afternoon was half gone when he rose from his study table. He had been at it all day, and all day the devils of dissatisfaction had rioted in his soul—or wherever it is that such devils are supposed to riot. Suffice it to say he could not fix his thoughts to his satisfaction onto the paper in front of him.

The three weeks had not been idle ones for young Dan Matthews.

He had made many pastoral calls at the homes of his congregation. He had attended committee meetings beyond number. Already he was beginning to feel the tug of his people's need—the world-old need of sympathy and inspiration, of help and spiritual nourishment, of courage and cheer; the need of the soldier for the battle-cry of his comrades, the need of the striving runner for the lusty shout of his friends, the need of the toiling servant for the "well-done" of his master.

Keenly sensitive to this great unvoiced cry of life, the young man answered in his heart, "Here am I, use me." Standing before his people he felt as one who, on the edge of a battlefield, longs to throw himself into the fight with all his heart. But it was as if his superior officers had ordered him to mark time, while his whole soul was eager for the command to charge.

"Why do people go to church?" he asked himself. What do men ask of their religion? Is it life changing? Or is their church life no different than if they belonged to a large social club? Are they looking out for the good of their neighbor, or rather seeking to bolster their own prestige and influence? And what have they the right to expect from their leaders, men such as he himself, who assume to lead them in their worship and direct their spiritual growth?

Already, in just three weeks as the minister of Corinth's Memorial Church, many questions like these were being shouted at him from the innermost depth of his consciousness. He felt he knew the answer to the latter question that his Master would give. He knew what manner of man should be ministering to the lost and struggling and poor and searching—nothing more than a man being formed into the image of Jesus.

But always between himself and those to whom he would give his life in ministry, those to whom he found himself wanting to speak when he took the pulpit, came the thought of his employers. And he found himself, while speaking to the people, nervously watching the faces of the Elders and their colleagues by whose permission he spoke.

So it came on this particular day that he was not satisfied with his work that afternoon, and he tossed aside his sermon to leave his study for the fresh air and sunshine of the open fields. From his roses the Doctor hailed him with a wave as he went down the street, but the boy did not stop, only answering with another wave of his hand. On this day Dan did not need the Doctor. He needed to be alone with his thoughts, and to pray.

Straight out into the country he went, walking fast, down one hill—up another, across a creek, over fences, through a pasture and into the woods. After an hour, at a pace hard enough to bring a sweat and tax his lungs, he felt better. The old familiar voices of hill and field and forest and stream soothed and calmed him. The physical exercise satisfied to some extent his instinct and passion for action.

Coming back through Old Town, and leisurely climbing the hill on the road that leads past the old school building now in disuse, known as the old Academy, he paused frequently to look back over the ever widening view of the countryside behind him, and to drink of the pure sun-filled air. At the top of the hill, reluctant to go back to the town that lay in front of him, he stood contemplating the ancient school building that held so bravely its commanding position at the edge of town, and yet looked so pitiful in its shabby old age. Then passing through a gap in the tumbled-down fence, and crossing the weed-filled yard, he entered the building.

For a while he wandered curiously about the time-worn rooms, reading the names scratched on the plaster walls, cut in the desks and seats, on the window casings, and on the big square posts that, in the lower rooms, supported the ceiling. He laughed to himself, as he noticed how the sides of these posts facing away from the raised platform at the end of the room were most elaborately carved. It suggested so vividly the life that had once stirred within the old walls.

Several of the names were already familiar to him. He tried to imagine the venerable heads of families he knew, as they might have been in the days when they sat upon these worn benches. Did Judge Strong or Elder Jordan, perhaps, throw one of those spit-balls that stuck so hard and fast to the ceiling? And did some of the grandmothers he had met giggle and hide their faces at Nathaniel's cunning evasion of the teacher's quick effort to locate the successful marksman? Had those staid pillars of the church ever been swayed and bent by passions of young manhood and womanhood? Had their minds ever been stirred by the questions and doubts of youth? Had their hearts ever throbbed with eager longing to know—to feel life in its fullness?

Dan seated himself at one of the battered desks and tried to bring back the days that were gone, and to see about him the faces of those who once had filled the room with the strength and gladness of their youth. He felt strangely old in thus trying to feel like a boy among those boys and girls of the days long gone.

If he was a boy again, back then, who among the lads of this classroom would be his best friend? Elder Jordan? He smiled. And who (the blood mounted to his cheek at the thought), who among the girls would be she whose face he would watch when she wasn't looking? Out of the mists of his revery came a face—a face that was strangely often in his mind since the first day he had arrived in Corinth. Several times he had caught passing glimpses of her. Once he had met her on the street and had nodded. And Dr. Harry, with whom he had already begun a deepening friendship, had told him much to add to his interest in her.

But for her to come into his mind in this dreamy sort of way—"What nonsense!" he said to himself, rising from the seat.

He strode to the window to clear his mind. But almost the next moment he drew back with a start. A young woman in the uniform of a trained nurse was entering the schoolyard below him.

# CHAPTER ELEVEN

# AN UNEXPECTED ASSAULT

Hope Farwell had heard a great deal about the new pastor of the Memorial Church.

Dr. Harry frequently urged her to attend services. Mrs. Mulhall, with whom she had become acquainted, was eloquent in Dan's praise. Mrs. Strong and the ladies who called at the house spoke of him often.

But for the first two weeks of her stay at Judge Strong's, the nurse had been confined so closely to the care of her patient that she had heard nothing to identify the preacher with the big stranger whom she had met at the depot the day of her arrival. By the time Miss Farwell began hearing of the new preacher, the interest brought about by his defense of Denny had already died down, and it chanced that no one mentioned the events of Fair day in her presence when speaking of him, while each time he had called at the Strong home the nurse had been either absent or busy.

Thus it was that so far as Miss Farwell herself knew she had never met the minister she had heard so much about. But she had several times seen the big fellow who had apologized at such length for running into her at the depot, and who had a short time later gone so quickly to the assistance of Denny. And indeed, how could she forget *him*, after what happened on the street. Yet it was quite natural that she never dreamed of connecting the young hero of the street fight with the Reverend Matthews of the Memorial Church.

Her patient had so far improved that the nurse was now able to leave for an hour or two most afternoons, and the young woman had taken the opportunity on this bright day to go for a walk just beyond the outskirts of town. Coming to the top of the hill she had turned aside from the dusty road, hoping to enjoy the view from the shade of a great oak tree that grew on a grassy knoll in the center of the school grounds.

Dan watched her as she made her way slowly across the yard, his eyes bright with admiration for her womanly grace as she stopped, here and there, to pick a wild flower from the tangle of grass and weeds. Reaching the tree, she seated herself, laid her parasol on the grass by her side, and began arranging the blossoms of the flowers she had gathered—pausing now and then to look over the rolling country of field and wood that, dotted by farm houses with their buildings and stacks, stretched away into the blue distance.

The young fellow at the window gazed at her almost dreamily. His blood tingled at the odd premonition that this woman was somehow to play a great part in his life. Nothing could have seemed more natural than that he should have come to this very spot this afternoon, as should she. He knew that he ought not to be thus secretly watching her. Therefore, he turned and left the building.

She started when he appeared a few moments later in the doorway of the old school, and half-arose from where she sat. Then recognizing him, she dropped back on the grass. There was a half-amused frown on her face, though her cheeks were red. She was indignant with herself that she should be blushing like a schoolgirl at the presence of this stranger whose name she did not even know.

"I beg your pardon, Miss Farwell," said Dan, already so ac-customed to being greeted by strangers that it never occurred to him that this lady did not know who he was, "I fear that I startled you."

She saw the sunlight on his shaggy, red-brown hair, and the fine poise of his well-shaped head, as she answered a bit shortly, "Yes, you did."

Woman-like she was making him feel her anger at herself. And also woman-like, when she saw his embarrassment at her blunt words and manner, she smiled.

"I am sorry," he said, but did not offer to go on his way, but remained standing where he was.

When she made no reply, but began rearranging her handful of blossoms, he spoke again, remarking on the beauty of the view before them, and ventured to ask if this knoll was a particular favorite spot of hers, adding that it was his first visit to the place.

"I have never been here before either," she answered.

The brief silence that followed was broken by Dan. "We seem to have made a discovery," he said. As she did not seem inclined to drive him away, or to go herself, Dan dropped to the grass nearby with an exclamation of satisfaction and pleasure.

Looking away over the landscape where the clouds and shadows were racing, and the warm autumn light lay on the varying shades of green and brown, he remarked, "When I see a scene such as that, on a day as bright and fragrant as this, or when I am out in the woods or up in the hills, I find myself wondering what men build churches for anyway. I fear I must be something of a pagan, for I often feel that I can worship God in his own temple far better than I can in those made by men." He laughed, but under the laugh there was a faint note of troubled seriousness.

She looked at him curiously. "You consider it heathenish to worship God outside a church? If it is, I fear that I too am a heathen."

He noted the words "I too," and realized instantly that she did not know who he was, but had understood from his words that he was not a church man. He felt he ought to correct her false impression, that he ought to tell her who and what he was, but he felt curiously reluctant to declare his calling.

The truth was, Dan Matthews did not want to meet this woman as a minister or a priest, but rather as a man. He had already learned how the moment the preacher was announced, the *man* was pushed to the background.

While he hesitated, she watched him with increasing interest. His words had pleased her. Now she waited for him to speak again.

"I suppose your profession does keep you from anything like regular church attendance," he said.

"Yes," she answered. "I have found that sick people do not as a rule observe a one-day-in-seven kind of religion. If they are spiritually inclined at all, they tend to attempt the practice of their faith on a more daily basis than that—not an unhealthy way to practice it in my opinion. But it is not my professional duties that keep me from church."

"You do not consider yourself a Christian then?"

"I did not say that."

"You said you were a heathen."

"Only *if* it is heathenish to worship God outside a church."

"We are back then to the matter of church. So you do not attend?"

"Decidedly not," she answered.

"I must admit to some surprise."

"Why is that?"

"I merely thought, of course, that you would be a member of some church."

"You thought *of course*." There was a touch of impatience in her quick reply. "And why *of course*, please?"

He started to answer, but she went on quickly. "I know why," she said. "It is because I am a woman, the weaker, one not supposed to be able to think freely about such things on my own, is that it?"

As she spoke the words, her voice contained none of the coarseness that commonly marks expressions of this kind. Dan was surprised to feel that her very passion when speaking emphasized the fineness of her character, as well as its strength.

"Because I am not a man, must I be useless?" she continued. "Is a woman's life of so little influence in the world that she should spend it in make-believe living as little girls play at being grown up, that I should have no right to think about and try to judge between truth and falsehood, and that I should not try to order my life by what I believe, that I should go along with everything that is commonly taught without trying to weigh the evidence for myself? Have I not as great a right to my paganism, as you would have my worship of God *outside* the church, as you have to yours?"

Again he saw his opportunity to say who he was, and realized that he ought to correct her mistake in assuming from his words that he was not a man of church affiliation. But again he passed it by, saying slowly instead: "I think your kind of 'paganism' must be a very splendid thing. No one could think of one dressed as you are, dedicated to helping the sick, as useless."

"I did not mean—"

"I understand I think," he said earnestly. "But won't you tell me why you feel as you do about the church?"

She laughed. "One would think from your awful seriousness that you were a preacher!" she returned. "Father Confessor, if you please—" she began mockingly, then stopped, arrested by the expression on Dan's face.

"Oh, I beg your pardon," she said. "Have I been rude? I meant no disrespect."

With a forced laugh he answered, "Oh no, indeed, not at all. It is only that your views of the Christian religion surprise me."

"My views of the Christian religion?" she repeated, very serious now. "I did not know that my views of Christianity had ever been mentioned."

Dan was bewildered. "But the church! You were speaking of the church as if you had no use for it whatever."

"And the church and Christianity are one and the same, is that it?" Again with a touch of sarcasm, more pronounced, "You will tell me next, I suppose, that most so-called 'ministers' truly *minister* to those whom they have been given—minister to their deepest needs, I mean. Aren't they really more like the directors of large social clubs, whose duty it is to preside over numberless activities?"

Dan was astonished and hurt. Such words as these were to his ears not only confusing, but amounted to little less than sacrilege.

He was shocked that they should come from one whose personality and evident character had impressed him so strongly. His voice was doubtful and perplexed as he said, "But is not the true church of Christ, which is composed of his true disciples, is not that Christian? Surely they can no more be separated than the sun can be separated from the sunshine. How can you talk of the church and Christianity as if they were not the same? And is not the ministry a vital part of that church?"

Seeing him so troubled, Miss Farwell wondered whether she understood him. She felt that she was talking too freely to this stranger, but his questions drew her on, and she was curiously anxious that he should understand her.

"I was not thinking of that *true* church, composed of the *true* disciples of Christ," she returned. "And that is just it, don't you see? It all depends on what 'church' you are talking about—the church of God, the *true* church, or the churches built by men. When I said what I did about the church, I was talking about the churches of men—the buildings, the clubs, the committees, the cliques, the politicking networks, the machinations—not the church of God made up by the uniting of the hearts of his people everywhere. The *true* church of God, that is so inseparable from the religion of Christ, is so far forgotten that it never enters into any thought of the churches of men at all. The sun always shines, it is true, but we do not always have the sunshine. There are dark and stormy days, you know, and sometimes there is an eclipse. To me these present days are the dark days, dark in the life of the *true* church, so dark that I wonder if it is not an eclipse, so dark that I wonder how much longer it will be before the sun of the *true* church begins to shine out again."

She paused, then added deliberately, "This selfish, wasteful, cruel, heartless thing that men have built up around their opinions, their whims, their ambitions, their greed, their self-righteousness, their doctrines—this huge empty structure they have built upon such flimsy pillars and which they wrongly call 'the church' has so come between the people and the true Christianity Christ brought to the earth, that men and women the world over now question whether indeed there is anywhere such a thing as a God or a true church at all."

Again Dan was silenced by her bold words, and by her passionate earnestness. He was all the more unsettled in that her manner did not convey the emotions of the usual religiously opinionated person mounting his high horse to wax eloquent on his favorite doctrinal theory. Rather her voice contained a certain note of sadness. It was as if she spoke to him professionally of the sickness of someone dear to her, and sought to keep her love for her patient from influencing her calm consideration of the case.

Such words and notions were entirely new to Dan. He had learned his Christianity in his backwoods home, from his mother Sammy and his father, and the man known to the region as the Shepherd of the Hills. But he had grown up knowing nothing of churches. He had been raised to believe and to practice that belief in the manner of his life. But he had never attended a church regularly as a youngster or a young man. He did not know of the Ally. All he knew of what he called "the church" was what the seminary had taught him. He accepted the denomination to which he belonged at its own valuation, highly colored by its own biased historians and interpreters. Its traditions he assumed were rooted in Christ. For those teaching him possessed not the slightest idea that they were in truth sending out to preside over their network of church-houses men who would soon be drawn into the webs spun by the religious spiders whose traditions were rather the offspring of the Pharisees.

Dan's next words were forced from him almost against his will. And his eyes had that wide questioning look so like that of his mother. "And the ministry?" he said.

"You ask if the ministry is not a vital part of the church, and your very question expresses conditions clearly," she answered. "What conception of Christianity is it that makes it possible for us to even think of the ministry as *part* of the church, or as some *job* within the church that some hold but most do not? The very pretext is false. Why, the true church *is* ministry! There can be no other reason for its existence. But don't you see how we have come to think of the ministry as we have come to think of the church? It has become merely an organizational term, devoid of the intrinsic *life* the word itself contains. It is to us, as you say, a part of this great organization that men have created and control."

Dan caught up a flower she had dropped and began picking it to pieces with trembling fingers.

"To me," he said slowly, "the minister is a servant of God. I believe, of course, that whatever work a man does in life he must do as his service to the race, and in that sense he serves God. But the ministry—" he reached for another flower, choosing his words carefully, "the ministry is, to me, the highest service to which a man may be called."

She did not reply, but looked away over the valley.

"Tell me, is it not so?" he said after a moment.

"If you believe it, then to you it is so," she answered.

"But you—" he urged further, "I want to know how *you* look upon the minister."

"Why should I tell you? What difference does it make what I think?"

"I don't know what difference it will make. But I would like to know."

"You forget that we are strangers." She smiled. "Let us talk about the weather; that's a safe topic."

"I *had* forgotten that we are strangers," he said with an answering smile. "But I am interested in what you have said because you—you have evidently thought a great deal about these things, and your profession must certainly give you opportunities for observation. So tell me, how do you look upon the minister and his work?"

She studied him intently before she answered. Then, as if satisfied with what she found in his face, she said calmly, "To me, the minister is the most useless creature in the world. He is a man set apart from all those who live lives of service, who do the work of the world. And then that he should be distinguished from these world-workers, these servers, by this noblest of all titles, this word that should equate all who bear it with the foot-washing Jesus—*a minister*—is the bitterest irony that the mind of the race has ever conceived."

Dan's face was now white as he answered, "But surely a ministry of the gospel is doing God's will, and is therefore serving God."

She answered, "Man serves God only by serving men. There can be no ministry but the ministry of man to man."

"But the minister is a man."

"The world cannot accept him as such, because his individuality is lost in the church to which he belongs. Other institutions employ a man's time, the church employs his life. He has no existence outside his profession. There is no outside the church for him. He is the representative of a denomination, not a servant of his people. The world cannot know him as a man, for he is all preacher."

"But the church employs him to minister to the world?"

"I cannot see that it does so at all. On the contrary, a church employs a pastor to serve itself. It employs him to be its *head*, so to speak, its leader, its company president. He is a public orator, a functionary, a facilitator of meetings and committees and men's meetings and women's organizations and youth groups. His job is to present a self-satisfied face to the world so that the appearance of the church is respectable. He is not hired to wash the feet of a church's members in *ministry*. To the churches Christianity has become a question of fidelity to a denomination and creed, not to the Spirit of Christ. The minister's standing and success in his calling, even the amount of his salary, depends upon his devotion to the particular views of the church that calls him and his ability to please those who are in power there and who pay him for pleasing them. His service to the world does not enter into the transaction any more than when you buy the latest novel of your favorite author, or purchase a picture that pleases you, or buy a ticket to hear your favorite musician. We do not pretend, when we do these things, that we are ministering to the world, or that we are moved to spend our money in these ways to serve God, even though there may be in the book, the picture, or the music, many things that will make the world better."

Dan moved uneasily.

"But the church is a sacred institution," he said. "You can hardly compare it with the institutions of men. Its purpose is holy, so different from other organizations."

"Which of the hundreds of different sects and denominations with their different creeds and doctrines and ideas do you mean by the church?" she asked. "Or do you mean all of them? And are all equally sacred, with the same holy purpose you speak of? If so, why are they at such variance with each other, and why is there such competition between them? How are these institutions—organized and controlled as they are by men—different from other institutions, organized and controlled by the same men? Surely you are aware that there are thousands of institutions and organizations in the world with aims as distinctly Christian as the professed object of the church. Why are these not as holy and sacred?"

"But the church is of divine origin."

"So is this oak tree. So is the material in that old building. So are those farms out in the valley there. To me it is only the Spirit of God in a thing that can make it holy or sacred. Surely there is as much of God manifest in a field of grain as in any of these churches. Why then is not a cornfield a holy institution, and why isn't the farmer who tends the field a minister of God?"

"So you would then condemn everyone in the church?" he asked, not without some bitterness in his tone. "I cannot think that—I know—" He paused.

"Condemn?" she answered questioningly. "Did I condemn?"

Her deep gray eyes were turned full upon him, and he saw her face grow tender and sad, while the sweet voice trembled with emotion. "Who spoke of condemnation? Are you not unfair? In my—" she spoke the words solemnly, "in my ministry, I have stood at the bedside of too many heroes and heroines not to know that the church is filled with the truest and bravest. And that—don't you see!—that is the awful pity of it all! That those true, brave, noble lives should be the cloud that hides the sun. As for the ministry, one in my profession could scarcely help knowing the grand lives that are hidden in this useless class set apart by the church to push its interests. The ministers are useless only because they are not free. They cannot help themselves. They are slaves, not servants. Their first duty is not service to the soul-sick world that so much needs their ministry but obedience to the whims of this hideous monster that they have created and now must obey or—" She paused.

"Or what?" he asked.

She continued as if she had not heard: "They are valued for their fidelity to other men's standards, never for the worth of their own lives. They are hired to give always the opinions of others, and they are denied the only thing that can make any life of worth—freedom of self-expression. The surest road to failure for them is to hold or express opinions of their own—especially if those opinions chance to cut across the grain of those who hold the reins of power and authority in the church. They are held, not as necessities, but as a luxury, like heaven itself, for which if men have the means to spare, they pay. They can have no real fellowship with the servants of the race, for they are set apart by the church, not *to* a ministry but *from* it. Their very personal influence is less than the influence of other good men because the world accepts it as professional. It is the way they earn their living."

"But do you think that the ministers themselves *wish* to be set apart in this way?" asked Dan. "I—I am sure they must all crave that fellowship with the workers, the common men and women of their town."

"I think that is true in many cases," she answered. "I am sure it is of the many grand, good men in the ministry whom I have known."

"Then you do think there are good men in the ministry?"

"Yes," she answered, "just as there are gold and precious stones ornamenting heathen gods and pagan temples, and their goodness is often just as useless. For whether they wish it or not the facts remain that their masters set them apart and they *are* separated, and I notice that most of them do not mind accepting gracefully the special privileges, and wear the title and all the marks of their calling that emphasize the distinction between them and their fellowmen."

"You wear a distinguishing dress," he said. "I knew *your* calling the first time I saw you."

She laughed merrily.

"What amuses you?" he asked, smiling himself at her merriment.

"Oh, it's so funny to see such a big man so helpless. Really, couldn't you find an argument of more weight? Besides, you didn't know my profession the first time you saw me. I only wear these clothes when I am at work, just as a mechanic wears his overalls—and they are just as necessary, as you know. The first time you—you bumped into me, I was dressed just like other people, and I had paid full fare too. Nurses don't get clergyman's discounts from the railroad."

With this she sprang to her feet. "Look how long the shadows are getting! I must get back to my patient."

As she spoke she was all at once painfully conscious again that this man was a stranger. What must he think of her? How could she explain that it was not her habit to talk so freely to men she did not know? She wished he would tell her his name at least.

Slowly, silently they walked together across the weed-grown yard. As they passed through the gap in the tumbledown fence, Dan turned to look back. It seemed to him ages since he had entered the schoolyard.

"What's the matter, have you lost something?" she asked.

"No. Well—that is . . . perhaps I have," he stammered. "But never mind, it is of no great importance. And anyhow, I could not find it if I looked. I think I will leave you here now," he added. "I'm not going back to town just yet. Goodbye."

Again she wondered why his face was so troubled.

She turned and headed down the street. He watched her go, until her blue dress, with its white trim, became a blur in the shadows. Then he struck out once more for the open country.

# CHAPTER TWELVE

# REFLECTIONS

Since that first chance meeting at the train depot when he had looked into the nurse's eyes and heard her voice only for a moment, Dan had not been able to put the young woman wholly out of his mind.

The incident on the street when she had gone to Denny, and the scene that followed in Denny's home had strengthened the first impression, while the meeting at the old Academy yard had stirred depths in his nature never touched before.

The very things she had said to him were so evidently born out of a nature great in its passion for truth and in its capacity for feeling, that even though her words were biting and stung, he could not but rejoice in the beauty and strength of the spirit they revealed.

The usual trite criticisms of the church Dan had heard, and he had already learned to think somewhat lightly of the kind of people who commonly make them. He could tell that Miss Farwell spoke out of her heart for truth's sake, and did not, like most, criticize for criticism's sake, and merely to build themselves up by tearing down another. This young woman—so wholesome, so good to look at in her sweet seriousness, so strong in her womanliness, so useful in what she called her ministry, so thoughtful, so earnest in desiring right to be done—this woman was, well, she was different.

Her words were all the more potent, coming as they did after the disquieting thoughts and the feelings of dissatisfaction that had driven him from his study that afternoon. The young minister could not at first rid himself of the awful suggestion that there might be a great deal of truth in the things she had said. After all, under the fine words, the platitudes and professions, the fact remained that he *was* earning his daily bread by being obedient to those who hired him. He had already begun to feel that his work was not so much to give what he could to meet the people's need as to do what he could to supply the wants of Memorial Church, and that his very chance to serve depended upon his satisfying these self-constituted judges. He saw, too, that these same judges, his masters, felt the dignity of their position heavily upon them, and would not be in the least hesitant to render their opinions and decisions. They would let him know what things pleased them and what things were not to their liking. Their opinions and commandments would not always be in definite words, perhaps, but they would be nonetheless clearly and forcibly given that they came in more subtle guise.

He had spoken truly when he had told Miss Farwell, as they parted, that he had lost something. And now, as he walked the country road, he sought earnestly to regain it, to find again his certainty of mind, to steady his shaky confidence in the work to which he had given his life.

Dan's character was strong, his conviction too powerful, his purpose too genuine, for him to be easily turned from any determined line of thought or action. Certainly it would require more than the words of a stranger to swing him far from his course, even though he felt that there might be a degree of truth in them.

And so, as he walked, his mind began shaping answers to the nurse's points, and gradually, out of the material of his school experience built upon the solid foundation of his upbringing, he attempted to build back again the old bulwark, behind which he would be able to laugh at his utter confusion of mind of the hour before.

But throughout this process Dan's admiration of the young woman's mind and character was not lessened. More than that, he felt that she had in some way given him a deeper view into her own life and thoughts than was due a mere stranger. He was conscious too of a sense of shame that he had, in a way, accepted her confidence under false pretense. He had let her believe he was not what he was. But, he argued with himself, he had not intentionally deceived her. And he smiled at last to think how she would enjoy the situation with him when she learned the truth.

How different she was from any of the women he had known in the church! They mostly accepted their religious views as they would take a doctor's prescription—without question.

And how like she was to his mother!

Then came the inevitable thought—what a triumph it would be if he could win such a character to the church. What an opportunity!

With that, already slipping off the high ground to which her probing questions had pointed him, the pastor again assumed the forefront and he began putting his thoughts in shape for a sermon on the ministry. Determined to make it the effort of his life, he planned how he would announce it next Sunday for the following week, and how, with Dr. Harry's assistance, he would perhaps secure her attendance at the service.

Meanwhile, Hope Farwell walked quickly along the street on her way home from her conversation under the old Academy oak tree. And as she went she was beset by many varied and conflicting emotions.

Recalling her conversation with the man who was to her so nearly a total stranger, she felt that she had been too earnest, too frank. It troubled her to realize how bare she had laid her deepest feelings. She could not understand how she had so completely forgotten her usual reserve. There was something in that young man, so tall and strong and lean-looking, that had called from her, in spite of herself, this exposition of her innermost life and thoughts.

It was as though she had flung wide open the door to that

sacred, inner chamber at which only the most intimate of her friends were privileged to knock. He had come into the field of her life in the most commonplace manner through the natural incident of their meeting. One would have thought the hour following such a meeting would be followed by conversation on such trivial and commonplace topics as usually occupy strangers upon such occasions, and that they would have parted strangers still.

But she felt that after this exhibition of herself, as she termed it in her mind, she at least was no stranger to him. And she was angry with herself, and ashamed, when she reflected at how deeply into her life she had allowed him to enter. Angry with him too, in a way, that he had gained this admittance with apparently no effort.

She reflected, too, that while she had so freely opened the door to him, and had admitted him with a confidence utterly inexcusable, he had in no way returned that confidence. She searched her memory for some word—some expression of his—that would even hint at what he thought, or believed, or was within himself, something that would justify her in feeling that she knew him even a little. But there was nothing. It was as though this stranger, whom she had admitted into the privacy of the inner chamber, had worn a mask and gown as he entered. No self-betraying expression had escaped him. He had not even told her his name. While she had laid out for his inspection the strongest passions of her life, had felt herself urged to show him all and had kept nothing hidden, he had looked and then gone away making no comment.

"Of course," she thought, "he is a gentleman, and he is cultured and refined, and a good man too." Of this much she was sure, but that was next to nothing. One does not talk as she had talked to a man just because he is not a ruffian or a boor. She wanted to know him as she had made herself known to him. She could not say why.

It had been three weeks since she had come to Corinth. The Judge's sister-in-law was improving rapidly, and her work was in all likelihood nearly finished. She would probably never meet the man again. What did it matter?

And yet somehow it *did*, somehow, seem to matter.

Of one thing she was sure—the man was well worth knowing. She had felt that there was a depth, a richness, a genuineness to him, and it was this feeling, this certainty of him, that had led her to such openness. Yes—she was sure there were treasures there— deep within, for those whom he chose to admit. She wished— why should she not confess it?—she wished that she might one day be thus admitted.

Hope Farwell was alone in the world, with not a single near living relative. She had only her friends, and friends to her meant more than to those who have others deared to them by ties of blood.

# CHAPTER THIRTEEN

# AN INVITATION

That same evening when Dr. Harry was leaving the Strong house after his visit to his patient, the nurse went with him to the door, as usual, for any word of instruction he might wish to give her privately.

"Well, Miss Hope," he said, "you've done it."

"What have I done?" she asked.

"Saved my patient in there. She would have gone without a doubt if you had not come when you did. It's your case all right."

"Then I'm glad I came," she said quietly. "And I may go back soon, may I not, Doctor?"

He hesitated as he slowly drew on his gloves.

"Must you return to Chicago, Miss Farwell? I—that is, we need you so much here in Corinth. There are so many cases, you know, where everything depends upon the nurse. There is not a trained nurse this side of St. Louis. I am sure I could keep you busy." There was something more than professional interest in the keen eyes that looked so intently into her own.

"Thank you, Doctor. You are very kind. But you know Dr. Miles expects me back. He warned me the last thing before I left that he was only lending me to you for this particular case. You know how he says those things."

"Yes," said the man grimly, "I know Miles. It is one of the secrets of his success, that he will be satisfied with nothing but the best. He warned me too."

He watched her keenly. *It would be just like Miles,* he thought, *to tell the young woman of the particular nature of the warning.* But Miss Farwell betrayed no embarrassing knowledge, and the doctor said, "You did not *promise* to return to Chicago did you?"

She answered slowly, "No, but he expects me, and I had no thought of staying beyond this one case."

"Well, won't you at least give the matter some serious thought? There are many nurses in Chicago. I don't mean many like you—" he added, interrupting himself hastily, "but here there is no one at all," and in his low-spoken words there was a note of interest more than professional.

She lifted her face frankly and let him look deep into her eyes as she answered, "I appreciate your argument, Dr. Abbott, and— I will think about it."

He turned his eyes away, and his tone was quite professional as he said heartily, "Thank you, Miss Farwell. I shall not give up hoping that we may somehow contrive to keep you. Good night!"

"Isn't he a dear, good man?" exclaimed the invalid, as the nurse reentered the sick room.

"Yes," she answered, "he is a good man, one of the best I think I have ever known."

The patient continued eagerly, "He told me the ladies could come here for their Aid Society meeting next week, if you would stay to take care of me. You will, won't you, dear?"

The nurse, busy with the medicine the doctor had left, did not answer at once.

"I would like it so much," came the voice from the bed.

Hope turned and went quickly to the bedside. "Of course I will stay if you wish it. I believe the meeting will do you good."

"Oh thank you, and you'll get to meet the new minister then for sure. Just to think you have never seen him, and he has called several times, but you have always happened to be out."

"Yes, I have managed to miss him every time," said Miss Farwell.

Something in the voice, always so kind and gentle, caused the sick woman to turn her head on the pillow and look at her nurse intently.

"And you haven't been to church since you have been here either."

"Oh, but you know I am like your good Doctor Abbott in that, and I can plead professional duties."

"Dr. Harry is always there when he can possibly go. Do you mind, dearie, if I ask you whether you are a Christian or not? I told Sapphira this afternoon that I knew you were."

"Yes," said Hope, "you are right. I cannot often go to church, but—" and there was a ring of seriousness in her voice now, "I am a Christian, if trying to follow faithfully the teachings of Christ is Christianity."

"I was sure you were," murmured the other. "Brother Matthews will be so glad to meet you. I know you will like him."

"But you will be in no condition for the visit of the ladies if I don't take better care of you now," the nurse answered. "Did you know that you are supposed to be sleeping now? You have had a busy day, and you are not going to speak another word except 'good night.' I am going to turn the light real low. And then I am going to sit here and tell you about my walk. You're just to shut your eyes and listen and rest . . . rest . . . rest."

And the low, sweet voice went on to tell of the flowers and the grass and the trees, the fields lying warm in the sunlight, with the flitting cloud-shadows, and the hills stretching away into the blue, until no troubled thought was left in the mind of the sick woman. And before long she was asleep like a child.

But as the nurse talked to make her patient forget, the incident of the afternoon came back, and while the patient slept, Hope Farwell sat going over again in her mind the conversation on the grassy knoll in the old Academy yard, recalling every word, every look, every expression.

What could be the man's work in life? He was no idler, she was sure of that. He had the air of a true worker, of one who was spending his life to some purpose. She wondered again at the expression on his face as she had seen it when they parted.

Then came again the question: Should she go back to the great city and lose herself in her work, or—she smiled to herself—should she yield to Dr. Abbott's argument and stay in Corinth a little longer?

# CHAPTER FOURTEEN

# THE LADIES' AID

The affairs of Memorial Church were booming. In only a month, Dan's presence seemed to have invigorated it with new energy.

In the more orthodox language of Elder Jordan, in an article to the official paper of the denomination: "The congregation has taken on new life, and the Lord's work is being pushed with a zeal and determination never before equaled. The audiences are steadily increasing. The interest is reviving in every department, and the world will soon see grand old Memorial Church taking first place in Corinth, if not the state. Already Reverend Matthews has been asked to deliver a special sermon to the L.M. of J.B.'s, who will attend the service in a body, wearing the full regalia of the order. Surely God has abundantly blessed the brethren in sending us such an able preacher."

The week following Dan's talk with Miss Farwell in the old Academy yard, the ladies of the Aid Society assembled early, and in unusual numbers, for their meeting at the home of Judge Strong. As the announcement from the pulpit had it—there was business of great importance to transact; also there was work on hand that must be finished.

The business of importance was the planning of a great entertainment to be given in the Corinth Social Hall, by local talent, both in and out of the church, for the purpose of raising money that the church still owed their former pastor. The unfinished work was a quilt of a complicated wheel pattern. Every spoke of each wheel contained the name of some individual who had paid ten cents for the honor. The hubs cost twenty-five cents. When finished, this "beautiful work of the Lord" (they always liked to call their work the Lord's work) was to be sold to the highest bidder, thereby netting a sum of money for the pulpit furniture fund nearly equal to the cost to anyone of the leading workers, for the society's entertainment, in a single afternoon or evening, for what would appear in the Sunday issue of the Daily Corinthian as a "social event."

It must be understood that not all the women enrolled as members of the congregation of Memorial Church belonged to the Ladies' Aid. Only the *workers* were active in that important part of the "Body of Christ." Many there were in the congregation, quiet, deeply, truly spiritual souls, who did not have the time for such service, but in the scheme of things as they were, such were not classed as "active" members. They were not of the inner circle. And everything depended on whether one was in this inner circle or not! Those who were not on the inside were reckoned as counting only on the roll of membership, but not in other ways.

The Ladies' Aid, then, represented the feminine half at least of the inner circle. So it was therefore the strength, the soul, the ruling power, the spirit of this Temple of God that assembled that afternoon at Judge Strong's big, brown house, on Strong Avenue, just beyond Strong Memorial Church.

The Ally came also. For the Ally never misses a Ladies' Aid meeting in Corinth.

Miss Farwell was there with her patient as she had promised, and Mrs. Strong took particular care that as fast as they arrived each one of her guests met the young woman.

To the women of the middle class, the trained nurse in her blue dress with white cap and apron was an object of unusual interest. They did not know whether to rank her with servants, stenographers, salesclerks, or teachers. And the Ally makes sure its people are always trying to classify everyone they meet into prescribed molds, the more easily to judge them.

But the *leading* ladies of the town (see the *Daily Corinthian*) were very sure of themselves, which the elongation of their noses indicated as they looked in the nurse's direction. This young woman worked for wages in the homes of people, waited on people. Therefore she was a working girl—a servant.

No one wasted much time with the stranger. The introduction was acknowledged with a word or a cool nod and an unintelligible murmur of something that meant nothing, or—worse—with a patronizing air, a sham cordiality elaborately assumed, which said plainly, "I acknowledge the introduction here, because this is the Lord's business. But be sure that you make no mistake and presume upon it should we chance to meet again."

When everyone had arrived, and those modern weapons of Christian warfare had been produced—needle, thread, and thimble—the quilt was attacked with a spirit that was worth at least half a column in the denominational weekly, while the sound of the conflict might almost have been heard as far as Widow Mulhall's garden where Denny was cheerily digging away with his one good hand.

To nurse Farwell sitting quietly—unobserved, but observing—there came a confused sound of many voices speaking at once, with now and then a sentence in a tone stronger than the common din. To her it sounded like the cackling of a yardful of hens, and she wondered how the fabric of some churches manages to hold together when gossip was the unifying thread throughout it all.

"She said the Memorial Church didn't believe in the Spirit anyhow, and that all we wanted was to get them in so we could get their money in our collection plates, and I said we believed in the Spirit as much as any church in town but we weren't going to fall all over ourselves about it . . . I told them Brother Matthews would surely be converting some of their folks before the year was out, if they kept on coming to our services . . . I says, says I—'Brother Matthews never said that; you'd better read your Bible. If you can show me in the Book where you get your authority for it, I'll quit Memorial Church right then and join yours' . . . Yes, all their people were out . . . Sure, he's their church clerk. I heard him say with my own ears that Brother Matthews was the biggest preacher that had ever been in Corinth . . . Well, you know what *she's* like—the mother I mean. Left Memorial two years ago 'cause she wanted deeper worship, so she said. I wouldn't trust that son of hers either. I quit going to his place right then, and told everyone I knew to do the same. No, it won't do to patronize those that are in rebellion against the Lord's work . . . I was glad to see her at the last meeting, though after the way she just sat there not saying a word, as if she expected *us* to make *her* feel welcome, I must say I'm not surprised not to see her back again today. And what do we need with her kind anyway, I say . . . I'll venture that sermon next Sunday on 'The Christian Ministry' will give them something to think about. That ought to show where *their* church is going wrong . . . The old Doctor never misses a service now. Wouldn't it be great if we was to get him to join? . . . Wasn't that solo the sweetest thing? . . Wish *he* would join— a good-looking man! We'd be sure of him then. . . .They would like mighty well to get *him* away from us if they could. But he'll stay around I think as long as Charity plays the organ!"

There was a laugh at this last from a group near the window, and Miss Charity blushed as she answered, "I've worked hard enough to get him, and I certainly intend to keep him if I can! I've been telling all the girls to be nice to him."

Someone nearer by said, in a low tone, "Of course there's nothing in all that! Charity's just keeping him in the choir to string him along. She wouldn't think of anyone but the preacher, I can tell you that. If Brother Matthews knows what's best for him, he won't miss that chance. I guess if the truth were known, old Nathan's about the best fixed of anyone in Corinth."

Sometimes a group would put their heads closer together and by the quick glances in her direction the nurse felt that she was contributing her full share to the success of the meeting. On one of those occasions she turned her back on the company to speak a few words to her patient who was sitting in an easy chair a little apart from the circle.

Mrs. Strong's sister's face was all aglow. "Isn't it fine!" she said. "I feel as if I had been out of the world for so long. It's so kind of these dear sisters to have the meeting here today so that I could look on and listen to all their news and talk. It's so good of you too, dear, to stay with me so they could come." She laughed. "Do you know, I think they're all a little bit afraid of you."

The nurse smiled and was about to reply when a sudden hush fell upon the room and her patient whispered excitedly, "He's come. Now you'll get to meet our minister!"

Mrs. Strong's voice in the hall could be heard greeting the new arrival, and answering her the deeper tones of a man's voice.

Miss Farwell started. Where had she heard that voice before? Then she felt him enter the room and heard the ladies greeting him. Something kept her from turning and she remained for another moment or two with her back to the room, watching her patient's face, as the eyes of the invalid followed the minister about the room.

Only Charity, of all the ladies, was noting the young woman's too obvious lack of interest.

The hum of quilting had already started back up again when Mrs. Strong's hand was placed lightly on the nurse's arm.

"Miss Farwell," she said, "I want you to meet our minister, Reverend Matthews."

An amused smile spread over Dan's face as he held out his hand. "I believe Miss Farwell and I have met before."

But the young woman ignored the outstretched hand, and her voice had an edge, as she answered, "It is possible, sir. I meet many strangers in my profession, you know, but I—I have forgotten you."

Charity was still watching with a suspicious gleam in her eye. At the minister's words she started, and a touch of color came into her pale cheeks. With Miss Farwell's answer the look of suspicion in her eyes deepened. What could it mean?

Dan's embarrassment was unmistakable. Before he could find

words to reply, the sick woman exclaimed, "Why, how strange! Do tell us about it, Brother Matthews. Was it here in Corinth?"

In a flash Dan saw his predicament. If he said he had met the young lady in Corinth, they would know it was impossible that she should have literally forgotten him. He understood the meaning of her words. These women would give them a hundred meanings. If he admitted that he was wrong and that he had not met her, there was always the chance of the people learning of that hour spent on the Academy grounds.

Meanwhile, the young woman made him understand that she realized the difficulties of his position, and all within earshot awaited his next words with interest. Looking straight into her eyes he said, "I seem to have made a mistake. I beg your pardon, Miss Farwell."

She smiled. It was almost as if he had deliberately lied, but it was the best he could do.

"Please do not mention it," she returned, with a meaning for him alone. "I am sorry that I will not be here next Sunday to hear your sermon on Christian ministry. Many of the women have urged me to attend. There is no doubt it will be interesting."

"You are leaving Corinth soon, then?" he asked.

At the same moment the patient and Mrs. Strong exclaimed almost together, "Oh, Miss Hope, we thought you had decided to stay. We can't let you go so soon."

She turned from the man to answer the invalid.

"Yes I must go. I did not know the last time we talked it over, but something has happened since that makes it necessary. I shall leave tomorrow. And now, if you will excuse me please, I will run away for a few moments to get my things together. You are doing so nicely, you really don't need me at all, and there is no reason I should stay longer—now that I have met the minister." She bowed slightly to Dan, and slipped from the room.

The women looked significantly at one another, and the minister too came in for his full share of the curious glances. There was something in the incident that they could not understand, and because Dan was a man they naturally felt that he was somehow

at the bottom of it. It was not long until Charity, under the pretext
of showing him a sacred song which she had found in one of Mrs.
Strong's books, led him to another room, away from the curious
crowd.

All week Dan had been looking forward to this meeting of the
Ladies' Aid Society, for he knew that he would see the nurse again.
Charmed by the young woman's personality and mind, and filled
with his purpose to win her to the church, he was determined, if
chance did not bring it about, to seek another opportunity to talk
with her. He had smiled often to himself, at what he thought
would be a good joke between them, when she came to know of
his calling.

Like many such jokes, it did not turn out to be so funny after
all. Instead of laughing with him, she had given him to understand
that the incident was closed, that there must be no attempt on his
part to continue the acquaintance—that, indeed, she would not
acknowledge that she had ever met him, and that she was so much
in earnest that she was leaving Corinth the next day because of
him.

"Really, Brother Matthews, if I have offended you in any way,
I am very sorry." Dan awoke with a start. He and Charity were
alone in the room. From the open door came the busy hum of the
workers in the Master's vineyard.

"I beg your pardon, what were you saying?" he said.

"I have asked you three times if you liked the music last Sunday."

Apologetically he answered, "Really, I am not fit company for
anyone today."

"I noticed that you seem troubled. Can I help you in any way?
Is it the church?" she asked gently.

He laughed. "Oh no, it's nothing that anyone can help. It's
myself. Please don't bother about it. I believe if you will excuse
me, and make my excuses to the ladies in there, I will go. I really
have some work to do."

She was watching his face so closely that she had not noticed
the nurse who passed the window and entered the garden. Dan
rose to his feet as he spoke.

"Why, Brother Matthews, the ladies expect you to stay for their business meeting, you know. They will think your leaving is very strange."

"Strange. There is nothing strange about it. I have more important matters that demand my attention—that is all. It is not necessary to interrupt them now, you can explain when the business meeting opens. They will excuse me I am sure, if they knew how important it was."

And before poor Charity had time to fairly grasp the situation he was gone, slipping into the hall for his hat, and out by a side door.

Miss Farwell, from meeting the minister, had gone directly to her room, but she could not go about her packing. Dropping into a chair by the window she sat staring into the tops of the big maples outside. She did not see the trees. Instead she saw a vast stretch of rolling country, dotted with farm buildings and stacks, across which the flying cloud-shadows raced. And about a half-mile away her eyes fell upon a weed-grown yard with a gap in a tumbledown fence, an old deserted school building, and the image of a big clean-looking man standing, with the sunlight on his red-brown hair.

She had known at the time he was fine and strong. He seemed made for important things. And he had let her go on—leading her to talk as she would have talked only to intimate friends who would understand. And then he had thought it all a joke! The gray eyes filled with angry tears, and the fine chin quivered. She sprang to her feet.

Why should she keep thinking about this stranger—this preacher? The room seemed to be closing in around her! She felt she could not stay another minute in the house—with those people downstairs. Catching up a book, she crept down the back way and out to a vine-covered arbor that stood in a secluded corner of the garden.

She had been in her retreat but a few minutes when the sound of a step on the gravel walk startled her. Then the doorway into the arbor was darkened by a tall, broad-shouldered figure, and a voice said, "May I come in?"

The gray eyes flashed once in his direction. Then she calmly opened her book, without a further glance or as much as a single sign to betray her knowledge of his presence.

"May I come in?" he asked again.

She turned a page, seeming not to hear.

Once more he repeated the same words slowly—almost apologetically. The young woman turned another page of her book.

Then suddenly the opening to the arbor was empty. Dan was halfway across the garden to the front of the house. Hope rose quickly from her place and started forward. Then she stopped, seeing Charity walk up to the minister as he strode toward the gate.

"Have you finished that important business so soon?" she asked sharply. Then with concern at the expression of his face, she added, "Won't you please tell me what is the matter?"

He tried to laugh and when he spoke, his voice was not his at all. The daughter of the church turned to watch her minister as he passed through the gate and walked down the street. Then she went slowly back the path to the arbor. She began to turn in at the doorway, but was startled to find a young woman crouched on the wooden bench weeping bitter tears—a book on the floor at her feet.

Quickly Charity drew back. Very quietly she went down the walk again. And as she went, she seemed all at once to have grown slightly whiter and thinner.

# CHAPTER FIFTEEN

# DR. HARRY'S CASE

The meeting of the Ladies' Aid Society adjourned and its members, with sighs and exclamations of satisfaction over work well done, separated to go to their homes—where there were suppers to prepare for hungry husbands, and children of the flesh.

Thus always in the scheme of things as they are, the duties of life conflict with the duties of religion. The faithful members of the Memorial Church were always being interrupted in their work for the Lord by the demands of the world. And as they saw it, there was nothing for them to do but to bear their crosses bravely.

The whistles in the factories blew for quitting time. The six o'clock train from the West pulled into the yards, stopped—puffing a few moments at the water tank—and thundered on its way again. On the street, businessmen and those who labored with their hands hurried from the scenes of their daily toil, while the country folk untied their teams and saddle horses from the hitch-racks to return to their waiting families and stock on distant farms.

A few miles out on the main road leading northward, the home-going farmers passed a tired horse hitched to a dusty, mud-stained top-buggy, plodding steadily toward the village. They all waved and hailed the driver of the rig heartily. It was Dr. Harry returning from a case in the backwoods country beyond Hebron.

The deep-chested, long-limbed bay, known to every child for miles around, was picking her own way over country roads, for the lines back to Dr. Harry's hand hung slack. Without a hint from her driver the good horse slowed to a walk on the rough places and quickened her pace again when the road was good, and of her own accord turned out for the teams passing from the other direction. The man in the buggy returned the greetings of his friends mechanically, scarcely noticing who they were.

It was Jo Mason's wife this time. Jo was a good fellow but wholly incapable of grasping the problem of the provision of daily life for himself and his brood. There were ten children in almost as many years. Understanding so little of life's responsibilities, the man's dependence upon his wife was pitiful, if not downright criminal. With tears streaming down his lean, hungry face, he had begged, "Do somethin', Doc! My God Almighty, you jest got to do somethin'!"

For hours Dr. Harry had been trying to do something. But out there in the woods, in that wretched, poverty-stricken home, with only a neighbor woman of the same class as Jo to help him, he had been fighting a losing battle.

And now while the bay mare was making her tired way home, he was still fighting—still trying to do something, even if only in his mind. His professional knowledge and experience told him that he could not win, that at best he could do no more than delay his defeat a few days, and his common sense urged him to dismiss the case from his mind. But there was something in Dr. Harry stronger than common sense, something greater than his professional skill. And so he must go on fighting until the very end.

It was nearly twilight when he reached the edge of the hill on the farther side of the valley. He could see the lights of the town twinkling against the dark mass of tree and hill and building, while on the faintly glowing sky the steeple of Memorial Church, the cupola of the old Academy building, and the courthouse tower were cut in black. Down into the dusk of the valley the bay picked her way, and when they had gained the hill on the edge of town it was dark. Now the tired horse quickened her pace, for the home barn and Uncle George were not far away. But as they drew near the big brown house of Judge Strong, she felt the first touch of the reins and came to a walk, turning in to the familiar hitching post with reluctance.

At that moment a tall figure left the Judge's gate to pass swiftly down the street in the dusk.

Before the bay mare quite came to a stop at the post, her master's hand turned her head into the street again, and his familiar voice bade her to go on. In mild surprise, she broke into a quick trot. The doctor thought he had seen his friend the minister coming from the Strong mansion. But how was Dr. Harry to know that Dan had only paused at the gate as if to enter, and then had passed on when he saw the physician turning in?

Farther down the street at the little white cottage near the monument, the bay mare was pulled again to a walk, and this time she was permitted to turn in to the curb and stop for a moment.

The old Doctor was sitting on the porch. "Hello!" he called out cheerily. "Won't you come in for a minute?"

"Not tonight, thank you, Doctor, but I mustn't," answered the younger man. At his words, his old ex-partner left his chair and came stiffly down the walk toward the buggy. When he was quite close, with one hand grasping the seat, Dr. Harry said to him in a low tone, "I've just come back from Masons'."

"Ah, hah," grunted the other, then inquiringly he added, "And—?"

"It's pretty bad."

The old man's voice rumbled up from the depth of his chest. "Nothing to do, eh?"

"Not much."

"You know I told you it was there. Been in her family way back. Seen it ever since she was a girl."

"I knew it was of no use, of course. But you know how it is."

The white head nodded in understanding as Dr. Harry raised his hand slowly to his eyes.

"Yes, I know, Harry. Jo take it pretty bad?"

"Couldn't do anything with him, poor fellow, and those children too—" Both men were silent. Slowly the younger man took up the reins. "I just stopped to tell you, Doctor."

"Well, you go home and rest. Get a good night's sleep whatever you do. You'll have to go out again, I suppose. Call me if anything turns up. But in the meantime, you've got to get some rest, Harry, do you hear!" He spoke roughly.

"Thank you, Doctor. I don't think I'll need to disturb you though. Everyone else is doing nicely. I can't think of anything else that is likely to call me out."

"Well, go to bed anyway."

"I will. Good night, Doctor."

"Good night, Harry."

The mare trotted on down the dark street, past the twinkling lights. The Doctor stood by the curb until he heard the buggy wheels rattle over the railroad tracks, then turned to walk stiffly back to his seat on the porch.

Soon the tired old horse was in the hands of old Uncle George, while Mam Liz ministered to the weary doctor. The old black woman lingered in the dining room, hovering about the table, calling his attention to various dishes, watching his face all the while with an expression of anxiety upon her own wrinkled countenance. At last Harry looked up at her with a smile.

"Well, Mam Liz, what is it? Haven't I been good today?"

"No, sir, you ain't. But 'tain't nothin' you done to other folks, Dr. Harry. It's what you all's doin' to yourself. Why, you's plumb tuckered out! You ain't slept in your bed for three nights 'ceptin' jest for an hour one morning when other folks was gettin' up, and only the Good Lord knows when you eats!"

The doctor laughed. "There, there, Mammy, you see me eating now all right, don't you?" But the old woman shook her head mournfully.

Harry continued, "One of your dinners, you know, is worth at least six of other folk's cooking. In fact—" he added seriously, "I believe I might safely say a dozen. Then he gave her a laughing description of his attempt to cook breakfast for himself and the ten children at the Masons' that morning.

The old woman was proudly indignant. "Them's poor triflin' white trash! To think o' you doin' that to such as them! What right's they got to be makin' you do that anyhow? They shore ain't got no claim on you—an' you ain't got no call to jump every time such as them snaps their fingers."

Dr. Harry shook his head solemnly.

"Now, Mam Liz, I'm afraid you're talking like an aristocrat. Why, you're not looking down your nose at white folks just because they're poor, are you?" he added with a wink.

With a "Humph!" she retorted, "You jest ain't got no call to be servin' such as them, that's all!"

"I'm afraid I do, Mam Liz," he returned slowly. "I'm afraid that's exactly what I have—a call to serve . . . whoever needs me."

He paused, looking away thoughtfully, then went on, but now more thinking aloud to himself, "Who knows why people have to live that way, or how they came to be? Whoever is responsible for the existence of such conditions isn't my problem to solve. The fact is, they are here. And while philosophers solve the problem of *why*, I am sure that we as individuals have a call to minister personally to their immediate needs."

The doctor's thoughts about a dilemma that was often in his mind was a little too much for the old servant. She watched him with a puzzled expression on her face.

"Talkin' 'bout ministers, the parson was here to see you yesterday evenin'."

"Brother Matthews? I'm sorry I was not at home."

"Yes, sir, I was sorry too. He's a right pious-looking man, he shore is. I done told him the Lord only knowed where you was or when you'd get back. He laughed and says he was shore the Lord wasn't far away wherever you was, and that I must tell you it was only a little call, nothin' of importance—so's you wouldn't bother 'bout it, I suppose."

Dr. Harry rose from the table. "Perhaps he will drop by this evening. No, this is prayer-meeting night." He stretched his tired body. "Perhaps I ought to go—"

The old woman interrupted him. "Now you look here, Dr.

Harry, you ain't goin' to leave this house tonight. You jest put on your slippers and set down in your chair an' smoke your pipe a little an' then go to bed. You ain't ate enough to keep a chicken alive, an' your eyes look like two holes burned in a blanket. I tell you, you's plumb tuckered!"

The weary physician looked through the door into the library, where the lamp threw a soft light over the big table. The magazines and papers lay unopened, just as they had been brought from the office by Uncle George. A book he had been trying to read for a month was lying right where he had dropped it to answer a call. While he hesitated at the door, the old black man came shuffling in with the doctor's pipe and slippers.

"Here they is—an' your mare's all taken care of—takin' her feed like a good one. I tell you, there ain't no better one on the road than her."

Dr. Harry laughed. "Uncle George, I have to agree with you there. And no doubt it's because you take such good care of her."

As he spoke he slipped out of his coat and Mam Liz, standing beside Uncle George, took it from his hand.

"Anything else, sir?" said Uncle George. Harry smiled and shook his head.

"Then good night, sir," said Uncle George, followed by the same from Mam Liz. They slipped noiselessly away as the doctor entered the library.

Is there, after all, anything more beautiful in life than the ministry of such humble ones, whose service to others is the deepest expression of their love?

Many of the Master's truths have been shamefully neglected by those into whose hands they were committed. Many of His grandest lessons are ignored by His disciples, who, ambitious for place and power—quarrel among themselves. Many of His noblest laws have been twisted out of all resemblance to His Spirit by those who interpret them to meet the demands of their own particular viewpoint and system. But of all the truths the Master has given to men, none perhaps has been more neglected, or abused, than the simple truth He illustrated so vividly when He washed His disciples' feet.

Left alone, Dr. Harry picked up one magazine after another, only to turn the leaves impatiently and—after a moment—toss them aside. He glanced at his medical journal and found it dull. He took up his book only to lay it down again.

Decidedly he could not read. The house with its empty rooms was so big and still. He seated himself at his piano, but he had scarcely touched the keys when he rose again to go to the window.

*Perhaps I should have gone to prayer meeting after all,* he thought. *I am not fit to be alone tonight. If I could only go to bed and sleep, but I feel as if I had forgotten how.* The strain of the day was visible on his worn and haggard face, and in his ears poor Jo's prayer still was ringing, "Do somethin', Doc! My God Almighty, you jest got to do somethin'!"

Turning from the window the doctor's eyes fell on his medicine case, which Uncle George had brought in from the buggy and placed near the hall door.

He picked up the case and went to the table, where he opened it with hesitating hand. There were drugs he gave to his patients to put them to sleep—why shouldn't he take one himself? "After all," he argued in his mind, "I would give it to a patient in my condition. I must have some rest!"

His thoughts were interrupted by the ringing of the doorbell.

Mam Liz's voice, in soft tones, came from the hall. "Yes, ma'am, he's home, but he's plumb tuckered out. Is you got to see him? You ain't wantin' him to go out again is you?"

Another voice answered, but the listening doctor could not distinguish the reply.

" . . . then come in, come in, ma'am. He's in the library."

A moment later the nurse stood in the doorway.

Dr. Harry rose to his feet. "Miss Farwell! I'm glad to see you."

They visited for a few moments, then the nurse told him why she had come—to bid him goodbye.

"But I thought you were going to stay!" he cried.

"I had thought of doing so," she admitted. "But something—something makes it necessary for me to go."

All his arguments and pleadings were in vain. Her only answer was, "I cannot, Dr. Abbott, truly I cannot." Nor would she tell him more than that it was necessary for her to go.

"But we need you so. There is no one to take your place, Hope—" Then he stopped.

She permitted him to look deep into her eyes. "I am sorry, Doctor, but I *must* go."

"Just one thing, Miss Farwell. You are not going because of—because of me?"

She held out her hand. "No, indeed, Doctor. Whatever you think, please don't think that."

He would have accompanied her home, but she would not permit it, and insisted so strongly that he retire at once, that he was forced to yield. But he would not say goodbye, declaring that he would be at the train station in the morning to see her off.

Coming home from prayer meeting, Mrs. Oldham found her husband still sitting on the porch. When she could not force him to listen to reason and go to bed, she left him to his thoughts. A little later the old Doctor saw the tall form of the minister turn in at the gate opposite. Then the light in the corner window flashed brightly. A few minutes more, and he saw a woman coming down the street, going toward Judge Strong's. Nearing the house across the way, she slowed her pace, walking very slowly. Under the corner window she almost stopped. As she went on she turned once to look back, then disappeared under the trees in the dusk.

It was almost morning when Miss Farwell was awakened by a loud knocking at the front door. Then Mrs. Strong came quickly upstairs to the nurse's room. The young woman was on her feet instantly.

"That old negro of Dr. Abbott's is here asking for you," explained Mrs. Strong. "He says Dr. Harry sent him and that he must see you. What in the world can it mean?"

# CHAPTER SIXTEEN

# THAT GIRL OF CONNER'S

Slipping into her clothing the nurse went down to the front door where Uncle George was waiting. A horse and buggy stood at the front gate.

"Evenin', ma'am, is you the nurse?" said Uncle George, lifting his cap.

"Yes, I am the nurse, Miss Farwell. Dr. Abbott sent you for me?"

"Indeed he did, ma'am—said I was to fetch you fast. Told me to say it was an emergency case, and that they needs you powerful bad over in Old Town."

The latter part of this speech was delivered to the empty door-way. The nurse was already back in her room.

The old black man rubbed his chin as he turned with a puzzled look from the open door to the horse and buggy and back to the door again. But before he had time to wonder what he should do being left alone as he was, Miss Farwell, fully dressed, was by his side again, and halfway to the gate.

"Come, let us go!" she urged.

"Yes, ma'am!" he answered, breaking into a trot for the rig, and climbing in by her side. "Come Jim, git!"

In two moments more the black horse was covering the ground

rapidly. The quick steady beat of the iron-shod feet and the rattle of the buggy wheels echoed loudly in the gray stillness of the morning. Above the tops of the giant maples that lined the road, the nurse saw the stars paling in the first faint glow of the coming day, while here and there in the homes of some early-rising workers the lights were already flashing on.

"Can you tell me something of the case?" asked the nurse.

"Case? Oh you mean the poor gal what tried to kill herself. Yes, Miss. She's that poor Conner gal, whose Daddy done killed Jack Mulhall, the town Marshall, you know. The Conners used to be nice folks, all except Jim. He'd drink too much sometimes an' then was plumb bad. An' since they took him off to jail an' Mrs. Conner died, the girl, she don't get along too good somehow. Since she left the hotel she's been livin' over in Old Town along with some colored folks, upstairs in the old town hall building. Liz an' me, we got friends, Jake Smith an' his folks, livin' in the same place, you see. Well, lately the gal don't appear to be doin' even as well as usual, an' the folks they been worried about her. Sometime last night, Jake an' Mandy they waked up hearin' a moanin' an' a cryin' in the poor girl's room. They called at the door but there ain't no answer. Then Mandy says to the folks what's been waked up an' is all standin' around the door that she ain't goin' to stand and stare doin' nothin' and she just forced open the door and goes in.

"Yes sir, Miss Nurse, Mandy said the girl was jest throwin' herself 'round the room an' screechin'. An' Mandy grabbed her just as she was about to jump out the window. The girl was burnin' up and Mandy sent Jake to me quick. I didn't want to wake Dr. Harry, Miss, 'cause he's so tired out, but I knew I had to, 'cause I didn't wake him once before when somebody wanted him, an' I ain't never done *that* no more! Yes sir, Master Harry Abbott he's a devil, Miss, when he's mad, just like his daddy. So I called him easy-like, but Lord—he's up an' dressed before I can hook up big Jim here to the buggy, an' we head for Old Town on the run. Quick as he was in the room he called out the window for me to drive quick as I can to the Judge's an' fetch you. An' that's all I know—'ceptin' Dr. Harry say it's an emergency case. We're almost there now. Go on Jim!"

While the trusty old black man was speaking, the big horse known as Jim was whirling them through the quiet streets of the town. As Uncle George finished they reached the top of Academy Hill, where Miss Farwell saw the old school building—ghostly and still in the mists that hung about it like a shroud, the tumbled-down fence with the gap leading into the weed-grown yard, the grassy knoll and the oak—all wet and sodden now, and—below, the valley—with its homes and fields hidden in the thick fog, suggestive of hidden depths.

"Is you cold, Miss? We's almost there now." The nurse had shivered as with a sudden chill as they had climbed to the top of the rise.

Turning sharply to the north a minute later, they entered the square of Old Town, where a herd of lean cows were just getting up from their beds to pick a scanty breakfast from the grass that grew where once the farmer folk had tied their teams, and in front of the ruined structure that had once been the principal store of the village.

Long without touch of painter's brush, the few wretched buildings that remained were the color of the mist. To the nurse—like the fog that hid the valley—they suggested cold mysterious depths of life, untouched by any ray of promised sun. And out of that dull gray emptiness, a woman's voice broke sharply through in a scream of pain.

"That's her, that's the poor girl now, nurse. Up there, where you sees that light."

Uncle George brought the big black horse to a stand in front of the ancient town hall and courthouse, a two-story frame building with the stairway on the outside. A group of blacks huddled at the foot of the stairs. They drew back as the nurse sprang from the buggy and ran lightly up the shaky old steps. The narrow, dirty hallway was crowded with more people. The odor of the place was not pleasant.

Miss Farwell pushed her way through and entered the room

where Dr. Harry, assisted by a big black woman, was holding his struggling patient on the bed. The walls and ceiling of the room— stained by the accumulated smoke of years—the rough bare floor, the window without shade or curtain, a rude little table and a chair or two, a little stove set on broken bricks, a handful of battered dishes and cooking utensils, a trunk, and the bed with its ragged quilts, all cried aloud the old, old familiar cry of bitter poverty.

Dr. Harry glanced up as she entered.

"Carbolic acid," he said quietly, "but she didn't get quite enough. I managed to give her the antidote and a hypodermic. We better repeat the hypodermic I think."

Without a word the nurse took her place at the bedside. When the patient had grown quiet under the influence of the drug, Dr. Harry dismissed the negro woman with a few kind words, and the promise that he would send for her if she could help in any way. Then when he had sent the others away from the room and the hallway he turned to the nurse.

"I am sorry I was forced to send for you, Miss Farwell," he said, "but you can see there was nothing else to do. I knew you would come immediately, and I dared not leave her without a white woman in the room."

He paused and went to the bedside. "Poor, poor little girl. She tried hard to die. And I'm afraid she will try again the moment she regains consciousness. These good black people would do anything for her, but she must see one of her own race to care also when she opens her eyes."

He paused, seemingly at a loss for words.

Miss Farwell spoke now for the first time. "Is she a good girl, Doctor?"

"Yes, she is a good girl," answered Dr. Harry positively. "It is not that, nurse."

"Then how—" Miss Farwell began, glancing around the room. "Then why is she here?"

No one ever heard Dr. Harry Abbott speak a bitter word, but there was a strange note in his voice as he answered slowly. "She is here because—because there seemed to be no other place for her to go. She has no one who—no one who will take her in. She did this because there seemed to be nothing else for her to do."

Then briefly he related the sad history of the good girl whose reputation the good church people of Corinth had turned against her.

"Dr. Oldham and I tried to help her," he said, "but some ugly stories got started and somehow Grace heard them. I suppose she thought we were part of it, and after that she avoided us."

For a little while there was silence in the room. When Dr. Harry again turned from his patient to the nurse, Miss Farwell was busily writing upon his tablet of prescription blanks with a stub of a pencil which she had taken from her pocket. The doctor watched her curiously for a moment, then arose, and taking his hat, said briskly: "I will not keep you longer than an hour Miss Farwell. I think I know of a woman I can get for today at least, and perhaps by tonight we can find someone else, or arrange it somehow. I'll be back in plenty of time, so don't worry. Your train does not leave until ten-thirty, you know. If the woman can't come at once, I'll ask Dr. Oldham to relieve you."

The nurse looked at him with smiling eyes. "I am very sorry, Dr. Abbott, if I am not giving you satisfactory service," she said.

The physician returned her look with amazement. "Not giving satisfaction! What in the world do you mean?"

"Why you seem to be dismissing me," she answered demurely. "I understood that you sent for me to take this case."

At the light that broke over his face she dropped her eyes and wrote another line on the paper in front of her.

"Do you mean—" he began, then stopped.

"I mean that unless you send me away," she answered, "I shall stay on duty."

"But Dr. Miles—that case in Chicago. I understood from you that it was very important."

She smiled at him again. "There is nothing so important as the thing that needs doing now," she answered. Then she went on slowly, turning her eyes toward the unconscious girl on the bed, "And I do seem to be needed here."

"And you understand there will be no—no fees for us in this case?" he asked.

The color rose to her face. "I know as well as you that our work is not always a question of fees, Doctor. I am surprised you would even bring it up. May I not collect my bill at the same time you receive yours?"

He held out his hand impulsively.

"Forgive me, Miss Farwell," he said, "but it is too good to be true. I can't say more now. You *are* needed here—you cannot know how badly. I—we all need you."

She gently released her hand, and then he continued in a more matter-of-fact tone. "I will go now to make a call or two so that I can be with you later. She will be alright for at least three hours. I'll send Uncle George with some breakfast for you."

"Never mind the breakfast," she said. "If you will have your man bring along these things, I will get along nicely."

She handed him the prescription blank. "Here is a list that Mrs. Strong will give him from my room. And here—" she gave him another blank, "here is a list he may get at the grocery store. And here—" she handed him a third, "is a list he may get at some dry goods store. I don't have my purse with me so he will need to bring me the bills. The merchants will know him of course—"

Dr. Harry looked from the slips in his hand to the young woman. "Miss Farwell," he said, "you really do not need to take the expense of—"

"This is my case now, you know, Doctor," she interrupted.

"It was mine first."

"Please, let me do my part to help."

He nodded and left her. A few moments later she heard the quick step of big Jim and the rattle of the wheels.

Two hours passed. A low knock sounded. The nurse opened the door to find Dr. Oldham standing in the narrow hall. The old physician was breathing heavily from his effort in climbing the rickety stairs. His arms were full of roses.

"Oh Doctor!" she exclaimed with delight, "just what I was wishing for!"

"Harry told me what you were up to. Thought I better come along in case you should need any help."

He drew a chair to the bedside, while the nurse with her sleeves rolled up returned to which his knock at the door had interrupted.

Clean, white sheets, pillows and coverings had replaced the tattered quilt on the bed. The litter about the stove was gone, and in its place was a big armful of wood neatly piled, the personal offering of Uncle George, who had returned quickly with the things she had sent for. The dirt and dust had vanished from the windows. The glaring light was softened by some sort of curtain material that the young woman had managed to fix in place. The bare old cupboard shelves covered with fresh paper were filled with provisions, and the nurse, washing the last of the dishes and utensils, was in the process of placing them carefully in order.

She finished as Dr. Oldham turned from the patient, and throwing a bright-colored cloth over the rough table, began deftly arranging the flowers he had brought in the best dish she could find in the place. Already the perfume of the roses was driving from the room that peculiar, sickening odor of poverty.

The old physician, trained by long years of service to habits of close observation, noted every detail in the changing room. Silently he watched the strong, beautifully formed young woman in the nurse's uniform as she bent over his flowers, and handled them with the touch of love on her face. And in the clear gray eyes shone the light that a few truly great painters have occasionally succeeded in capturing in their pictures of the mother of Jesus.

The keen old eyes under their white brows filled, and the Doctor turned hastily back to the figure on the bed. A worn figure it was—thin and looking old, with lines of care and anxiety, of pain and fear, of dread and hopelessness. Only a faint suggestion of youth was left, only a hint of the beauty of young womanhood that might have been. Nay, that *would* have been—that *should* have been.

Miss Farwell started as the old man suddenly let out an exclamation and stood erect. He faced the young woman with blazing eyes and quivering face—his voice shaking with passion, as he said, "Nurse, you and Harry tell me this is suicide." He made a gesture toward the still form on the bed. "You will tell the people that this poor child wanted to kill herself, and the people will call it suicide too."

He paused, and his voice mounted. "But by God—it's murder!" he went on. "Murder—I tell you! She did not want to take her life. She *wanted* to live, to be strong and beautiful like you. But this community, with its churches and Sunday schools and prayer meetings and its religious socializing that insists that everyone be just like they think they ought to be, wouldn't let her. They denied her even the privilege of working for the food she needed. They refused help, they refused compassion, they refused even a word of sympathy. They shunned her and hounded her into this stinking hole to live in poverty. She may die, Nurse, and if she does—as truly as there is a Creator who loves His creatures—her death will be on the heads of the cruel, pious, self-worshiping, self-righteous, spiritually-rotten, proud, churchified people in this town!" The old man dropped into his chair exhausted by his passionate outburst.

For a few moments there was no sound in the room except the heavy breathing of the physician. The nurse stood gazing at him—trying to take in what he had just said.

Then the figure on the bed stirred. The sick girl's eyes opened and stared about wildly, questioningly through the room. With a low word to the Doctor, Miss Farwell went quickly to her patient.

# CHAPTER SEVENTEEN

# THE MINISTER'S OPPORTUNITY

When Dan left Miss Farwell in the summer house at Judge Strong's, he went straight to his room.

Two or three people whom he met on the way turned when he had passed to look back at him. Mrs. James talking over the fence with her neighbor wondered aloud why he did not return her greeting. Denny hailed him joyfully from his garden, but Dan did not slow his pace.

Reaching his own gate, he nearly broke into a run, flew up the stairway, rushed into his room, then closed and locked his door. He stood, breathing hard and smiling grimly at the foolish impulse that had made him act for all the world like a thief escaping with his booty.

He puzzled over the strange feeling that possessed him, the feeling that he had taken something that did not belong to him. At length the thought struck him that there might be, after all, good reason for the fancy. Perhaps it might indeed be more than just his imagination.

Pacing back and forth the length of his little study, he recalled every detail of that meeting in the Academy yard. And as he remembered how he had consciously refrained from making his position known to the young woman—not once, but several times when he thought of speaking up—and how his questions, combined with the evident false impression that his words had given her, had led her to speak thoughts she would never have dreamed of expressing had she known him, the conviction gradually grew that he had indeed, like a thief, taken something that did not belong to him. He realized that more and more his silence must appear to her as premeditated, and he reflected that her fine nature would shrink from what she could not but view as a low trick no gentleman would play.

His face grew hot with shame and guilt. No wonder, he told himself, that he had instinctively shrunk from looking into the faces of the people he had met on his way home, and had fled to the privacy of his rooms.

Dan did not spare himself that afternoon. He came in for his full share of self-condemnation. And yet beneath all the self-scorn he could not help feeling, there was a deeper subconscious conviction that he was not really—at heart—guilty of the thing with which he charged himself. Not guilty because the thing had not been intentional. The very conviction, though felt but dimly, made him all the more unsettled. He had the hopeless feeling of one caught in a trap—of one convicted of a crime he was guilty of in the eyes of the law, but which he knew he had unwittingly committed, without intent of hurt.

And, in fact, Dan was less guilty by a higher law than he was making himself. In so closely analyzing the woman's thoughts and feelings, and in taking so completely her point of view, he neglected to consider his own motives thoroughly. He could not realize how true to *himself* he had actually been. For the impulse that had prompted him to deny his calling was, in fact, a true instinct of his own strong manhood—the instinct to be accepted or rejected for what he was within himself, rather than for the mere accident of his calling and position in life.

One thing was clear. He must see Miss Farwell again.

She must listen to his explanation and apology. She must somehow understand.

For apart from his interest in the young woman herself, there was that purpose of the minister to win her to the church. That she was a Christian there could be little doubt from her words. But Dan had not yet come to the point where *Christian* and *church member* could be distinguished from one another. It was a monstrous thought that he himself should be the means of strengthening her feeling against the cause of the church to which he had given his life. The cause of Christ was not yet foremost in Dan's spiritual economy, but rather the cause of the church.

So he had gone to Judge Strong's home early that evening and determined to see her. But at the gate, when he saw Dr. Harry turning in as if to stop, he had passed on in the dusk. Later at prayer meeting his thoughts were far from the subject under discussion. His own public petition was so faltering and uncertain that Elder Jordan watched him suspiciously.

The next day Dan was putting the finishing touches to his sermon on "The Christian Ministry" when his landlady interrupted him with the news of the attempted suicide in Old Town. When he heard that the girl had at one time been a member of his congregation, he went at once to learn more of the particulars from Dr. Oldham.

He found his old friend, who had returned from the scene half an hour before, sitting in his big chair on the front porch gazing at the cast-iron monument across the way. Still absorbed in the enormity of the crime that had been committed against the poor girl, as he thought, by the well-to-do religious citizenry of the town, the Doctor returned only monosyllables or grunts and growls to the young man's questions.

Plainly the Doctor did not wish to talk. His face was dark and forbidding, and under his scowling brows, his eyes—when Dan caught a glimpse of them—were hard and fierce. The young man had never seen his friend in such a mood, and he could not understand.

Dan did not know that the kindhearted old physician had just learned from his wife that the girl with the bad reputation had called at the house to see him just a few hours before she had made the attempt to end her life, and that she had been sent away by the careful Martha, with the excuse that the Doctor was too busy to see her.

Neither could the boy know how the old man's love for him was keeping him silent, lest, in his present bitter frame of mind, he say things that would strengthen that undefined something which they each felt had come between them.

Suddenly the Doctor turned his gaze from the monument and flashed a meaning look straight into the brown eyes of the young minister.

"She was a member of your church," he said. "Why don't you go see her? Ask the nurse if there is anything the church can do."

Dan nodded in agreement. As he turned to go down the walk, Dr. Oldham added, "Tell Miss Farwell that I sent you." Then smiling, he growled to himself, "You'll get move valuable material for that sermon on the ministry there than in your study, if I don't miss my guess!"

The thought that he was to see the nurse again danced in Dan's brain as he walked through the town. How strangely the opportunity had come! The young minister felt that the whole thing had, in some mysterious way, been planned. In the care that the church would give this poor girl, the nurse would see how wrongly she had judged the sacred institution. She would be forced to listen to him now. Surely God had provided him this opportunity, both to redeem himself, and to redeem the church in Miss Farwell's eyes!

Poor Dan! Just now his heart and mind were too full of his own desire to win this young woman to the church to think of Grace and her attempted suicide. Dan was yet thoroughly orthodox.

So in the brightness of the afternoon, the pastor of Memorial Church went along the street that, in the gray chill of the early morning, had echoed the hurried steps of the doctor's horse. The homes—so silent when the nurse had passed on her mission—were now full of life. The big trees—dank and still then—now stirred softly in the breeze, and rang with the songs of their feathered inhabitants. The pale stars were lost in the infinite blue, and the sunlight warmed and filled the air, flooding street and home and lawn and flower with its golden beauty. Dan paused at the top of Academy Hill. For him no shroud of mist wrapped the picturesque old building, no fog of mysterious depth hid the charming landscape.

Recalling the things the nurse had said to him there under the oak on the grassy knoll, and thinking of his sermon which he had written to answer her charges—he smiled. It was a good sermon, he thought with honest pride—strong, logical, convincing.

With a confident stride he continued on his way.

# CHAPTER EIGHTEEN

# DAN SEES SOMETHING MORE

Miss Farwell was alone with her patient.

Dr. Harry, who had returned soon after the girl regained consciousness, had gone out into the country, promising to look in again during the evening on his way home. The old Doctor, finding that there was no need for him to remain, had left a few minutes later.

Except to answer their direct questions, the sick girl had spoken no word. She lay motionless—her face toward the wall. Several times Miss Farwell tried to gently arouse her, but except for a puzzled, half-frightened, half-defiant look in the wide-open eyes, there was no response, though she took her medicine obediently. But after Miss Farwell bathed the girl's face, brushed and braided her hair, and dressed her in a clean, white gown, the frightened defiant look gave place to one of wondering gratitude. And a little later she seemed to fall asleep.

She was still sleeping when Miss Farwell, who was standing by the window watching a group of children playing ball in the square, saw a man approaching the group from the direction of the village. The young woman's face flushed as she recognized the unmistakable figure of the minister.

An angry light shone in the gray eyes. She drew back from

the window with a low exclamation. As if in evident answer to his question, a half-dozen hands pointed toward the window where she had been standing. From within the room she watched him coming toward the building.

*What should she do*, she wondered. Her first angry impulse was to refuse to let him in. What right did he have to attempt to see her after all that had happened!

Then she thought—perhaps he was coming to see the sick girl. She had no right to refuse to admit him, when it could in no way harm her patient. The room, after all, was Grace's home, and she was only there in her professional capacity.

Miss Farwell began to feel that she was playing a part in a mighty drama, that the cue had been given for the entrance of another actor. She had nothing to do with the play except to act well her part. It was not for her to arrange the lines or manage the parts of the other players. The feeling possessed her that, indeed, she had somewhere rehearsed the scene many times before.

Stepping quickly to the bed she saw that her patient was still apparently sleeping. Then she stood trembling, listening to the steps in the hall as Dan approached.

He knocked a second time before she could summon strength to cross the room and open the door.

"May I come in?" he asked.

At his words—the same he had spoken a few hours before in the garden — the nurse's face grew crimson. She made no answer, but in the eyes that looked straight into his, Dan read a question and his own face grew red as he said, "I called to see your patient. Dr. Oldham sent me."

"Certainly, come in." She stepped aside and the minister entered the sickroom. Mechanically, without a word, she placed a chair for him near the bed, then crossed the room to stand by the window. But he did not sit down.

Presently Dan turned to the nurse. "She is asleep?" he asked in a low tone.

Miss Farwell's answer was calmly, unmistakably professional. Looking at her watch she answered, "She has been sleeping nearly two hours."

"Is there—will she recover?"

"Dr. Abbott says there is no reason why she should not, if we can turn her away from her determination to die."

Dan had always been intensely in love with life, from his earliest days when he romped the hills with his father or the Shepherd, learning the secrets of the animals and their ways, getting to know the mysteries of life hidden yet vital throughout the mountain region that was his home. He had a strong, full-blooded young man's horror of death. He could think of it only as a fitting close to a long and useful life, or as a possible release from months of sickness and pain. That anyone young, and in good health, with the world of beauty and years of usefulness before them, with the opportunities and duties of life calling, that such a one should willfully seek to die was a monstrous thought to him. In many ways Dan Matthews, young minister from the Ozarks, was still an innocent. He was only beginning to sense vaguely the great forces that make and mar humankind.

At the calm words of the nurse he turned quickly toward the bed with a shudder. "Her determination to die!" he repeated in an awed whisper.

Miss Farwell was watching him curiously.

Then half to himself he whispered, "Why should she possibly wish to die?"

"Why should she wish to live?" rejoined the nurse. The cold, matter-of-fact tone of her voice startled him.

He turned toward her perplexed and wondering. "I—I do not understand you," he said after a moment.

"I don't suppose you do," she answered soberly. "I doubt it is possible for you to understand. How could you? Your ministry is a matter of schools and theories, of doctrines and beliefs, of knowledge and histories and interpretations and sects. *This* is a matter of life."

"My church—" he began, remembering his sermon.

But she interrupted him. "Your church does not understand either. It is so busy defending its doctrinal positions, feeding the hunger to gather religious facts, promoting its cliquish social fraternity, and earning money to pay its ministers and keep up its programs that it has no time for such things as this."

"But they do not know," he faltered. "I did not dream that such a thing as this could happen right here, in our own town—that someone that used to be in our *own* church could—" He looked about the room, unable to complete the sentence, and then at the still form on the bed. He shuddered.

"You are a minister of Christ's gospel, and you are ignorant of these things? And yet this is not an uncommon case at all. I could tell you of many similar things I have seen, though not all of them have chosen to die. This girl could have made a living, had she degraded herself. I suppose you understand me. But she is a good girl. So she saw nothing for it but this. All she asked was a chance—only a chance. But none of the good people of this town would give it to her."

The minister was silent. He had no words to answer.

The nurse continued. "What right do you have, Mr. Matthews, to say that you do not understand? It is your business to understand—to know. And your church—what right does it have to plead ignorance of the life about its very doors? If such things are not its business, what business could it possibly have, that institution that professes to exist for the salvation of men—that hires men like you, as you yourself told me, to minister to the world? What right, I repeat, do you or your church have to be ignorant of these everyday conditions of life, of these hurts, of this poverty, of the emotional scars caused by the self-righteousness of what is professed to be a sacred institution ordained by God? Dr. Abbott must know his work. I must know mine. Our teachers, our legal and professional men, our public officers, our mechanics and laborers must all know and understand their work. The world demands it of us. And the world is beginning to demand that you and your church should know your business, too."

As the nurse spoke in low tones, her voice was filled with sorrowful, passionate earnestness.

And Dan, big Dan Matthews, newly ordained yet still such a babe in the spiritual woods, sat like a child before her—his face white, his brown eyes wide with question. His own voice trembled as he tried to answer, "But the people are not beasts. They do not realize. At heart, they—*we* are kind. We in the church do not *mean* to be carelessly cruel. Surely you believe that, Miss Farwell?"

She turned from him wearily, as if in despair at trying to make him understand.

"Of course I believe it," she answered. "But how does that affect the situation? The same thing could be said, I suppose, of those who crucified Christ, and burned the martyrs at the stake. The fact that they do not *mean* to be heartless does not alter the fact that great wrong is being done. It is this system that has enslaved the people, that feeds itself upon the strength that should be given to their fellowmen. They give so much time and thought and love to their churches and creeds and meetings and experiences and gatherings that they have nothing left—nothing for girls like these." Her voice broke and she went to the window.

In the silence Dan gazed at the form on the bed—gazed as if fascinated. From outside came the shouts of the children.

"Is there no one who cares?" Dan said at last, in a hoarse whisper.

"No one has made *her* feel that they care," the nurse answered, turning back to him. Her manner and tone were cold again.

"But you," he persisted. "surely *you* care?"

The gray eyes filled and the full voice trembled as she answered, "Yes, of course I care. How could I help it? And if only we can make her feel that we—that *someone* wants her, that there is a place for her, that there are those who need her!"

She went to the bedside and stood looking down at the still form. "I can't—I won't—I won't let her go."

"Let us help you, Miss Farwell," said Dan. "Dr. Oldham suggested that I ask you if the church could not do something. I am sure they would gladly help if I were to tell them of the situation."

The nurse wheeled on him with indignant, scornful eyes.

He faltered, not expecting such a reaction to his offer of help. "This is the church's work, you know."

"Yes," she returned, and her words stung. "You are quite right, this *is* the church's work."

He gazed at her as she continued hotly. "You have made it very evident, Mr. Matthews, that you know nothing of this matter, nothing of what is truly needed here, nothing of the true reason why this girl is in this state! Oh, I have no doubt that your church members would respond with a liberal collection if you were to picture to them what you have seen here this afternoon in an eloquent public appeal. Some, in the fullness of their emotions, would offer their personal service. Others I am sure would send flowers. But I suggest that for your own sake, before you present this matter to your church you ask Dr. Oldham to give you a full history of the case. Ask him to tell you why Grace Conner is trying to die. And now you will pardon me, but in consideration of my patient, who may waken at any moment, I dare not take the responsibility of permitting you to prolong this call."

Too bewildered and hurt to attempt any reply, he left the room. She stood listening to his steps as he went slowly down the hall and out of the building.

From the window she watched as he crossed the old square, watched as he passed from sight up the weed-grown street.

The cruel words had leaped from her lips unbidden. Already she regretted them deeply. She knew instinctively that the minister had come from a genuine desire to be helpful. She should have been more kind. But his unfortunate words had brought to her mind in a flash the whole hideous picture of the poor girl's broken life. And the suggestion of such help as the church would give now came with such bitter irony that her outburst had followed without her stopping to weigh her words.

The situation was not at all new to Hope Farwell. Her profession placed her constantly in touch with such so-called "ministries," which came after the fact and too late. She remembered a saloon keeper who had contributed liberally to the funeral expense of a child who had been killed by its drunken father.

But as she reflected, Hope realized she had never lashed out in such cruel anger as she just had to the minister. *Was she growing bitter*, she wondered. All at once her cheeks were wet with hot tears.

# CHAPTER NINETEEN

# THE TRAGEDY

Dan found the Doctor sitting on the porch just as he had left him. He walked heavily up the path between the roses, while the Doctor observed him closely. The young minister did not sit down.

"Well?" said the Doctor.

Dan's voice was strained and unnatural. "Will you come over to my room?" he asked.

Without a word, the old man rose and followed him.

In the privacy of his little study, after they were comfortably seated, Dan said, "Doctor, you had a reason for telling me to ask Miss Farwell if the church could do anything for that poor girl. And the nurse told me to ask you about the case. So I want you to tell me about her—*all* about her. Why is she living in that wretched place? Why did she try to kill herself? I want to know about this girl as you know her—as Miss Farwell knows."

The old physician made no reply, but sat silently studying the young man who had already risen again from his chair and now paced up and down the room.

When his friend did not speak, Dan said again, "Doctor, you must tell me. I'm not a child. What is this thing that you should so hesitate to tell me about? You must tell me."

"I guess you are right," returned the other slowly.

The room was silent another minute or two, then the Doctor began, and told of Grace's upbringing in the church, and how the church had ostracized her when she became offensive to it.

To Big Dan, born with the passion for service in his very blood, and reared amid the simple surroundings of his mountain home, where the religion and teaching of the old Shepherd had been felt for a generation, where every soul was a neighbor—with a neighbor's right to the assistance of the community, and where no one was made to suffer for the accident of birth or family, but stood and was judged upon his own life and behavior, the story of Grace Conner was a revelation almost too hideous in its cruelty for him to believe.

When the Doctor finished there was a tense silence in the minister's little study.

Trained under the influence of his parents, and from them receiving the highest ideals of life and his duty to the race, Dan had been drawn irresistibly by the theoretical self-sacrificing heroism and traditionally glorious ministry of the church. In the ideal as he had envisioned it, the church was the place for him truly to help and minister to souls hurting in life. To Dan the church had represented the compassion of Christ being lived out in the highways and byways of the world. To him the church—the organized, tightly structured, denominationalized, and traditional church—was Christ's body in today's world. For Dan's experience had been sorely limited. He had not been in many churches. He had not been part of the politics and power struggles which went on hidden from view. He had never confronted intractable eldership. Dan had never met the Ally.

Now, for the first time in his life, he found himself face to face with existing conditions, with the church as it was today, not as it was established to be. No theory, no ideal, no self-sacrificing and glorious ministry confronted him at this moment, but actual practice. Not the traditional, but the actual.

It was, indeed, a tragedy. Both what had happened to poor Grace, and what the awful revelation was now doing within young

Dan. Had he indeed studied and prepared and now given his life for an institution that was nothing at all what he had envisioned it?

The young man's face was drawn and white. His eyes—wide with that look of question—burned with a light that his old friend had not seen in them before—the light of suffering—of agonizing doubt.

In his professional duties the Doctor had been forced to school himself to watch the keenest suffering unmoved, lest his emotions bias his judgment—upon the accuracy of which depended the life of his patient. He had been taught to cause the cruelest pain with unshaken nerve by the fact that a human life under his knife depended upon the steadiness of his hand. But his sympathy had never been dulled—only controlled and hidden. So, long years of contact with what might be called a disease of society had accustomed him to the sight of conditions—the revelation of which came with such a shock to the younger man.

But the Doctor could still appreciate what the revelation meant to the boy. Knowing Dan from his childhood, familiar with his home-training, and watching his growth and development with personal, loving interest, the old physician had realized how singularly susceptible his character was to the beautiful beliefs of the church. For it is often the most innocent, those with good motives and pure hearts, who get swept into the coterie of the church without suspecting its result. Most, however, when hints of the truth begin to show themselves, close their mind to them, and do not allow their eyes to be opened. Thus, they cross the line from their former goodness and innocence, and make themselves partners with the Ally.

Dan now stood at that crossroads. His eyes were being opened.

The Doctor had foreseen this moment, and knew something of the suffering which would inevitably come to his friend when he should be brought face to face with the raw, naked truths of life. And Dan, as he sat now searching the rugged but kindly face of his friend, realized faintly why the Doctor had shrunk from talking to him of the sick girl.

Slowly Dan—as one in perplexing, troubled thought—aimlessly went to the window. Standing there, he looked out with unseeing eyes on the cast-iron monument on the opposite corner of the street. Then he moved restlessly to the other window, and, with eyes still unseeing, looked down into the little garden of the crippled boy—the garden with the big rock covered with moss and vines in its center. Then he went to his study table and stood idly moving the books and papers about.

His eye mechanically followed the closely written lines on the sheets of paper that were lying just as he had left them that morning. He paused. Then the next moment, with one quick movement, he crushed the pages of the manuscript in his powerful hands and threw them into the wastebasket.

He faced the Doctor with a grim smile. "My sermon on 'The Christian Ministry,' " he said.

# CHAPTER TWENTY

# TO SAVE A LIFE

"Nurse!"

Hope Farwell turned quickly. The girl on the bed was watching her with wide eyes.

She forced a smile. "Yes, dear, what is it? Did you have a good sleep?"

"I was not asleep. Oh Nurse, is it true?"

Hope laid a firm, cool hand on the hot forehead, and looked kindly down into the wondering eyes.

"You were awake while the minister was here?"

"Yes, I heard it all. Is it—is it true?"

"Is what true, child?"

"That you care . . . that anyone cares?"

Miss Farwell's face shone now with a mother-look. She lowered her head until the sick girl could see straight into the deep gray eyes. The poor creature gazed into them hungrily.

"Now don't you know that I care?" whispered the nurse.

Grace burst into tears, grasping Hope's hand in both her own. With the reviving hope of life, she clung to it convulsively.

"I'm not what you think, Nurse," she sobbed. "I've always tried to be good, even when I was so hungry. But they—they talked so cruelly about me, and made people think I was bad, until

I was ashamed to meet anyone. Then they put me out of the church, and nobody would give me work in their homes, and they drove me away from every job and every room I got, until there was no place but this. Oh Nurse, I didn't want to do it—I didn't want to do it. But I was sure no one cared—no one!"

"They did not mean to be cruel, dear," said the nurse softly. "They did not understand. You heard the minister say they would help you now."

The girl grabbed Miss Farwell's hand with a shudder.

"They put me out of the church. They turned their backs on me when I needed help the most. I don't want to see any of them. Don't let them come! Promise me you won't let them in."

The other calmed her. "I will take care of you, dear. And no one can put you away from God, you must remember that. The church may shun you, but God *never* does."

"Is there a God, do you think?" whispered the girl. "After what they did, I stopped believing in their God. If He was anything like them, I didn't want to know Him."

"Yes, yes, dear. God is with us all the time. He is here with us right now! And he is *nothing* like those people in the church who hurt you. All the cruelty in the world can't take God away from us if we hold on to Him. We all make mistakes, you know, dear—terrible mistakes sometimes. People with the kindest hearts sometimes do cruel things without thinking. I suppose even those who crucified Jesus were kind and good in their way. When they went home to their families at night, they were probably not wicked and cruel every moment. Only they didn't understand what they were doing, you see. By and by you will learn to feel sorry for these people, just as Jesus wept over those whom He knew were going to torture and kill Him. But first you must get well and strong again. You will now, won't you, dear?"

"Yes, Nurse," Grace whispered. "I'll try now that I know you care." So the strong young woman with the face of the mother Mary talked to the poor outcast girl, helping her to forget, turning her thoughts from the sadness and bitterness of her experience to the gladness and beauty of a possible future. And when the sun lighted up the windows on the other side of the square with flaming fire, and all the sky was filled with the glory of his going, the sick girl slept, still clinging to her nurse's hand.

In the twilight Hope Farwell sat in earnest thought. Deeply spiritual—as all true workers for others must be—she sought to know her part in the coming scenes of the drama in which she found herself cast.

She still felt she should leave Corinth. Her experience with Dan had made the place unbearable to her. And how was she to turn her back on the multitude of opportunities for ministry in the city with Dr. Miles?

But what of Grace Conner? This girl so helpless, so alone, so buffeted and bruised, who had been tossed senseless at her very feet by the wild storms of life. Hope Farwell knew the fury of the storm. She had witnessed before the awful strength of those forces that had so recently overwhelmed Grace Conner. She knew too that there were many others struggling hopelessly in the pitiless grasp of circumstances beyond their strength.

As one watching a distant wreck from a place of safety on shore, the nurse grieved deeply at the relentless cruelty of these ungoverned forces, and mourned at her own powerlessness to check them.

But especially she felt responsible for this poor girl who had been cast within her reach. Here was work at her hand. This she could do and it must be done now, without hesitation or delay. She could not prevent the shipwrecks. She could, however, perhaps save the life of this one who had felt the fury of the storm. It was not Hope Farwell's way to theorize about the causes of the wreck, or to speculate as to the value of inventions for making more efficient the life-saving service, when there was a definite, immediate, personal something to be done for the bit of life that so closely touched her own.

There was no doubt in the nurse's mind now but that the girl would live and regain her health. But what then? She would be shown compassion as long as she was sick. But once she was well, would the people not still look down upon her as before? Who among them would give her a place to live or a job when she was no longer an object of ostentatious charity? Her very attempted suicide would mark her in the community more strongly than ever, and she would be met on every hand by suspicion, distrust, and cruel curiosity.

Then indeed she would need a friend—someone to believe in her and love her! What use would it be to save the life tossed up by the storm, if only to set it adrift again? As Hope meditated in the twilight, the conviction grew that her responsibility could end only when the life was safe, and Grace growing strong again in confidence and faith.

It is, after all, a little thing to save a life. It is a great thing to make it safe. Indeed, in a larger sense a life is never saved until it is safe.

When Dr. Harry called, later in the evening as he had promised, he handed the nurse an envelope.

"Mr. Matthews asked me to give you this," he said. "I met him just as he was crossing the square. He did not want to come in, but turned back toward town as soon as he had given it to me."

He watched her curiously as she broke the seal and read the brief note.

I have seen Dr. Oldham and he has told me about your patient. You are right—I cannot present the matter to my people. I thank you for making so many things clear to me. But this cannot prevent my own personal ministry. Please use the enclosed for Miss Conner, without mentioning my name. Please, do not deny me this opportunity.

The "enclosed" was a bill, large and generous.

Miss Farwell handed the letter to Dr. Harry with the briefest explanation possible. For a long moment the doctor sat in somber silence, then, making no further comment than asking her to use the money as the minister had directed, he questioned her as to the patient's condition. When she had finished her report he drew in a long breath.

"Well, I think we are all right now, Nurse. She will get over this and be as good as ever in a week or two. *Physically*, that is. As to the rest . . ." he added with a questioning look, "who can say if she will recover from that?"

# CHAPTER TWENTY-ONE

# ON FISHING

"Come, boy," said the Doctor, "let's go fishing. I know a dandy place about twelve miles from here. We'll coax Martha to fix us a bite of breakfast and start at daylight. What do you say?"

The two were together again later that same day, after Dan's walk to Old Town with his note, this time sitting on the Doctor's porch.

"But I can't," said Dan. "Tomorrow is Saturday and I have nothing now for Sunday, now that my sermon is in the wastebasket back in my room."

"You'll find a better one when you get away from all this," grunted the Doctor. "Older men than you, Dan, have fought this thing all their lives. Don't think that you can settle it in a couple of days' thinking. Take time to fish a little. It'll help clear your brain. There's nothing like a running stream to wash out the confusion and set one's thoughts going in fresh channels. I want you to see Gordon's Mills."

The evening was spent in preparation, eager anticipation, and discussion of what equipment they would use. As they overhauled flies and rods and lines and reels, and recalled the many delightful days spent as they proposed to spend the next day, the young man's thoughts were led away from the agony in his soul. At daylight, after a breakfast of their own cooking—partly prepared the night before by Martha, who unquestionably viewed the minister's going away on a Saturday with doubtful eyes—they were off.

When they had left the town far behind, following the ridge road in the clear air of the early day, and at last entered the woods, the Doctor laughed aloud as Dan burst forth with a wild boyish yell.

"I couldn't help it," he said. "It's so good to be out in the woods with you again. I feel as if I were being recreated already."

"Then yell again," said the physician with another laugh. "I won't tell."

Gordon's Mills, on Gordon's creek, lay in a deep, narrow valley, shut in and hidden from the world by many miles of rolling, forest-covered hills. The mill, the general store and post office and the blacksmith shop were connected with Corinth, twelve miles away, by a daily stage—a rickety old spring wagon that carried the mail and any chance passengers. Pure and clear and cold, the creek came welling up to the surface of the earth full-grown, from vast, mysterious, subterranean caverns in the heart of the hills. From the brim of its basin it rushed, boiling and roaring along to the river two miles distant, checked only by the dam at the mill. For a little way above the dam the waters lay still and deep, with patches of long mosses, vines and rushes, waving in its quiet clearness, forming shadowy dens for lusty trout, while the open places—shining fields and lanes—reflected, as a mirror, the steep green-clad bluff, and the trees that bent far over until their drooping branches touched the gleaming surface.

As the two friends tramped the little path at the foot of the bluff, wading occasionally, with legs well-braced, in the tumbling torrent, and sent their flies hither and yon to be snatched by the hungry inhabitants of the stream, Dan felt the life and freshness and strength of God's good world entering into his being. At dinnertime they built a little fire to make their coffee and broil a generous portion of their catch. Then lying at ease on the bank of the great spring, they talked as only those can talk who get close enough to the great heart of Mother Nature to feel strongly their kinship with her and with their fellows.

After one of those long silences that come so easily at such a time, Dan tossed a pebble far out into the big pool and watched it sink down, down, down until he lost it in the depths.

"Where does it come from?" he asked.

"Where does what come from?"

"This stream. You say its volume is always the same—unchanged by heavy rains or long draughts. How do you account for that?"

I don't account for it," rejoined the Doctor with a twinkle in his eye. "I merely fish in it."

Dan laughed. "And that," he said slowly, "is your philosophy of life."

The other made no answer.

Choosing another pebble carefully, Dan said, "Speaking as a preacher—won't you please elaborate."

"Speaking as a practitioner—you try it," returned the Doctor. The big fellow stretched himself out on his back, with his hands clasped beneath his head. He spoke deliberately.

"Well," Dan began, "let's try this: You do not know where your life comes from, and it goes after a short course, to lose itself with many others in the great stream that reaches—at last, and is lost in—the Infinite."

The Doctor seemed interested. Dan continued, half talking to himself. "Thus, it is not for you to waste your time in useless speculation as to the unknowable source of your life-stream, or in seeking to trace it in the ocean. It is enough for you that it is, and that, while it runs its brief course, it is yours to make it yield its blessings. For this you must train your hand and eye and brain— you must be in life a fisherman."

"Very well done!" said the Doctor, "for a preacher. Stick to the knowable things, and don't bother with the unknowable. That is my law and my gospel. But if your parishioners heard you, they would be scandalized to hear such liberal theology coming from your lips, without the cross and the blood and the atonement coming in for their fair share of your interpretation of the meaning of this stream."

"I was speaking metaphorically, you know, Doctor. I beg you not to quote me in front of the Elder or the Judge."

Dr. Oldham let out a great laugh.

"And if you question my interpretation," Dan retorted, "now let's watch the practitioner make a cast."

"Humph!" replied the Doctor, paused a moment, then added, "Why don't you stop it?"

"Stop what?"

The other pointed to the great basin of water that—though the stream rushed away in such volume and speed—was never diminished, being constantly renewed from its invisible, unknown source.

The young man shook his head, awed by the contemplation of the mighty, hidden power.

"No more can the great stream of love," said the Doctor—a poet now—"that is in the race for the race and that finds expression in sympathy and service be finally stopped. Fed by hidden, eternal sources it will somehow find its way to the surface. Checked and hampered, for the moment, by obstacles of circumstances or conditions, it is not stopped, for no circumstance can touch the source. And love will keep coming—breaking down or rising over the barrier, it may be—cutting for itself new channels, if need be. For every Judge Strong and his kind there is a Hope Farwell and her kind. For every cast-iron, ecclesiastical dogma there is a living, growing, truth."

---

Dan had indeed had many new things to think about this week!

And his sermon the next day, given in place of the one announced, did not please all of the people present in the Memorial Church. It was the first time since his coming that some wondered aloud concerning the source of his "sermon material."

"It was all very fine and sounded very pretty," said Martha Oldham on her way past him in the greeting line. "But I would like to know, Brother Matthews, where does the church come in? The Word clearly tells us, you know, not to forsake the assembling together of the saints."

# CHAPTER TWENTY-TWO

# COMMON GROUND

The following Tuesday morning Dan was at work bright and early in Denny's garden. Many of the good members of Memorial Church would have said that Dan might better have been at work in his study.

The ruling classes in this congregation that theoretically (like all churches like to *think* of themselves, although most do so wrongly) had no ruling classes were beginning to hint among themselves of a humiliation beyond expression at the spectacle, now becoming so common, of their minister working with his coat off like an ordinary laboring man.

He should have more respect for the dignity of the cloth! At least, if he had no pride of his own, he should have more regard for the feelings of his membership. Besides this, they did not pay him to work in anybody's garden!

The grave and watchful keepers of the faith who held themselves responsible to the God they thought they worshiped, for the belief of the man they had employed to prove to the world wherein it was all wrong and they were all right, watched their minister's growing interest in this Catholic family with increasing uneasiness.

The rest of the church, who were neither of the class nor of the keepers, but merely passengers, as it were, in the Ark of Salvation, looked on with puzzled interest. It was a new move in the game that added a spice of ginger to the play not wholly distasteful. From a safe distance the "passengers" kept one eye on the "class" and the other on the "keepers" with occasionally a stolen glance at Dan, and waited nervously for their cue.

The world outside the fold awaited developments with amused and breathless interest. Everybody secretly admired the stalwart young worker in the garden, and the entire community was grateful that he had given them something new to talk about. Memorial Church was filled at every service.

Meanwhile, utterly unconscious of the speculation that was focused on him, Big Dan continued digging his way among the potatoes, helping the crippled boy to harvest and prepare for market the cabbages and other vegetables that grew in the plot of ground under his study window, never dreaming that there was the least interest either to church or town in the simple neighborly kindness. Dan would probably not have admitted it at the time, but the hours spent in the garden, with Denny enthroned upon the big rock, and Deborah calling out an occasional cheery word from the cottage, were by far the most pleasant hours of the day for the young minister.

Every nerve and muscle in the splendid warm-blooded body of this young giant of the hills called for action. The one mastering passion of his soul was the passion for deeds—to do, to serve, to be used. He had felt himself called to the ministry by his desire to accomplish a work that would be of true and vital worth to the world. He was already conscious of being somewhat out of place with the regular work of the church: the pastoral calls—which meant visiting day after day in the homes of the members to talk with the women about nothing at all, while the men of the household were away laboring, with brain or hand, for the necessities of life; the meetings of the various women's groups and societies— where the minister himself was the only man present, and the talk was all women's talk; the committee meetings—where hours were spent in discussing the most trivial matters with the most ponderous gravity, as though the salvation of the world depended upon the color of the pulpit carpet, or who should bake a cake for the next potluck. It was gradually becoming all Dan could do to continue enduring the endless "business" of the church without seeing the least hint that any true *kingdom business* was being done. He felt more like a company chairman than a minister of the Gospel.

For nearly a week now, Dan had found little time to touch the garden, and he was resolved this day to make good his neglect. An hour before Denny was up, the minister was ready for his work. As he went to get the garden tools from the little lean-to woodshed, Deborah called from the kitchen, " 'Tis early you are this morning. It's not many that are up at the crack of day so they can do somebody else's work for them."

The minister laughingly dodged the warmhearted expressions of gratitude he saw coming. "I've been shirking lately," he said. "If I don't do better than this, the boss will fire me! How is he?"

"Fine, sir, just fine! He's not up yet. You'll hear him yelling at you out the window as soon as he sees what you're at."

"Good!" exclaimed Dan. "I'll get ahead of him this time. Perhaps I can get such a start before he comes that he'll let me stay awhile longer. It wouldn't be pleasant to get my discharge."

Passing laborers and businessmen on the way to work smiled at the coatless figure in the garden. Several called out pleasant greetings. The paperboy looked curiously over the fence, and when the Doctor came out on the porch he looked across the street to the busy gardener and smiled with satisfaction to himself as he turned to his roses.

Dan's mind was not altogether occupied that morning by the work at which his hands were engaged. Neither was he thinking only of his church duties, or planning a sermon. As he bent to the earth under his fingers, his thoughts strayed continually to the young woman whom he had last seen at the bedside of the sick girl in the poverty-stricken room in Old Town. The beautiful freshness and sweetness of the morning and the perfume of the dewy things seemed subtly to suggest her. Thoughts of her seemed somehow to fit in with the gardening which was so pleasant to him.

He called to mind every time he had met her. The times had not been many, and in certain ways they were still virtual strangers. But every occasion had been marked by something that seemed to fix it in his memory as unusual, making their meeting seem far from commonplace. He still had that feeling that she was to play a large part in his life. He was confident that they would meet again. He was wondering where and how, when he looked up from his work to see her coming toward him, dressed in a fresh nurse's uniform of blue and white.

Dan stood speechless, watching as she came toward him, picking her way daintily among the beds and rows of the garden, holding her dress carefully, her beautiful figure expressing health and strength and joyous, tingling life in every womanly curve and line.

There was something wonderfully intimate and sweetly suggestive in the picture they made that morning, these two—the strong young woman in her uniform of service going out in the glow of the early day's sun to meet the stalwart coatless man in the garden, to interrupt him in his earthy labor.

"Good morning," she said with a smile. "I have been watching you from the house, and decided that you were working altogether too industriously, and needed a breathing spell. Do you do everything so energetically?"

It is sadly true of most men today that the more you cover them up the better they look. Our civilization demands a coat, and the rule seems to be: the more civilization, the more coat.

Dan Matthews was one of those rare men who looked good in his shirt sleeves. His shoulders and body needed no shaped and padded garments to set them off. The young woman's eyes, in spite of her calm self-possession, betrayed her admiration as he stood before her so tall and straight—his powerful shoulders, deep chest, and great muscled arms so clearly revealed.

But Dan did not see the admiration in her eyes. He was so bewildered by the mere fact of her presence that he failed to note this interesting detail.

He looked toward the house, then back to the young woman's face. "You were watching me from the house?" he repeated. "I did not know that you—"

"Were your neighbors?" she finished for him. "Yes, we are. Grace and I moved yesterday. You see," she continued, "it was not good for her to remain in that place, and alone. It could never remind her of anything but suffering. She needed a change. I knew that Mrs. Mulhall had a room for rent, because I had thought of taking it before I decided to go back to Chicago."

She blushed as she recalled the thoughts that had led her to the decision, but then she went on resolutely. "The poor girl has such a fear of everybody that I thought it would help her to know that Mrs. Mulhall and Denny could be good to her, even though it was Denny's father, that her father—Well, you know."

Dan's eyes were shining. "Yes, I know," he said.

"I explained to Mrs. Mulhall and, like the dear good soul she is, she understood at once and made the poor child feel better right away. There is such forgiveness under that roof! I thought too that if Grace were living here with Mrs. Mulhall it might help the people to be kinder to her. Then someone will give her a chance to earn her living and she will be all right. The people will soon act differently when they see how Mrs. Mulhall has forgiven her and loves her, don't you think?"

Dan could scarcely find words. She was so entirely unconscious of the beautiful thing she was doing.

"And you?" he asked. "You are not going away after all?"

"Not until she gets a place. She will need me for a while, until she finds a home, you know. And Dr. Harry assures me there is plenty of work to keep me busy in Corinth in the meantime. So Grace and I will keep a little apartment at Mrs. Mulhall's. Grace will do the work while I am busy. It will make her feel less dependent, and," she added frankly, "it will not cost so much that way. And that brings me to what I came out here to say."

She paused. "I wish to thank you, Mr. Matthews," she went on after a moment, "for your help—for the money you sent. The poor child needed so many things, and—I want to beg your pardon for—for the shameful way I treated you when you called. I knew better, and Mrs. Mulhall has been telling me how much you have done for them. I want—"

"Please don't, Miss Farwell," interrupted Dan, "I understand. You were exactly right. I know now." Then he added slowly, "I want you to know, though, Miss Farwell, that I had no thought of being rude when we talked in the old Academy yard."

She was silent and he went on. "I hope I can make you understand that I am not the ill-mannered cad that I seemed. I—you know, this *ministry*," he emphasized the word with a smile, "is so new to me—I am really inexperienced—and I suddenly found myself in a situation, that day with you, I had never been in before."

She glanced at him quickly.

"I had never heard such thoughts as you expressed," he continued, "and I was too puzzled to realize how my silence would appear to you when you knew."

"Then this is your first church?" she asked.

"Yes," he said. "I am barely three months out of seminary! And I am beginning to realize how terribly ignorant I am of life. You know, I was born and brought up in the backwoods. Until I went to college I knew nothing except our simple country life. At college I knew only books and students. Then I came here."

As he talked the young woman's face cleared. It was something very refreshing to hear such a man declare his ignorance of life with the simple honesty of a boy. She held out her hand impulsively.

"Let's forget it all," she said. "It was a horrid mistake."

"And we are to be friends?" he asked, grasping her outstretched hand.

Without replying the young woman quietly released her hand and drew back a few paces. She was trembling. She fought for self-control.

There was something about this man! What was it? The touch of his hand? Hope Farwell was frightened by emotions new and strange to her.

She found a seat on the big rock, and ignoring his question tried to lead their conversation along a new path. "So that's why you are so big and strong, and know so well how to work in a garden," she said. "I thought it was strange for one of your calling. But now I see how natural it is."

"Yes," he smiled. "It is very natural—more natural for me than preaching. But tell me—don't you think we should be friends? We are going to be now, aren't we?"

The young woman answered with quiet dignity. "Friendship, Mr. Matthews, means a great deal to me, and to you also, I am sure. Friends must have much in common. We have nothing, because—because everything I said to you at the Academy, to me is true. You are part of a church system that I can never believe in. We live in two different worlds."

"But it is for myself—the man and not the minister—that I ask it," he urged.

She watched his face closely. Then she answered, "But you and your ministry are one and the same. Your life *is* your ministry. You are your ministry, and your ministry is you."

"But we will *find* common ground!" he exclaimed. "Look here, we have already found it! This garden—Denny's garden! We'll put a sign over the gate, 'No professional ministry shall enter here! ' The 'Preacher' lives up there." He pointed to his window. "The man, Dan Matthews, works in the garden here. To the man in the garden you may say what you like about the parson up there. We may differ, of course, but we may each gain something, as is right for friends, for we will each grant to the other the privilege of being true to self."

She hesitated. Then slipping from the rock and looking him full in the face, she said, "I warn you it will not work. But for friendship's sake, I am willing to try."

Neither of them realized the deep significance of the terms, but in the days that followed, the people of Corinth had much more to talk about. The Ally was well-pleased, and saw to it that the ladies of the Aid Society were not long in deciding that something must be done.

# CHAPTER TWENTY-THREE

# THE WARNING

It happened two weeks to the day after Dan and Miss Farwell had spoken in Denny's garden.

The Ally had been busy to some purpose. The Ladies' Aid Society, having reached the point of declaring that something must be done, did something. Thus followed the inevitable. The Elders of Memorial Church, in their official capacity, called on their pastor.

Dan was in the garden when the Elders came. Working with his fingers in the dirt, dirt owned by a Catholic, did not strengthen his cause in the eyes of the Elders.

The Doctor's wife declared that Dan spent most of his time in the garden now, and that, when there, he didn't do much of anything anymore because that nurse was always helping. Good Martha has the fatal gift of telling a bit of news so vividly that it gains much in the telling. Though not always much in the way of truth.

On that particular afternoon, Miss Farwell was in the garden with the minister, and so was Denny, while Grace Conner and Deborah Mulhall were sitting on the front porch of the little cottage. Though neither of the church fathers turned their heads as they passed, neither of them failed to see the two women on the porch and the three friends in the garden.

"For the love of Heaven, look there!" exclaimed Deborah in an excited whisper. "They're turning in at the minister's gate, and him out there in the 'taters in his shirt, digging in the ground, and talking with Denny and Miss Hope. I don't doubt there's something stirring to take them to his door today. I'll have to run and tell him!"

But Dan had seen them and was already on his way to the front gate, pulling on his coat as he went. From the other side of the street the Doctor waved his hand to Dan in encouragement, as the young man walked hastily down the sidewalk to overtake the church officials at the front door.

Truly in this denominational circus, odd yokefellows are sometimes set to run together. The efforts of the children of light to lead the church indeed often equal the efforts of the children of darkness. They will clap the church's ecclesiastical harness upon anything that—by flattery, bribes, or intimidation—can be led, coaxed, or driven to pull at the particular congregational chariot to which the tugs are fast!

Two more different men it would be difficult to imagine. When the people of Corinth speak of Judge Strong's religion, or his relation to the Memorial Church, they wink—if the Judge is not looking. When Elder Jordan is mentioned, their voices always have a note of respect and true regard. Elder Strong is always called "The Judge"; Nathaniel Jordan was known far and wide as "Elder Jordan." Thus does the community, as communities have a way of doing, touch the heart of the whole matter.

Dan recognized instinctively the difference in the characters of these two men. Yet he had found them always of one mind in all matters concerning the church. He felt the subtle antagonism of Judge Strong—though he did not realize that the reason for it lay in the cunning instinct of a creature that recognized a natural enemy in all such spirits as his. He felt, too, the regard and growing appreciation of Elder Jordan. Yet the two churchmen were in perfect accord in their "brotherly administration."

When the officials met in Dan's study that day, their characters were unmistakable. The minister's favorite chair creaked in dismay as the Judge settled his heavy body, and twisted this way and that in an open effort to inspect every corner of the apartment with his narrow, suspicious eyes. The older churchman sat by the window, studiously observing something outside.

Dan felt that strange feeling of uneasiness familiar to every schoolboy when called upon unexpectedly for a private interview with the principal. The Elders had never visited him before. It was all too evident from their bearing that they had come today on matters of painful importance.

At last Judge Strong's wandering eye came to rest upon Dan's favorite fishing-rod standing in a corner behind a bookcase. The young man's face grew red in spite of himself. It was impossible not to feel guilty of something in the presence of Judge Strong. His very bearing spoke of reproof.

The silence was broken by the Judge's metallic voice. "I see that you follow in the footsteps of the early disciples in one thing, at least, Brother Matthews. You go fishing." He gave forth a cold laugh that, more than anything else, betrayed the real spirit he laughed to hide.

It was a remark characteristic of Judge Strong. The words seemed to say one thing, while the subtle implication was of another meaning entirely. On the surface it was but the mild jest of a churchman, whose mind—he would have you to think—dwelt so habitually on the sacred Book, that even in his lightest vein he could not but express himself in terms and allusions of religious significance.

Beneath the surface, however, the words carried an accusation, a condemnation, and—that most hideous of all hateful things in God's eyes—a religious sneer. Following his comment, the faint gleam in the Judge's eye betrayed his intent: he sat in the eager, expectant, self-congratulatory manner of a dog that has treed his quarry. He was still the *judge*, in the tradition of St. Matthew, not St. Judge Strong the elder. His method had been skillfully chosen—for he was a master at it—to give him this advantage: it made his meaning clear while it gave no possible opening for a reply to the real idea his words conveyed. His listener was thus forced into an embarrassed silence of self-condemnation, securing the Judge all the more solidly in his assumed position of pious superiority. The Judge—as are many religious personages occupying roles of feigned power and supposed importance—was well-practiced in his art.

Dan forced a smile. He felt that the Judge's laugh demanded it. "Yes," he said, "I am scriptural when it comes to fishing. Dr. Oldham and I had a fine day at Gordon's Mills a few weeks ago."

"So I understand," said the other with heavily implied meaning. "I suppose you and the old Doctor have some interesting talks on religion?"

It was impossible not to feel the weight of innuendo under the words. It was as impossible to answer. Dan's face flushed slightly again as he said, "No, actually we rarely discuss the church."

"No?" said the Judge.

"The Doctor and I have known one another for years. We have many other things to talk about."

"I should think you would find him a good subject to practice on. Perhaps, though, he practices on you with his unbelief, eh?" Again he laughed.

The false assumption about his friend nettled Dan. He opened his mouth to speak to his defense, but was interrupted by Elder Jordan.

"Ahem, ahem!" came the usual warning that old Nathaniel was about to speak. Dan sat back and turned to the good old man with a feeling of relief. At least Nathaniel Jordan's words would bear their face value. "Perhaps, Brother Strong, we had better tell Brother Matthews the object of our call," he said.

The Judge leaned back in his chair with the air of one about to be pleasantly entertained. He waved his hand with a gesture that said as plainly as words, *All right, Nathaniel, go ahead. I'm here if you need me, so don't be uneasy! We have this fox up the tree already. If you find yourself unequal to the task, depend upon me to help you out.*

The minister waited.

"You must not think, Brother Matthews," began Elder Jordan

hesitantly, "that we called because we think there is anything which could actually be called *wrong*. But we, ahem—we thought it best to give you a, ahem—a brotherly warning before the situation becomes, ah, shall we say—more serious. I'm sure you will take it in the spirit in which it is meant."

The Judge stirred uneasily in his chair, bending upon Dan such a look—had he been a judge in the judicial rather than the spiritual sense—as he might have cast upon a convicted criminal. He signified his assent to the Elder's statement, and Nathaniel proceeded:

"You are a young man, Brother Matthews. I may say a talented young man, and we are very hopeful for your success in this community and, ahem—for the standing of Memorial Church. Some of our ladies feel—I may say that *we* feel that you have been a little, ah—careless about some things of late. Elder Strong and I know from past experience that a preacher—a young, unmarried preacher—cannot be too careful. Not that we have the least idea that you mean any harm, you know—not the least in the world. But people will talk and—ahem, well . . . ahem!"

Dan stared at the good Elder in bewilderment. He was so clearly mystified by the Elder's remarks that the poor old man found his duty even more embarrassing than he had anticipated. He had made every attempt to be forthright, yet the young man had not a clue as to his meaning.

But Dan had not long to wait for clarification. The next instant Judge Strong again assumed the offensive, and proceeded to throw a flood of light upon the situation in his characteristic manner. "That young woman, Grace Conner, has a mighty bad name in this town," he said. "And the other one, her friend the nurse, is a stranger. She was in my house for a month, and—well, some things about her look mighty peculiar to me. She hasn't been inside a church since she came to Corinth. I would be the last man in the world to cast suspicion on anyone's character, but—"

He let the unspoken remainder of the sentence be finished with a shake of his head, and an expression of pious doubt on his crafty face that said he could, if he wished, tell many dark secrets of Miss Hope Farwell's life.

Dan was on his feet instantly, his face flaming and his eyes gleaming with indignation. But even as his mouth opened in support of Hope Farwell's work and ministry, he suddenly remembered who these men were, and his relation to them in the church.

"I beg your pardon," he said slowly, and dropped back into his chair, clenching his big hands in an attempt to maintain his self-control.

Elder Jordan broke in nervously. "Ahem, ahem! You understand, Brother Matthews, that the sisters—that *we* do not think that you mean any harm, but your standing in the community, you know, is such that we must shun every appearance of evil. The reputation of the church, you understand—we are ambassadors for Christ, you remember, and we, ahem—that is, we felt it our duty to call."

Big Dan Matthews—humble and innocent and without guile—had never met that spirit, the Ally, and he therefore did not now know how to answer his masters in the church. On the one hand, he tried to feel that their mission to him was of grave importance. But on the other he was tempted to laugh outright; their ponderous dignity seemed so ridiculous.

"Thank you, sir," he at last managed to say seriously. "I think it is hardly necessary for me to attempt any explanation."

He was still fighting for self-control and chose his words carefully. "I will certainly consider this matter in prayer," he added.

When the overseers of the church were gone, the young pastor walked the floor of the room trying to grasp the true significance of the situation. For still he found himself alternating between fits of bewilderment and righteous anger. Gradually the real meaning of the Elders' visit grew upon him. Because his own life was so big, so broad, because his ideals and ambitions were so high, so true to the Spirit of Christ whose service he thought he had entered, he could not believe what his senses were clearly telling him.

He might have found some shadow of reason, perhaps, for their fears regarding his friendship of the girl with the bad reputation, had the circumstances been other than they were, and had he not known who it was who gave Grace Conner her bad name.

But that his friendship for Hope Farwell, whose selfless heart and beautiful ministry to the downtrodden was such an example of the Spirit of Jesus Christ himself, and that her care for the poor girl should be so quickly construed into something evil—his mind positively refused to entertain the thought. He felt that the visit of his church fathers was unreal. He walked around as one dazed by an unpleasant dream. They could not possibly have meant what it seemed they were implying, he said to himself. Could he possibly have mistaken their intent?

To come from the pure, wholesome atmosphere of his home, and the inspiring study of the history of Christianity, prepared, as he thought, to follow in the footsteps of the saints of old into the true ministry of the life-changing Gospel of Jesus Christ—to come from that into such a twisted, distorted, hideous corruption of the church policy and spirit, was, to Dan, like coming from God's sunny hillside pastures to the gloom and stench of the slaughter pens. He was stunned by the pettiness, the meanness, the self-righteousness, and the judgmental spirit that had prompted the "kindly warning" of these two leaders of the church.

Slowly he began to see what that spirit might mean to him.

Dan did not possess wide experience. He had not visited many churches—large, small, rich, poor, of every denomination and persuasion, pentecostal, evangelical, liberal, and conservative. He had not traveled the length and breadth of the country, and had not spent a lifetime discerning the modes of operation in all the infinite varieties of Christian assemblies. If he had, he would not have been so shocked. For he would have known that Judge Strong and Elder Jordan and the women of the Ladies' Aid were not such unique personalities in the annals of organized and churchified Christendom, but were mere "types," representative of their counterparts in ten thousand congregations across the land.

No man of ordinary intelligence could long be in Memorial Church, without learning that it was ruled by a ring, a clique, an inner circle, as truly as any political body was ever so ruled by those holding the reins of power. Nor in this was Memorial Church unlike its countless brother and sister congregations throughout the land. In some the power is wielded by a visible few. In others by an invisible network—many of whose members do not even realize that *they* are the kingmakers, *they* are the destroyers of the Grace Conners in their midst, *they* are those who unknowingly sit in judgment upon those who would enter their company to effect change and speak bold words of truth, *they* are those who make or break the lives and futures and reputations of the Dan Matthews' who come among them, never knowing that their attitudes and subtle words and stray glances and insinuations have the force to elevate into or topple from positions of great influence. Truly the Ally has many allies who know not what cause they really serve. In still other congregations, and these not a few, the power—whether visible or under the surface, whether recognized as such by newcomers or only those who have endured its effect for ten, fifteen, or twenty years, whether intentional or unintentional—is in the grip of interconnected familial relationships, whose dynasties and patriarchs and matriarchs and crown princes and princesses and heirs occupy the role of a ruling elite as certainly as the Hapsburgs walked the courts of Austria.

Dan Matthews understood all too clearly that his position in Memorial Church depended upon the "bosses" then in control. And he saw additionally that his final success or failure in the calling he had chosen depended upon the standing that should be given him by this, his first pastorate. If he was given the stamp as a "black sheep" here, he could scarcely hope to occupy another meaningful pulpit again. His desire to speak, minister, and *live* the truth, he now realized had to be subordinated to his efforts to "please" those who held his life in their grip. His whole future depended upon these two men, who had shown themselves, each in his own way, so easily influenced by the low, condescending, and self-righteous tales of a few idle-minded church gossips who loved the shade, not the light of truth.

Alone in his room, his brain tumbling about through realizations too heartbreaking to believe, as one in the dark stepping without warning into a boggy hole, Dan's mind groped for firmer ground.

As one standing alone on a wide plain, seeing on the distant horizon the threat of a gathering storm, and shuddering at the shadow of a passing cloud, Dan stood staring blankly out his window—a feeling of loneliness and dread heavy upon him.

He longed for companionship, for someone to whom he could go and open his heart.

But to whom in Corinth could he go? These two men who had just "advised him" were, theoretically, supposed to be his spiritual counselors. To them he was supposed, and had expected in his inexperience, to look for advice and help in church matters— these men, old in the service of the church and town. But what of matters more personal? He knew how *they* would answer his troubled thoughts, and he did not relish such an interview as opening his mind to them would surely bring to pass.

He shrugged his shoulders and smiled grimly. The Doctor? He smiled again. Dan little dreamed how much that keen old fisherman already knew, from a skillful baiting of Martha, about the visit of the Elders that afternoon. And his knowledge of Dan's character from very childhood enabled the physician to guess more than a little of the thoughts that occupied the young man pacing the floor of his room.

But the Doctor would not do for the young man that day.

Dan went again to the window and this time looked down on the garden. The nurse was still there, helping crippled Denny with his work. The minister's hoe was leaning against the big rock, just as he had left it when he had caught up his coat.

Should he go down? What would she say if he were to tell her of the Elders' mission?

Something caused Miss Farwell to look up just then, and she saw him. She beckoned to him playfully, guardedly, like a schoolgirl.

Smiling, he shook his head. No, she was not the one to tell. More than ever, in that moment Dan felt very much alone.

# CHAPTER TWENTY-FOUR

# DR. HARRY PRESENTS ANOTHER SIDE

The friendship between Dan and Dr. Abbott had grown rapidly, as was natural, for the two men had much in common.

In a town as small as Corinth, there are many opportunities for even the busiest men to meet, and scarcely a day passed that the doctor and the preacher did not at least exchange greetings. As often as their duties permitted they got together, sometimes at the office or in Dan's small apartment, or during an evening at Harry's home, or driving miles out into the country behind the bay mare or big Jim—the physician to see a patient, and the minister to act as the "hitching post."

Harry was just turning from the telephone that same evening when Dan entered the house.

"Hello, Parson!" he cried heartily. "I was just trying to call you. I couldn't think of anything to do to anybody else, so I thought I'd have a try at you." Glancing at his friend's depressed-looking face, he added, "That wasn't such a bad guess either!"

Dan half-smiled with a grim expression.

"You look like you need to have something fixed!" the doctor went on. "What did you do, swallow a bottle of vinegar? Or is it your liver?"

He led the way into the library.

"Isn't the liver where you medical men consign emotional disorders, and other ailments of the nerves and psyche?" laughed Dan.

"And anything else we don't know what to do with!"

"Well, it can't be my liver, then. Don't you know those in my calling aren't supposed to have that disease?"

He pushed an armchair to face the doctor's favorite seat by the table.

Harry chuckled as he reached for his pipe and tobacco. "You don't need to have an ailing liver yourself to suffer from liver troubles. Speaking professionally, my opinion is that you preachers, as a class of men, are more likely to suffer from other people's livers than from your own, though it is also true than the average parson has more of his own than he knows what to do with."

"You are most perceptive," replied Dan.

The other struck a match.

"And what do you doctors prescribe when it *is* the other fellow's liver causing the difficulty?" asked Dan.

"There's a difference of opinion in the profession. The old Doctor, for instance, pins his faith to a split bamboo with some flies or a can of bait."

"And you?" Dan was smiling now.

The answer came through a cloud of smoke. "Just a pipe and a book."

"I fear your treatment would not agree with my constitution," said Dan. "My system does not permit me to use the remedy you prescribe."

"You mean the pipe?" A puff of smoke punctuated the remark. The physician was closely watching his friend's face now. "Pardon me, Brother Matthews, I meant no slur upon your personal convictions—"

"Brother Matthews!" interrupted Dan sharply. "I thought we agreed to drop all that! It's bad enough to either be dodged or shunned or spoken to in reverent tones like I was eighty years old and wearing white robes by every man and woman in town, without your rubbing it in. As for my personal convictions, they have nothing to do with the case. In fact, my *system* does not permit me to have personal convictions!"

Dr. Harry's eyes twinkled. "This system of yours seems to be in a bad way, Dan. What's wrong with it?"

"Wrong with it! Wrong with the system, the organization? Man, don't you know that to even suggest there might be something *wrong* would be heresy? How can there be anything wrong with the system? Doesn't it relieve me of any responsibility in the matter of right and wrong? Doesn't it take from me all such burdens as personal convictions? Doesn't it fix my standards of goodness, and then doesn't it make goodness itself my profession? You poor fellow, you and the rest of the merely "human"—you have to choose whether to be good or not! Thanks to the system of which I have become a part, *my* goodness is a matter of business. I am paid for being good! The system says that your pipe, and perhaps your book, and my gardening, and Hope Farwell's ministry, are all bad—sinful. I have nothing to do with it. I only obey and draw my salary."

"Oh well," said Harry calmly, "there is always the old Doctor's remedy. It's probably better on the whole."

"I tried that the other day," said Dan.

"Worked, didn't it?"

Dan grinned in spite of himself. "At first the effects seemed to be very beneficial, but later I found that it was, er—somewhat irritating, and that it slightly aggravated the complaint."

The doctor was smiling now. "Suppose you try a little physical exercise occasionally—working in the garden, or—"

Dan threw up his hands with a tragic gesture. "Suicide!" he cried.

Then both lay back in their chairs and howled with laughter.

"That does a fellow good!" said Dan after a while.

"I think I have located your liver trouble," said Harry with a final chuckle. "When did they call?"

"This afternoon. But how did you know?"

"I've been expecting it for several days. I guess you were about the only person in Corinth who wasn't."

"Why didn't you tell me?"

"If I can avoid it, I never tell a patient of a coming operation until it's time to operate. Then it's all over before he has a chance to be nervous about it."

Dan shuddered. The laugh was all out of him now. "I have certainly been on the table this afternoon," he said. "I need to talk it out with someone. That's what I came to you for."

"Perhaps you had better tell me the particulars," said Harry quietly.

Dan told him the whole story, and when he had finished they had both grown very serious.

"I was afraid of this, Dan," said Harry. "You'll need to be very careful from now on—very careful."

Dan started to reply, but the doctor checked him.

"I know. I know how you feel. What you say about the system and all that is all too true. And you haven't seen the worst of it yet, by a good deal."

"Do you mean to tell me that Miss Farwell will be made to suffer because she has taken an interest in that poor girl?" asked Dan.

"If Miss Farwell continues to live with Grace Conner at Mrs. Mulhall's, there's not a respectable home in this town that will receive her," answered the doctor bluntly.

"My God! Are the people blind?" exclaimed Dan. "Can't the church see what a beautiful, Christlike thing she is doing?"

"You know Grace Conner's history," said Harry coolly. "What reason is there to think it will be different in Miss Farwell's case, so far as the attitude of the community is concerned?"

Dan could keep his seat no longer. He rose and walked the floor in agitation. Then suddenly he turned on the other and demanded, "Then am I to understand that in the end my friendship with Miss Farwell will mean for me—"

Dr. Harry was silent. Indeed, how could he suggest, ever so indirectly, that the friendship between Dan and Miss Farwell should be discontinued. If the young woman had been anyone else, or if Dr. Harry himself did not find her so—

*But why attempt explanation*? he said to himself.

The minister continued pacing up and down the room, stopping now and then to face the doctor, who sat still in his chair by the library table, quietly smoking his pipe.

"I just can't believe this, Harry! It's not really my friendship with Miss Farwell, is it? It goes beyond that. It is the spirit of it all that matters." Dan paused, but then resumed almost as quickly. "I never dreamed that such a thing could be. That Grace Conner's life should be ruined by the wicked carelessness of these people seems bad enough. But that they should take the same attitude toward Miss Farwell, simply because she is seeking to do the Christian thing that the church itself will not do—it is monstrous!"

He turned impatiently to resume his restless movement. Then, when his friend continued not to speak, he continued slowly, as though the words were forced from him against his will. "And to think that they could be so unmoved by the suffering of that poor girl, their own victim, and be so untouched by the example of Miss Farwell. And then that they should give such grave consideration and be so influenced by absolutely groundless and vicious idle gossip! And that the church should be in the hands of such mean and small people!"

He confronted the doctor again and his face was red. "My whole career as a Christian minister depends upon the mere whim of these people, who are moved by such a spirit as this. No matter what motives may prompt my course, they have the power to prevent me from doing my work. This is one of the strongest and most influential churches in the denomination. They can give me such a name that my very future, my whole lifework will be ruined. What can I do?"

"You must be very careful, Dan," repeated Dr. Harry slowly.

"Careful! And that means, I suppose, that I must bow to the people of this church—ruled as they are by such a spirit—as to my lords and masters—that I shall have no other God but this congregation, that I shall deny my own conscience for theirs, that

I shall go about the trivial nonsensical things they call my pastoral duties in fear and trembling, that my ministry is to cringe when they speak and do their will regardless of what I feel to be the will of Christ! If that is what the call to the ministry means, I am beginning to understand some things that have always puzzled me greatly."

He dropped wearily back into his chair.

"Tell me, Doctor," he asked, "do the people in general see these things? Do they realize this stranglehold the small band of policymakers exerts?"

"It seems to me that everyone who is able to think must see them to some degree, though many blind themselves to the truth, thinking they are thus being 'faithful' to God's anointed, I suppose."

"But if some do see them, why did no one tell me? Why didn't the old Doctor explain the real condition of the church?"

"As a rule it is not a safe thing to attempt to tell a minister these things. Would you have listened if he had tried to tell you earlier? Or would you have misunderstood his motives because he is not a church man? The Doctor loves you, Dan."

"But you are a church man, Harry. You are even a member of the board of my own congregation. If men like you know these things, why are you in the church at all?"

Silently Dr. Harry refilled and lit his pipe, deliberating over his reply. The membership of every church may be divided into three distinct classes: those who *are* the church, those who *belong to* the church, and those who are members, but neither are, nor belong to its ruling elite. Dr. Harry was a member.

Or seen another way, the three classes might be viewed in such a manner: those who serve the Ally, even if unknowingly; those active participants who see the Ally-servers, but who are willing to overlook the Ally's work while trying to avoid it themselves; and the mere attenders and functionaries who are too far from the center and thus remain forever oblivious of the Ally's grip. There is another class as well—those who see the Ally and try to awaken their fellows to the need to root out its influence from their midst.

These, however, generally do not remain long in any congregation. They are driven out by the first group. From this vantage point, Dr. Harry fell into the second class. Dan was sounding dangerously like one of the fourth. And thus came the doctor's injunctions toward care.

"Dan," answered the physician at length, "I suppose it is very difficult for a man such as you to understand the spiritual dependence of people like myself. I see the church's lack of appreciation for true worth and character. I know the vulgar, petty scheming and wire-pulling for place and position and power, the senseless craving for notoriety. I know that if a minister is not part of the problem himself and desires to do good, he is often at the mercy of some of the most self-seeking spirits in his congregation. But, Dan, because we love the cause we do not talk of these things even to each other, for fear of being misunderstood. It is useless to talk of them to our ministers, for they dare not listen. Why, man, I never in my life dreamed that I would talk to my pastor as I am talking to you!" He smiled. "I suppose I was afraid that they would tell Judge Strong, and that the church would throw me out. And with most of them, that is probably exactly what would have happened. I am not sure but that even you will consider me unsafe, and avoid me in the future," he added with a chuckle.

Dan smiled at his words, though they revealed so much to him.

Dr. Harry went on. "We remain in the church, and give it our support, I suppose, because we are dependent upon it for our religious life, because we know no religious life outside of it."

He paused, gave a puff or two at his pipe, clearly thinking. When he finally continued it was with a pensive tone. "Perhaps that is not good, to be dependent upon a system rather than an inner spirituality that can derive strength from God alone. I have not really thought about this before, so I can speak for no one but myself. So I say, perhaps this church life which men like myself need is not the best way. Christ, I don't suppose, needed man nor church but found his life solely from God. But many of us lesser mortals would be spiritually lost without the organization which is the church. We know of no religious life outside it. And we love its teaching in spite of its practice. We are always hoping that someone will show a better way for its teachings to be put into practice."

Again he stopped. He looked at Dan, but his visitor was quiet now and seemed content to allow him to continue.

"I don't know how or when the change in the church will come, Dan," he said. "But I am confident that it will come, and it will come from men like you—some of the ministry, some from the laity, but men with the highest ideals. But it all will take time, Dan, and you must be careful, mighty careful."

# CHAPTER TWENTY-FIVE

# A PARABLE

"Miss Farwell."

The nurse looked up from the sewing in her hands. "Yes, Grace, what is it?"

"I think I'd like to try to find some work today. Mrs. Mulhall told me last night that she had heard of two women who need help. It may be that one of them will take me. I think I ought to try."

This was the third time in the last few days that the girl had talked of getting out and working again. Under Miss Farwell's personal care, she had recovered rapidly from her terrible experience, both physically and mentally. Yet the nurse felt she was not yet strong enough to meet a possible rebuff from the community, especially one that had been so reluctant in the past to treat her with any degree of kindness or consideration. The girl's spirit had been cruelly hurt. She had an unhealthy, morbid fear of the world that would cripple her for life if it could not somehow be overcome.

Miss Farwell felt that Grace Conner's only chance to do that was to win for herself a respectable place in the very community where she had suffered such ill-treatment. But before she faced the people again she must be prepared. The sensitive, wounded spirit must be strengthened, for it could not bear many more blows. How to accomplish that was the problem now occupying Hope Farwell's thoughts and prayers.

Hope dropped her sewing in her lap. "Come over here by the window, dear, and let's talk about it."

The young woman came and seated herself on a stool at the feet of her companion. In actual years the two were nearly the same age, yet in so many ways Hope had become to her as an elder sister.

"Why are you so anxious to leave me, Grace?" asked the nurse with a smile.

The girl's eyes—eyes that would never now be wholly free from that shadow of fear and pain—filled with tears. She put out a hand impulsively, touching Miss Farwell's knee. "You know it isn't that I want to leave you," she said, with a little catch in her voice.

The eyes of the stronger woman looked down to reassure her. "What is it then?"

The girl's face was downcast and she picked nervously at the fold of her friend's skirt. "It's nothing, I guess . . . only I feel that I—that I oughtn't to keep being a burden to you a day longer than I can help."

"I thought that might be it," returned the other. Her firm, white hand slipped under the trembling chin. She gently lifted the girl's face until Grace was forced to look straight into her deep gray eyes. "Tell me, dear," said Hope, "why do you feel you are a burden upon me?"

There was silence for a moment in the room. "I—I don't know," said the girl at length.

The nurse smiled.

"I'll tell you why," she said, and then paused. There was a grave note in her voice as she spoke, still holding the girl's face toward her own.

"It is because you have been hurt so deeply," she went on after a moment. "This feeling is one of the scars of your experience. All your life you will need to fight that feeling—the feeling that you are not wanted. And you *must* fight it—fight it with all your might. You will never overcome it entirely, for the scar of your hurt is there to stay. You will always suffer at times from the old fear. But, if you will, you can conquer it! Though it will always be with you, you can overcome it so that it will not spoil your life. And in the end you can, with God's help, turn it into good. You will be even stronger and more compassionate as a result of that very past of pain. You can conquer it. And you *must*—for your own sake, and for my sake, and for the sake of the wounded lives you are going to help heal—help all the better because of your own hurt. The day will come when you will even rejoice at what you had to suffer, for the help it will bring to others. Do you understand, dear?"

The other nodded. But she could not speak. There were tears in her eyes. The very idea that *she*, lowly Grace Conner—that *she* would ever be a help to anyone else, was inconceivable. Yet deep in her being she so desperately wanted to believe it might be true!

"You will eventually be going back out into the world to find a place for yourself. And of course, that is the right thing to do," Hope continued. "And if possible, it will be best for you to find a place here in Corinth. But it is not going to be easy, Grace. It is going to be hard, very hard, and you will need to know that no matter what other people make you feel, you have a place in my life, a place where you belong."

She paused, thinking, then said, "Let me try, if I can, to explain that in a way you will never, never forget."

For a few minutes the nurse looked away out of the window, up into the leafy depths of the big trees, and into the blue sky beyond, while the girl watched her eyes with a wondering, hungering earnestness. When Miss Farwell spoke again she chose her words carefully.

"Once upon a time a woman was walking in the mountains. By chance she discovered a wonderful mine of gold, of such vast wealth that there was nothing in all the world like it for richness. And because she had found it, the mine belonged to the woman. But it was not her desire to hide her discovery, nor to hoard and accumulate the gold only for herself. She desired instead for her discovery to benefit mankind. There was such wealth that she knew she could share and share and share it, and still have an abundance. And thus the wealth of the mine went out into the world for men and women everywhere to use, and thus, in the largest sense, the riches the woman found belonged to all mankind. But still, because she had found it, the woman always felt that it was hers. And so, through her discovery of this vast wealth, and the great happiness it brought to the world, the mine became to the woman the dearest of all her possessions—dearer because it had gone out to others than it could ever have been had she kept it to herself."

Miss Farwell stopped, then looked down at the face she loved. "Tell me, Grace," she asked, "do you think that anyone could ever replace the mountains, the ocean or the stars, or any of these wonderful, wonderful things in the great universe, if they were to be destroyed? Could anyone ever do again what God did when He created the world?"

"No," came the girl's answer with a puzzled tone.

"And do you think, Grace, that anything in all this beautiful world is of greater importance—of more value to the world—than a human life, with all its marvelous power to think and feel and love and hate and so leave its mark on all life, for all time?"

Again came the answer, "No, I don't suppose so."

"Well, here is what I am trying to say, dear. The feeling you will have, and I'm sure have had many times already, of worthlessness—the feeling that the world would be better off without you—the feeling that you don't make a difference to anyone—the feeling that you have no value—all those feelings are not true! Nothing in all the world that God has created is so wonderfully full of worth as *every* human soul he has made. It is impossible that anyone could ever take your place! You have a place in the world—a place that is yours because God put you in it, just as truly as he put the mountains, the seas, the stars in their places. And that is why you must feel that you have a right to your own life-place, and why you must hold it, no matter what others say

or do or think—because your place is of great value to God and
to the world. And, Grace—look at me, child—do you think that
anything in all the universe is dearer to the Father than a human
life that is so wonderful and so eternal in its power? So life should
be the dearest thing in all the world to us. Not just the life of each
to himself, but every life—any life, the dearest thing to all. I think
this was true of Jesus. I think it should be true of all Christians. I
believe this with all my heart."

There was silence for a little while. Then Hope went on again.

"Now, Grace, you are the mine I was talking about—a wonderful, rich mine full of untold amounts of gold. And I am the
one who found you. Your life, the most wonderful, the dearest
thing in all the world—it belongs to me! And as the mine brought
the woman great joy because it blessed the world, now you will
fulfill my joy when you are standing tall and strong and ministering to others and sharing your wealth with the world. But you
will always be dearest of all to me! And I never want you to forget
that! As I said, whatever anyone says or does or makes you feel,
in *my* heart you are a mine of gold. When others threw your life
aside, when you yourself tried to throw it away, I found it. I took
it. It is one of my prized possessions. And it is the dearest thing
in all the world to me, because it is so great a thing, because no
other life can take its place, and because it is of such great worth
to the world—greater worth than any gold mine. Do you see?"
the calm voice was now vibrant with deep emotion.

Looking up into those gray eyes that shone with such love into
her own, Grace Conner began to realize the mighty truth that *she*
had worth in the eyes of God—a truth so powerful that in time it
would mold and shape her own life into a life of beauty and power.

"So, dear," the nurse continued, "when you go out into the
world again, and people make you feel the old hurt—as they
will—you must remember the woman who found the mine. They
may not see the gold yet. But you must remember that I see it,
and I know that it is going to be a blessing to the world. So never
mind that they don't see it yet. Feeling that you belong to me and
to all life, you will not let people rob you of your place in the

world. You will not let them rob me of my great wealth. And now you must try the very best you can to get work here in Corinth. But if you should fail to find it, you won't let that matter too much. You'll keep your place right here with me just the same, won't you, Grace, because you are mine, you know, and it may take a while for other people to see what a wealth of gold I have discovered."

The girl looked long and earnestly into the face of the nurse, and Miss Farwell understood what she could not say. Suddenly the girl caught her friend's hand, kissed it, then rushed from the room. Miss Farwell wisely let her go without a word. But her own eyes were full.

She turned to the open window to see the minister coming in at the gate.

# CHAPTER TWENTY-SIX

# DAN CONSIDERS OPTIONS

Dan did not take his usual path leading to the garden, but walked straight to the porch. His face was serious as he asked Miss Farwell if he could come in when she answered the door.

She welcomed him, and at once took up the thread of conversation which the visit of the Elders had interrupted the day before. But it was clear Dan's mind was busy with other thoughts, and soon they were facing an embarrassing silence. The young woman gazed thoughtfully at the monument across the street, while Dan moved in his chair uneasily. At last the big minister broke the silence.

"I don't know what you will think of me for coming upon the errand that brought me," he said, "but I sincerely want you to believe that I am trying to do what is best."

She looked at him with a questioning expression, inviting him to continue.

"I learned something yesterday," Dan went on, "that I feel you ought to know, and there seems to be no one else to tell you . . . so I came."

"Go on, please."

Dan then proceeded to tell her of the Elders' visit and his talk with Dr. Abbott, including the talk that was beginning to circulate concerning the nurse and the pastor. A time or two Miss Farwell's cheeks and brow grew crimson, but she quickly managed to regain her composure.

"So you see," he finished with a grim smile, "I did not come to you with this for fun."

"You don't seem to be particularly enjoying it," she agreed. "I can easily understand how this talk might have serious results for you. You remember I warned you that you could not leave the preacher on the other side of the fence. But of course you can easily avoid any trouble with your people if you only stop—"

She paused, checked by the expression on his face.

"I did not come here to discuss the trouble for *me*," he said, with an earnest, almost desperate tone. "Please believe me. Don't you see how this idle, silly talk is likely to harm *you*? You know what the gossip in this town did for Grace Conner. It is serious, Miss Farwell, believe me, or I would not have told you about it at all."

"I realize that," she said quietly. "Already it has begun. Though he has not said it in so many words, I believe Dr. Abbott has begun to find that some people will not employ me because of the things that are being said. I could tell something was wrong—instead of telling me of possible cases and assuring me of work, as he did at first, he has been saying lately, 'I will let you know if anything turns up.' "

"I hope you do not think that Dr. Abbott—"

She interrupted him with quiet dignity. "Certainly I do not think any such thing. You and Dr. Abbott have been very considerate. But really, you must not be troubled about this gossip. I am not exactly dependent upon the good people of Corinth, you know. I can go back to Chicago at any time. Perhaps," she added slowly, "considering everything, that would be the wisest thing to do, after all."

"But you do not need to leave Corinth," said Dan eagerly. "This talk, you know, is all because of your companion's reputation."

"You mean the reputation the people have given her."

"So far as the situation goes, it amounts to the same thing. It is your association with her. If you could arrange to board with some other family—"

Again she interrupted him. "Grace needs me, Mr. Matthews. Surely you cannot think for a moment that I would desert her for the sake of what people think of me."

"But it is all so unjust," he argued. "How can you afford to place yourself before the community in such a wrong light?"

Miss Farwell's face shone first with surprise and disappointment, then a flash of the old irritation. She was shocked to hear him speak so. She had come to think that his spirit was larger than the stock policies of his profession. Her first reaction was to respond in a scornful, cutting reply. Yet somehow she knew he was not being true to himself. Therefore, the words that finally came from her mouth carried a note of sadness.

"In even suggesting such a thing, are you not advocating the doctrines of the people who are responsible for this problem, rather than the teachings of Christ? Aren't you now speaking professionally? Haven't you forgotten our agreement to leave the preacher on the other side of the fence?"

Dan's embarrassment was obvious. "Miss Farwell, please do not misunderstand me. I did not mean that I consider Grace . . . that I agree with what these people—it is only that I cannot stand the thought of your being so misjudged because of this beautiful Christian service. I was only seeking a way out of the trouble for you."

"I will not misunderstand you," she said gently. "But there is only one way out, as you put it."

"And that?"

"For me to continue my ministry—with Grace, and whomever like her God gives me."

Dan sprang to his feet and crossed the room to her side.

"What a . . . you are simply—!" he exclaimed impulsively, then calmed as he struggled for words. "You are a very unusual woman," he finally said in a steady voice.

She trembled. Something about this man moved her strangely.

An awkward pause followed while Dan resumed his seat.

"But my way out will not help you," she said at length. "You must think of *your* ministry and *your* future as well."

"I thought we agreed not to talk of my profession."

"But we must. You must consider what the result will be if you are seen with me—with Grace and me," she added, catching herself quickly. "Can the pastor of Memorial Church afford to associate with two women of such doubtful reputation? What will your church think?"

She was smiling to herself as she spoke, but her tone also carried much earnestness. She wanted him to know how well she understood his position. She wondered if he himself understood it. "You see," she insisted, "you will need to find a way out for yourself too."

"I am not looking for a way out," he growled.

"Ah, but you should. You must consider your influence. Consider the harm to your church. You must remember your position in the community. You cannot afford to—to risk your reputation."

She chose her words carefully. She had to be sure within herself. Thus she pressed him further and further against the wall. The stock argument sounded strange coming from her. Unconsciously she had repeated almost the exact words of Elder Jordan. She saw Dan's hands clench, and the great muscles in his arms and shoulders swell. But deliberately she went on.

"It is not necessary for you to continue our little friendship," she said. "You can stay on the other side of the fence. I—that is, Grace and I will understand. You have too much at stake. You—"

"Miss Farwell," he interrupted, "I can't imagine what you think of me to say such things! I had hoped that you were beginning to look upon me as a man, not merely as a preacher. I had even dared to think that our friendship was growing to be something more than just a little friendly acquaintance. If I am mistaken, I will stay on the other side of the fence. If I am right—if you do care for my friendship," he finished slowly, "then I will try to serve my people faithfully, but I will not willingly shape my life by their foolish, wicked whims. Denny's garden may get along

without me, and you may not need what you call 'our little friendship,' but I need Denny's garden, and—I need you."

Her face shone with gladness. "Forgive me," she said. "I was
only trying to be sure that you understood some things clearly."

At her rather vague words, he said, "I am beginning to understand a good many things."

"And understanding them, will you still come to—" She
smiled. "Will you still come to work in Denny's garden?"

"Yes," he answered with a boyish laugh, "just as if there were
no other place in all the world where I could get a job."

She watched him a few minutes later as he swung down the
walk, through the gate, and away up the street under the big trees.

As she watched him, she could not keep from repeating his
words in her mind, "I need you . . . just as if there were no other
place in all the world. . . ."

She wondered how much they meant.

# CHAPTER TWENTY-SEVEN

# A LABORER AND HIS HIRE

The Doctor could tell that his young friend Dan Matthews was struggling for a place to set his feet—groping for something, he knew not what.

With all the eager confidence of the newly graduated, this young shepherd had come from the denominational granary to feed his flock with a goodly armful of theological husks. And decently good husks they were too. It must be remembered that while Dan had been so raised under the teachings of his home that his ideals and ambitions were to an unusual degree genuinely Christlike, he knew nothing of life other than the simple ways of the country neighborhood where he was born. He knew little of churches. Therefore, while it was natural and easy for him to accept the husks from his church teachers at their face value—since he was wholly without the fixed prejudice that comes from family church traditions—it was just as natural and easy for him to discover quickly, when once he was face to face with his hungry flock, that the husks were husks.

From the charm of the historical glories of the church as pictured by the church historians, and from the equally captivating theories of speculative religion as presented by teachers of schools of theology, Dan had been brought suddenly into face to face contact with real people and actual conditions and practical daily life.

In his experience of the past weeks there was no charm, no glory, no historical greatness, no theoretical perfection. There was meanness, shameful pettiness—repulsive, shocking. There was judgment, self-centeredness, bigotry, vanity, pharisaic vanity and self-contentment. Dan was compelled to recognize the real problems and needs that his husks could not satisfy. They had been forced upon him by living people and real situations that could not be ignored. And Big Dan was big enough to see that the husks did not suffice—and he was consistent enough to stop giving them out. Yet the young minister felt pitifully empty-handed to supply anything of his own in their place.

The Doctor had foreseen even before he had stepped off the train in Corinth that Dan would soon reach the point in his ministerial journey where he was now standing—the point where he must decide which of the two courses open to him he should choose. He was standing, as it were, at a fork in the road. And which path young Dan decided to take would no doubt determine the course of his future for the rest of his life.

Before him, on the one hand, lay the easy, well-worn path of obedience to the traditions, policies, and doctrines of Memorial Church and its denominational leaders. The path was wide, easily visible, and stretching out straight before him, with many able souls lined up all along its sides to help him keep to the middle of the course without wavering to the right or left.

Off to one side wound another path. It was narrow, more difficult to see, and quickly disappeared into the woods, where the course of its direction was impossible to determine. And there were no intrepid souls standing alongside the path to help him find his way along it. To walk in this direction would mean stepping out alone, although there were many waiting to offer their encouragement in the woods, just beyond his sight, where the path quickly widened. But he would not be able to see such until he had left the fork behind and struck out along the lonely path himself.

This was the harder and less-frequented way of truthfulness to himself and his own convictions.

Would he lower his individual standard of righteousness and wave the banner of his employers, preaching not the things that he believed to be the teachings of Jesus but the things he knew would meet the approval of the church rulers? Or would he preach the things that his own prayerful discernment told him were needed if his church was to be, indeed, the temple of the Spirit of Christ? Dan knew he must decide whether he would bow to the official board that paid his salary . . . or to God.

That was the question facing young Dan Matthews. And with a great amount of satisfaction, the Doctor saw him beginning one by one to throw down the husks of tradition.

Dan's next sermon was entitled "The Fellowship of Service," and in tone and theme it was very different from the sorts of things with which he had begun his preaching in Corinth. It was received by the Elders and ruling classes with silent, uneasy questioning. Others were puzzled no less by the new and unfamiliar note, but their faces expressed a kind of doubtful satisfaction. Thus, for both reasons, scarcely a person in the entire congregation mentioned the sermon as they greeted the minister at the close of the service. One of the exceptions happened to be a big, broad-shouldered young farmer whom Dan had never seen before.

Elder Strong was nearby and introduced him. "Brother Matthews," he said in the pious voice of the official church, "you must meet Brother John Gardner. This is the first time he has been to church for a long while."

The two young men shook hands, each measuring the other with admiring eyes.

"Brother John used to be one of our most active members," the Judge continued, "but for some reason he has fallen behind. We never could exactly understand it." He finished with a patronizing laugh, which unmistakably conveyed the notion that he *did* in fact understand it well enough if he chose to reveal it, and that the reason was anything but complimentary to Brother John.

The big farmer's face grew red at the Judge's words. But instead of retorting, he ignored the Elder and spoke out honestly to Dan. "I'm afraid he is right," he said, "and I may as well tell you the truth that I wouldn't be here even today except that I am caught late with my harvesting and short of hands. I drove into town this morning to see if I could pick up a man or two. I didn't find any, so I waited over until church, thinking that I might run across someone here."

Dan smiled. The husky fellow was so uncompromisingly forthright and outspoken—unashamed of who and what he was. It was like a breath of air from the minister's own home hills. It was so refreshing Dan wished for more.

"And have you found anyone?" he asked.

"No," replied Gardner, "but I'm glad I came anyway. Your sermon was mighty interesting to me. I couldn't help thinking, though, that these sentiments about Christian service would come a heap more forceful from someone who actually knowed what a day's work was. My experience has been that the average preacher knows about as much about the lives of working people as I do about theology."

"You may be right," said Dan. "Though admitting it saddens me. However, I do not think you can say it is true in all cases. Many preachers do in fact come from the working classes."

"If he comes from them, they take mighty good care that they stay away from them after they start their preaching," replied the other. "But I've got something to do besides starting an argument now. I don't mind telling you, though, that if I could see you pitch wheat once in a while, when crops are going to waste for lack of help, then I'd feel that maybe we was close enough together for you to preach to me."

With the words, the farmer turned abruptly and pushed his way through the crowd toward a group of working-men who stood near the door.

The Doctor had never commented to Dan on his sermons. But that night as they walked home together, something made Dan feel his old friend was pleased. And Dan could not help feeling encouraged himself. The encounter with the blunt young farmer had been so refreshing that he was not the least depressed in spirit as he commonly was after the perfunctory, meaningless, formal compliments and handshaking that usually closed his services.

"The people did not seem to like my sermon today," commented Dan.

"They were too stunned to like it," grunted the Doctor.

"Do you think they will feel differently when they recover?" asked Dan with a laugh.

"In my own practice," said the old man dryly, "I never prescribe medicine to suit a patient's taste, but to cure him."

Dan understood him. They were silent for a few steps.

"What do you know of the farmer John Gardner?" asked Dan at length.

"A mighty fine fellow."

"Seems to be," agreed Dan thoughtfully. "Where does he live?"

The Doctor told him. "I wouldn't call on him till the harvest is over, if I were you," he added. "He won't have any time to give you, and he'd tell you so."

---

The sun was just up the next morning. John Gardner was hitching his team to the big hay wagon. Already the smoke was coming from the stack of the threshing engine that stood with the machine in the center of the field. The crew had begun making their way to the field from the cook-wagon. Two hired men, with another team and wagon, had already begun and were gathering a load of sheaves to haul to the threshers.

The house dog barked fiercely. The farmer paused and looked over toward him to see what was the cause. He saw a big man turning into the barn lot from the road.

"Good morning!" called Dan cheerily. "I was afraid I would be too late." He walked up to the young fellow who stood staring at him—too astonished to speak.

"Do you still need a hand or two?" asked Dan. He was dressed in a rough suit of clothes—a worn flannel shirt and an old slouch hat—Dan's fishing outfit.

With a slow smile, John turned and continued hooking up his trace and gathering his lines. "Do you mean to say that you walked out here from town this morning to work in my harvest field," he said, "—a good eight miles?"

"That's what I mean."

"What for?" asked the farmer bluntly.

"For the regular wages," returned Dan. "But with two conditions."

"And they are?"

"That no one on the place shall be told that I am a preacher. And that—for today at least—I pitch against you. If by tonight you are not satisfied with my work, you can discharge me without pay for the day." As Dan spoke, he faced the rugged farmer with a look that made him understand that his challenge of the night before had been accepted.

The blue eyes gleamed.

"I'll take you on," he said. Then calling to his wife, "Mary, give this man some breakfast." Then again to Dan, "When you get through, come out to the machine."

He sprang on his wagon and Dan turned toward the kitchen.

"Hold on a minute," John shouted back as the wagon began to move. "What'll I call you?"

"Just by my name," answered the other over his shoulder. "Call me Dan."

All that day the two men worked, each determined to handle more sheaves of grain than the other. Before noon the spirit of the contest had infected the whole workforce. Every hand on the place fell to their tasks as if on a wager. The threshing crew were all from distant parts of the country, and no one knew who it was that had so recklessly matched his strength and staying power against John Gardner, the acknowledged champion among the farmers for miles around.

Bets were freely laid. Rough but good-natured chaff flew from mouth to mouth. And now and then a hearty yell echoed over the field. But the two men in the center of the contest remained silent, scarcely exchanging a word.

In the afternoon the stranger slowly but surely forged ahead. His stamina still held and the quantity sent to the thresher by his hand did not slacken. John rallied every ounce of his strength but could not keep the pace—his giant opponent gained steadily. When the last load came in, the farmer threw down his pitchfork before the whole crowd and held out his hand to Dan.

"I'll give it up," he said heartily. "You're a better man with the wheat than I am stranger, wherever you come from!"

Dan took the offered hand while the men cheered lustily. But the light of battle still shone in the minister's eyes.

"Perhaps," he said, "pitching wheat is not your best game. I'll offer to match you tonight for anything you want—wrestling, running, jumping, or go up against you at any time for any other work you can name."

John slowly looked him over and shook his head. "I know when I've had enough," he said laughing. "Perhaps some of the boys here—" He turned to the group.

The men grinned as they measured the stranger with admiring glances. "We don't know where you come from, pardner," drawled one, "but we sure know what you can do. Ain't nobody in this outfit hankerin' to tackle the man that can work John Gardner down."

At the barn the farmer drew the minister to one side. "Look here, Brother Matthews," he began.

But the other interrupted sharply. "My name is Dan, Mr. Gardner. Don't go back on the bargain."

"Well then, Dan, I won't. And after this my name is John. But I started to ask if you really meant to stay out here and work for me this harvest?"

"That was the bargain, unless you are dissatisfied and want me to quit tonight."

The farmer rubbed his tired arms. "Oh, I'm satisfied all right!" he said grimly. "I just can't understand you, that's all."

"Perhaps if you were a preacher, you would understand it clearly enough."

The big farmer laughed. "Well, come on in to supper." He led the way to the house.

For three days Dan fairly reveled in the companionship of those rough, hardworking men, who gave him full fellowship in their order of laborers. When the fields had been cleared he went back to town.

John drove him in, and the two chatted like the good comrades they had come to be. Within sight of the town, however, a silence began to descend upon them. Their remarks grew formal and forced.

Dan felt as if he were leaving home to return to a strange land where he would always be an alien. Stopping in front of his door, the farmer said awkwardly, "Well, goodbye, Brother Matthews, come out whenever you can."

The minister winced at the designation, but did not protest. "Thank you," he returned. "I have enjoyed my visit more than I can say." His voice sounded sad, and the stalwart farmer could make no reply. He drove quickly away without another word or backward glance.

In his room Dan sat down by the window, thinking about the next day and what the church called his "work"—the pastoral visits, the committee meetings, groups like the Ladies' Aid. At last he stood up and stretched his great body to its full height with a sigh. Then he drew his wages from his pocket and placed the money on the study table. He stood for a long time contemplating the pieces of silver as if they could answer his thoughts.

Again he went to the window and looked down at Denny's garden that throughout the summer had yielded its strength to the touch of the crippled boy's hand. Then from the other window he gazed at the cast-iron monument on the corner—gazed until the grim figure seemed to threaten him with its uplifted arm.

Slowly he turned once more to the coins on the table. Gathering them one by one, he placed them carefully in an envelope. Seating himself, he wrote on the little package, "The laborer is worthy of his hire."

# CHAPTER TWENTY-EIGHT

# THE WINTER PASSES

The harvest time passed and the winter came. With the new year Memorial Church began to look forward to the great convention of the denomination which was to be held in a distant city.

All through the months, the new note begun in the fall had continued dominant in Dan's preaching, and indeed in all his work. His manner in the pulpit changed. All the little formalities and mannerisms—tricks of the ecclesiastical trade—disappeared. He discarded the formal robe of the clergyman, and began wearing instead his one suit of dark blue.

It was impossible that the story of those three days in John Gardner's harvest field should not get out eventually. Memorial Church was crowded at every service. Some remained merely curious. Other hearts responded, even though many of them could not yet grasp the full significance of the preaching and life of this manly fellow, who, in spite of his profession, was so much a man among men.

But the attitude of the church fathers and the ruling class remained one of doubt and suspicion, however much they could not ignore the manifest success of their minister. In spite of their misgivings, their hearts swelled with pride and satisfaction as they saw their church's attendance forging ahead of all other congregations in the town. And try as they might, they could fix upon nothing unchristian in his teaching. They could not point to a single sentence in any one of his sermons that did not unmistakably harmonize with the teaching and Spirit of Jesus.

It was not so much what Dan preached that worried these pillars of the church. It was what he did not preach that made them uneasy. They missed the familiar pious sayings and platitudes, the time-worn sermon subjects that had been handled and rehandled by every preacher they had ever sat under. The old path—beaten so hard and plain by the many "bearers of glad tidings"—the safe, sure ground of doctrine and theology, even the familiar, long-tried type of prayer, all were quietly but persistently ignored by this calm-eyed, broad-shouldered, strapping young minister who was often so much in earnest in his preaching that he forgot to talk like a preacher.

Unquestionably, decided the fathers, this young giant was "unsafe." Wagging their heads wisely, under their breath they predicted dire disasters. Yet openly and abroad they continued to boast of the size of their audiences and their minister's oratorical power.

Nor did these keepers of the faith fail to make Dan feel their dissatisfaction. By hints innumerable, by carefully withholding words of encouragement, by studied coldness, they made him understand that they were not pleased. Every plan for practical Christian work that Dan suggested (and he suggested many that winter) they coolly refused to endorse, while requesting that he give more careful attention to the long-established activities and traditions.

Without protest or bitterness Dan quietly gave up his plans. And except in the matter of his sermons, he yielded to their demands. Never was there a word of harshness or criticism of the church or its people in his talks, only firm but gentle insistence upon the great living principles of Christ's teaching. And in his presence, the people often knew the feeling the Doctor was conscious of—that this man was, in some way, that which they might have been. This feeling saddened some of his hearers with regret. Others it inspired with hope and filled them with a determination to discover that best part of themselves. To still others it was a rebuke, the more stinging because so unconsciously given, and they were filled with anger and envy.

Meanwhile, the attitude of the people toward Hope Farwell and the girl whom she had befriended remained unaltered. But now Deborah and Denny as well came to share in their displeasure. Dan made no change in his relation to the nurse and her friends in the little cottage on the other side of the garden. In spite of constant hints, insinuations, and reflections on the part of his church masters, he calmly and deliberately threw down the gauntlet before the whole scandal-loving community. Everyone respected and admired him—for this is the way with the herd—even while it abated not one whit its determination to ruin him the instant chance afforded the opportunity.

So the spirit that lives in Corinth—the Ally—waited. The power that had put the shadow of pain over the life of Grace Conner now waited for Hope and Dan, until the minister himself should furnish the motive that should call it into action.

Dan felt it—felt his enemy stirring quietly in the dark, watching, waiting. And as the weeks passed, it came to be noticed that there was often in the man's eyes and in his voice a great sadness— the sadness of one who toils at a hopeless task, the sadness of one who suffers for crimes of which he is innocent, the sadness of one who fights for a well-loved cause with the certainty of defeat.

Because of the very fine sense of Dan's nature, the situation caused him the keenest suffering. It was all so different from the life which he had looked forward to with feelings of joy. Everything seemed to him so unjust.

Many were the evenings that winter when the minister went to see Dr. Harry or old Doctor Oldham. And in those hours the friendships with the two physicians grew still deeper and more enduring. As the one had been, so the other became—a friendship that would last for all time. Many times too, Dan fled across the country to the farm of John Gardner, there to spend the day in the hardest toil, finding in the ministry of labor something that met his need. But more than these was the friendship of Hope Farwell, and the influence of her life and ministry.

It was inevitable that the very attitude of the community should force these two friends into closer companionship and sympathy. In judging them so harshly for the course each had chosen—chosen because to them it was right and the only course possible to their spiritual ideals—the people drove them to a fuller dependence upon each other.

Because of his own character and his conception of Christ, Dan understood, as perhaps no one else in the community possibly could have, just why the nurse clung to Grace Conner and the work she had undertaken. At the same time, he felt that she grasped, as no one else, the peculiarly trying position in which he so unexpectedly found himself in his ministry. And feeling that Dan alone understood her, Hope realized as clearly that the minister had come to depend upon her as the one friend in Corinth who appreciated his true situation. Thus, while she gave him strength for his fight, from him she drew strength for her own.

The gossip about them had not again been mentioned between Hope and Dan, though it was impossible that they should not know the attitude of the community toward them both. That subtle, un-get-at-able power—the Ally—that is so irresistible, so certain in its work, depending for results upon words with double meanings, suggestive nods, tricks of expression, sly winks and meaning smiles, while giving its victims no opportunity for defense, never leaves any doubt as to the object of its attack.

The situation was never put into words by these two, but they knew, and each knew the other knew. And their respect, confidence, and regard for each other grew steadily, as it must with all good comrades under fire. In those weeks and months, each learned to know and depend upon the other, though neither realized to what extent.

So it came to be that it was not Grace Conner alone that kept Hope Farwell in Corinth, but the feeling that Dan Matthews also depended upon her—the feeling that she could not desert her comrade in the fight—or, as they had both come to feel, *their* fight.

Hope Farwell was not a schoolgirl. She was a strong, full-blooded, perfectly developed workwoman, matured in body and mind. She realized what the continued friendship of this man might mean to her—realized it fully and was glad. Dimly too, she saw how this that was growing in her heart might bring great pain and suffering—lifelong perhaps.

Her profession had trained her to almost perfect self-control. There was no danger that she would let herself go. Her strong, passionate heart would never be given its freedom by her, to the hurt of the life upon which it fixed its affections. She would suffer the more deeply for that very reason. There is no pain so poignant as that which is borne in secret. But still she was glad! Such a strange thing is a woman's heart!

Dan himself, though given to deep thought, was not given overmuch to self-analysis. Few men are. He felt; he did not spend time reasoning within himself. Neither did he look ahead to see whither he was bound. Such a strange thing too is the heart of a man!

# CHAPTER TWENTY-NINE

# DEBORAH'S TROUBLE

Gradually the long winter came to an end. New life stirred in blade and twig and branch, and mystical calls went out to the hearts of men.

When the first days of the spring bass-fishing season came, the Doctor coaxed Dan away for three days. Up the river they went, beyond Gordon's Mills, where the roaring trout brook entered the larger stream.

It was well on toward noon the morning that Dan and the Doctor left that Miss Farwell found Deborah in tears, with Denny trying in vain to comfort her.

"Come, come, Mother, don't be takin' it so," Denny was saying as the nurse passed the open door of the little kitchen. "It'll be all right somehow."

The widow sat in her low chair, her face buried in her apron, swaying back and forth and shaking with sobs. Denny looked up and saw the nurse. There was appeal in his eyes.

"Come, Mother, look! It's Miss Hope come to see you. We'll make it through all right, Mother."

Miss Farwell went to Denny's side and together they managed to calm the good woman after a few minutes.

"I'm sorry to be goin' on so, Miss Hope, but I—but I—" She began to break down again.

"Won't you tell me the trouble, Mrs. Mulhall?" urged the nurse. "Perhaps I can help."

"Indeed, dear heart, don't I know you've trouble enough of your own without your loadin' up with Denny's an' mine besides? Ain't I seen how you been put to it the past months to make both ends meet for you an' Gracie, poor child. An' you all the time fightin' to look cheerful an' bright, so as to keep her heartened up? Many's the time, Miss Hope, I've seen the look on your own sweet face, when you thought nobody'd be noticin'. An' every night Denny an' me's prayed the Blessed Virgin to soften the hearts of the people in this danged town. But it does look like God had clean forgotten us altogether. I can't help thinkin' it would be different somehow if only we could go to mass somewhere like decent Christians ought."

"You and Denny have helped me more than I can ever tell you, dear friend," said Hope, "and now you must let me help you, don't you see?"

"It's glad enough I'd be to let you help, if it was anything you could fix. But nothin' but money'll do it, an' I can see by them old shoes you're wearin', an' you goin' with that old coat all winter, that you ain't earned but just enough to keep you an' Gracie alive."

"That's true enough," returned Hope cheerfully, "but I am sure it will help you just to tell me the trouble."

With a little more urging, at last the nurse drew from them the whole pitiful story.

At the time of Jack Mulhall's death, Judge Strong had held a mortgage on the little home with but a small amount remaining to be paid. But with her husband's income gone, Mrs. Mulhall had been unable to continue paying down the principal. By careful planning, however, the widow and her son had managed to pay the interest promptly and had thus been able to hold on to the house. Though he coveted the place, the Judge had not dared to push the payment of the mortgage too soon after the marshall's death. Jack Mulhall had been popular in town, and he feared public sentiment. But sufficient time had now gone by, thought the Judge, for the public to forget their officer who had been killed on duty. And having received Grace Conner and Miss Farwell into her home, Deborah Mulhall was now included to some extent in the damaging comments circulating through the righteous community. Thus the crafty Judge saw his opportunity. He knew that the people themselves would never go to the length of putting Deborah and her crippled son out of their little home. But he was certain he had nothing to fear from the sentiment of the community should he do so under the guise of legitimate business.

The attitude of the people toward her boarders had kept Deborah from being able to earn as much as usual, and for the first time ever she found herself unable to make the interest payment during the first week of April when it fell due. Indeed, it was only by the most rigid pinching of pennies that they would be able to make their bare living, until the mid-summer months when Denny's garden should again begin to bring them something.

Their failure to pay the interest gave the Judge just the reason he had been looking for to push for the payment of the debt. Everything had been done in precise legal form. The eviction notice came by special messenger. The interest now being delinquent, unless they paid the amount in full, Deborah and Denny would have to leave the premises the next day. The widow had gone to see the Judge. But she had already exhausted every resource. Promises and pleadings were useless, and it was only at the last hour she had given up.

"But have you no relatives, Mrs. Mulhall, who could help you?" asked Hope. "No friends? Perhaps Dr. Oldham—"

Deborah shook her head. "There's only me an' Brother Mike in the family," she said. "Mike's a bricklayer an' would give the coat off his back for me. But he's movin' about so over the country from job to job, bein' single, you see, that I can't get a letter to him. I did write to him where I heard from him last, but my letter came back. He don't write often, you see, thinkin' Denny an' me is all right. I ain't seen him since he was here to help put poor Jack away."

For a few minutes the silence in the little room was broken only by poor Deborah's sobs, and by Denny's voice as he tried to comfort his mother.

Suddenly the nurse sprang to her feet. "There *is* someone!" she cried. "I knew there must be, of course. Why didn't we think of him before?"

Mrs. Mulhall raised her head, a look of doubtful hope on the tear-wet face.

"Mr. Matthews!" said Hope.

Deborah's face fell. "But, child, the minister's away with the Doctor. I saw 'em leave just this mornin'. An' what good would he be able to do even if he was here? He's got no money himself."

"I don't know what he'd do, but I know he'd do something. He's that kind of man," declared Hope with such conviction that, even against their better judgement, Deborah and Denny could not help taking heart.

"And he's not so far away but that he can't be reached," added Hope. Later that afternoon, the dilapidated old hack of a coach from Corinth to Gordon's Mills carried a passenger, dressed in the gray–blue uniform of a nurse.

# CHAPTER THIRTY

# A FISHERMAN

In the crisis of Deborah's trouble, Hope had turned to Dan impulsively. When she was powerless in her own strength to meet the need, she looked confidently to him.

But now that she was actually on the way to him, with Corinth behind her and the long road over the hills and through the forests in front of her, she had time to think. And as she did, the conscious object of her journey forced itself on her thinking.

The thing that the young woman had so dimly foreseen for herself of her friendship with this man, she now saw more clearly, as she realized how much she had grown to depend upon him—upon the strength of his companionship. She had learned almost without knowing it to watch for his coming, and to look often toward the corner window of the house on the other side of the garden!

But, she asked herself, was her regard for him anything more than a natural admiration for his strong character, as she had seen it revealed in the past months? Their peculiar situation had placed him more in her thoughts than any man had ever been before. Wasn't this all? The possibility had not yet become a certainty. The revelation of Hope Farwell to herself was yet to come.

The hack, with its one passenger, arrived at Gordon's Mills

about four o'clock. Miss Farwell climbed down from the ancient vehicle in front of a typical country hotel, went inside, and inquired for Dr. Oldham.

The slouchy, slow-witted proprietor of the place passed her inquiry on to a group of natives who were lounging on the porch, and one, whose horse was hitched in front of the blacksmith shop across the way, gave out the information that he had seen the Doctor and the big parson at the mouth of the creek as he came past an hour earlier. He added that he reckoned "they wouldn't be back in till dark, fer they was a-ketchin' a right smart bunch of bass."

"Is it far from here?" asked the nurse.

"Somethin' less than a mile, ain't hit, Bill?"

Bill allowed, "Hit war about that. Mile an' a quarter to Bud Jones', Bud calls hit."

"And the road?"

"Ain't no road, miss. Foller the creek—can't miss hit."

After the vague words, accompanied with points in the right direction from the rest of the men, Miss Farwell set out, every eye in the place watching her until she disappeared around the first bend.

As she drew near the river, the bank of which was marked by a high bluff on the other side, the young woman began to feel a growing sense of apprehension over what she had impulsively done. What would Mr. Matthews think of her coming to him in such a way? And Dr. Oldham—

Already she could feel the keen eyes of the old physician, with their knowing twinkle, fixed upon her face. The Doctor always made you feel that he knew so much more about you than you knew about yourself.

Coming to the river at the mouth of the creek, she saw them. Half hidden by the upturned roots of a fallen tree, she stood still and watched.

They were on the downstream side of the creek. Dan, with rubber boots that came to his hips, stood far out on the sandy bar, braced against the current that tugged and pulled at his great legs.

The Doctor stood farther down, on the bank.

She watched Dan with the curious interest a woman always feels when watching a man who, while engaged in a man's work or play, is unconscious of her presence.

She saw the fisherman as he threw the line far out, with a strong, high swing of his long arm. As she continued to watch, a lusty bass—heavy and full of fight—took the hook. She saw the man stand motionless, intent, alert, at the instant he first felt the fish. Then came the skillful turn of his wrist as he struck—quick and sure. She stared as one captivated with breathless interest as—bracing himself—the fisherman's powerful figure became instinct with life. With the boiling water grasping his legs, clinging to him like a tireless wrestler seeking the first unguarded moment, and with the plunging, tugging, rushing giant at the other end of the silken line, fighting with every inch of his spring-steel body for freedom—Dan made a picture to bring the light of admiration to any woman's eyes.

And Hope Farwell was very much a woman.

Slowly but surely, the strength and skill of the fisherman prevailed. The master of the waters gradually came nearer and nearer the hand of his conqueror. The young woman held her breath while the fish made its last mad attempt to wriggle free, and then—when Dan held up his prize for the Doctor standing on the bank, who had been in the middle of the fight with his whole soul—then at last she forgot her embarrassment. She sprang into full view upon the trunk of the fallen tree, and shouted and waved her congratulations.

Dan's footing momentarily wavered in shock, and he struggled to keep from dropping the fish!

The Doctor's old eyes were not so quick to recognize the woman on the log. He was amazed to see his companion go splashing, stumbling, and plowing through the water toward the shore.

"Hope . . . Miss Farwell!" gasped Dan, floundering up the bank, the big fish still in his hand, the shining water streaming from his high boots, his face glowing with healthful exercise—and something else perhaps. "What good fortune brings you here?"

At the eagerness that shone in his eyes and sounded in his voice, the woman's face had grown rosy red. But by the time the fisherman had gained his footing and come toward her, the memory of her mission had driven every other thought from her mind. Briefly she told him of Deborah's trouble, and a few moments later the Doctor—crossing the creek higher up—joined them. As they talked, Hope saw all the light and joy go from Dan's face. In its place came a look of sadness and determination.

"Doctor," he said, turning to Dr. Oldham, "I must go back to Corinth with Miss Farwell tonight. We'll get a team and buggy at the Mills."

The old man grumbled heartily. *Why hadn't the foolish Irishwoman let them know her trouble before?*

Still muttering, he drew from his pocket a book and hastily signed a check. "Here, Dan," he said, "use this if you have to. You understand—don't hesitate if you need it."

Reluctantly the younger man took the paper. "I don't think it will be necessary," he replied. "It ought not to be necessary for you to do this, Doctor."

"Humph!" grunted Doctor Oldham. "There's a lot of unnecessary things that have to be done from time to time. Hustle along, you two. I'm going back after the mate to that last one of yours!"

Dan and the nurse walked back to the hotel, stopped there long enough for a hurried late lunch, then started for Corinth in the gathering dusk with a half-broken team and a stout buggy.

As the light went out of the sky and the mysterious stillness of the night came upon them, they too grew quiet, as if no words were needed. They seemed to be passing into another world—a strange dream-world where they were alone. The things of everyday, the commonplace incidents and happenings of their lives, drifted far from their thoughts. They talked but little. There was so little to say. Once Dan leaned over to tuck the lap robe carefully about his companion, for the early spring air was chilly when the sun went down.

So they rode until they saw the lights of the town. Then it all came back to them with a rush. The woman drew a long breath.

"Tired?" asked Dan. There was that in his voice that brought tears to the gray eyes—tears that he could not see because of the dark.

"Not a bit," she answered cheerfully in spite of them. "Will you see Judge Strong tonight?" She had not asked him what he was going to do.

"Yes," he said. When they reached the big brown house, he drew the horses to a walk. "I think, if you are not too tired, I had better stop now. I will not be long."

There was something in his voice that made her heart jump with sudden fear. She was instantly reminded of what she had felt at times when Dr. Miles at the hospital had told her to prepare to assist him in an operation. But no fear showed itself in her voice.

Dan hitched the team, then—leaving her waiting in the buggy—went up to the house. She heard him knock. The door opened, sending out a flood of light. He entered. The door closed.

She waited in the dark.

# CHAPTER THIRTY-ONE

# A MATTER OF BUSINESS

At the prayer meeting of the Memorial Church earlier that evening, Judge Strong had prayed with a fervor unusual even for him. And in church circles the Judge was rated mighty in prayer. In fact, the good Elder's religious capital was mostly invested in good, safe, public petitions to the Almighty—such investments being rightly considered by the Judge as "gilt-edged," for whatever the ultimate returns, it was all profit.

Theoretically the Judge's God noted "even the sparrow's fall," and in all of his public religious exercises, the Judge stated that fact with clearness and force. Making practical application of his favorite text, the Judge never killed sparrows. His everyday energies were spent in collecting mortgages, acquiring real estate, and in like harmless pursuits, that were—so far as he had observed—not mentioned in the Word, and presumably, therefore, were passed over by the God of the sparrow.

So the Judge prayed that night, with pious intonations asking his God for everything he could think of for himself, his church, his town, and the whole world. And when he could think of no more blessings, he unflinchingly asked God to think of them for him, and to give them all abundantly—more than they could ask or desire. Reminding God of His care for the sparrow, he pleaded with Him to watch over their beloved pastor, "who is absent from his flock in search of—ah, enjoying—ah, the beauties of nature—ah, and bring him speedily back to his needy people, that they may all grow strong in the Lord."

Supplementing his prayer with a few solemn reflections, as was expected from an Elder of the church, the Judge commented on the smallness of the company present, lamented the decline of spirituality in the churches, declared the need for a revival of the New Testament Gospel and the preaching of the truth as it is found in Jesus Christ. He roundly scored those who were absent, seeking their own pleasure, neglecting their duties while the world was perishing, and finished with a plea to the faithful to assist their worthy pastor—who, unfortunately, was not present with them that evening—in every way possible. Then the Judge went home to occupy the rest of the evening with some pressing matters of business.

In the Strong mansion the room known as the library was on the ground floor in a wing of the main building. As rooms have a way of doing, it expressed unmistakably the character of its tenant. A bookcase, with a few spick-and-span books standing in prim, cold rows behind the glass doors—which were always locked—leaned against one wall. The key to it was somewhere, no doubt. There were no pictures on the walls, except for a fancy calendar—presented with the compliments of the Judge's banker—a poorly done portrait of the Judge's father in a cheap gilt frame, and another calendar, compliments of the Judge's grocer.

The furniture and appointments were in harmony—a table with a teachers' Bible and a Sunday school quarterly lying on it, a big safe wherein the Judge kept his various mortgages and papers of value, and the Judge's desk, being the most conspicuous piece of furniture of all. It is a significant comment on the Elder's business methods that in the top right-hand drawer of his desk he kept a small caliber gun ready for instant use, and that the window shades were always drawn when the lamps were lighted. A good churchman he may have been, but the Judge was a prudent businessman first and foremost, and took no chances.

Sitting at his desk the Judge heard the front doorbell ring and his wife direct someone to the library. A moment later he looked up from his papers to see Dan standing before him.

The Judge was startled. He had thought the young man far away. Then too, the Judge had never seen the minister dressed in rough trousers, belted at the waist, wearing a flannel shirt under a torn and mud-stained coat, and with mud-splattered boots that came nearly to his hips. The slouch hat completed the unexpected picture. Nor could the faint odor of fish be ignored. Dan looked big in any garb, and as the Judge saw him that night he seemed a giant. And this giant had the look of one come in haste on business of the most urgent kind.

Was it the look on Dan's face that made the Judge think impulsively of that top right-hand drawer?

Forcing his usual dry, mirthless laugh, he greeted Dan with forced effusiveness, urging him to take a chair, and declaring that he hardly knew him, that he thought he was at Gordon's Mills fishing. Then he entered at once into a glowing description of the splendid prayer meeting they had held that evening in the minister's absence.

Ignoring the invitation to be seated, Dan walked slowly to the center of the room, and standing by the table, stared intently at the man behind the desk. The patter of the Judge's talk died away. The presence of the man by the table seemed to fill the whole room. The very furniture became suddenly cheap and small. The Judge himself seemed to shrink, and a foreboding came over him of something about to happen. Swiftly he reviewed in his mind several recent deals. What could it be that made the minister look at him so? "Well," he said at last, when Dan did not speak, "won't you sit down?"

"Thank you, no," answered Dan. "I can only stay a minute. I called to see you about that mortgage on Widow Mulhall's home."

"Ah, I see . . . well?"

"I want to ask you, sir, if it is not possible for you to reconsider the matter and grant her a little more time."

So that was all it was, the Judge thought. His countenance visibly relaxed, as he answered curtly, "Possibly, but—but to do so would not be proper business. The mortgage is due, you see." He paused briefly, then looked up at Dan and added, "Do you—ah, consider this matter as falling under your—ah, pastoral duties? The woman is a—"

"I will undertake to see that the mortgage is paid, sir," interrupted Dan earnestly, ignoring the Judge's question, "if you will give me a little time."

The Judge's reply was cold. "My experience with ministers' promises to pay has not been reassuring, and, as an Elder in the church, I may say that we do not employ you to undertake the payment of other people's debts. The people might not understand your interest in the widow's affairs."

Again Dan ignored the other's answer, though his face went white and his big hands crushed the slouch hat they held with a mighty grip. He attempted to explain what it would mean to the widow and her crippled son to lose their little home and the garden—almost their only means of support.

The face of the Judge remained unmoved. He was acting in a manner that was fully consistent and legitimate. Any banker or mortgage holder would do the same. He had considered the whole matter very carefully. As for the hardship, some things in connection with business were inevitable.

Dan argued further, his voice pleading, then sad, then trembling. When the uselessness of his efforts were altogether too evident for him to continue the conversation, he turned sadly toward the door.

Something caused the Judge to say, "Don't go yet, Brother Matthews. You see, being a minister, there are some things that you don't understand. You are making a mistake in—"

He caught his breath. Suddenly he became aware of Dan's purpose. Instead of leaving the room, Dan was closing and locking the door.

He now turned and came back in three quick strides. This time he placed his hat on the table. When he spoke his voice was still low—intense—shaking with emotion.

"You say, sir, that some things are inevitable. Perhaps you are right."

There was something frightening in his manner now that made the powerful man in the chair tremble. He started to speak, but Dan silenced him.

"You have said quite enough, sir. Don't think that I too have not fully considered this matter. I have. Now—turn to your desk there and write a letter to Mrs. Mulhall granting her another year of time."

The Judge tried to laugh. But his dry lips made a strange sound. Suddenly with a quick movement he jerked open the drawer by his right hand and seized the weapon. Dan leaped to within easy striking distance, reached across the huge desk, and had the man's wrist clutched in his vice-grip in less than a second. With a clunk, the gun dropped from his hand and back into its place of hiding.

"Shut that drawer!"

The Judge obeyed.

"Now write!"

"I'll have the law on you! You dare burst into my home, hold me against my will, and attack me physically," said the Judge, rubbing his wrist as if to remove the redness Dan had inflicted.

Dan laughed bitterly. "Considering what you were about to attempt, Judge," he said, "my attack, as you call it, hardly seems worthy of note."

"I'll put you out of the Christian ministry! I'll have you arrested if you assault me again. I'll—"

"I have considered all that too," said Dan. "Try it, and you will stir up such a feeling that the people of this community will drive you out of the country. You can't do it and live in Corinth, Judge Strong. You have too much at stake in this town to risk it. You cannot afford to have me arrested for this, sir. And if the whole truth came out, it would not go well for you—pulling a pistol on a man of the cloth who had come to you to plead for the cause of a widow and cripple. Write that letter and no one but you and I will ever know of this incident. Refuse, or fail to keep the promise of your letter, and no power on earth shall prevent me from seeing that justice is done! I can hardly believe that you could come from a prayer meeting to rob that crippled boy of his garden—"

Suddenly the Judge opened his mouth to call out for help. But reading his purpose in his eyes, Dan reached across the desk again and took one of the Judge's slight shoulders in his huge hand before he could utter a sound. For one of the first times in his life, the Judge found himself intimidated by another mortal. The squeeze of his shoulder, and the penetrating look of Dan's eyes into his was enough to silence him utterly.

Slowly Dan released his grip. Casting him a final look of hatred, the Judge picked up the pen that lay on the desk, and wrote as Dan had ordered him.

With the letter in his pocket, Dan stood silently before his adversary for a moment. When he spoke again, his voice was full of pain.

"I deeply regret this incident, Brother Strong," he said, "more than I can say. I am sorry you forced me to this. Yet I have no apology to make for my actions. You have my word that no one shall know, from me, what has occurred here this evening. When you have time to think it all over I am sure you will see the wisdom in not carrying the matter further. You cannot afford it. A moment's reflection will show you that it is in your best interest to keep it quiet as well."

When the Judge lifted his head he was alone.

"Did I keep you waiting too long?" asked Dan when he had again taken his place by Miss Farwell's side.

"Oh no. But tell me, is everything all right?"

"Yes. Judge Strong has kindly granted our friends another year. That will give us time to do something."

Arriving at the house he gave Hope the letter for Deborah. "And here," he said, "is something for you." From under the seat he drew the big bass.

When Dan returned to Gordon's Mills with the buggy and team the next morning, he gave back the Doctor's check. "The

Judge listened to reason," he said, "and decided not to press it." And that was all the explanation he ever made, though it was by no means the end of the matter.

Even Dan himself did not realize what he had done. He did not realize how potent were the arguments he had used to convince the Judge.

The young minister had at last furnished the motive the Ally had been waiting for!

# CHAPTER THIRTY-TWO

# THE DAUGHTER OF THE CHURCH

Dan was right. Judge Strong could not afford to make public the facts connected with the young man's visit to him that evening. But while the Judge was held both by his fear of Dan and by his own best interests from moving openly against the man who had so effectively blocked his well-laid plans for acquiring another choice bit of Corinth real estate, there were other ways, perfectly safe, by which he might make the minister suffer.

Judge Strong had not been a ruling elder in the church for so many years without learning the full value of the spirit that makes Corinth its home. The Elder was a past master in directing the strength of the Ally to the gaining of his own ends.

Thus when he learned of Hope's trip to Gordon's Mills, and the long ride in the night alone with Dan, the Judge smiled to himself. It would be so easy to discredit Dan now!

In the two days before the next weekly meeting of the Ladies' Aid Society, it so happened that the good Elder took it upon himself to have quiet confidential talks with several of the most active members of the congregation. In these talks the Judge did not openly charge the minister with wrong conduct, with any neglect of his duties, or with any unfaithfulness to the sacred doctrines. No indeed! The Judge was not such a bungler in the art of directing the strength of the Ally in serving his own ends. But nevertheless, each good sister, when the interview was ended, felt that she had been entrusted with the confidence of the very inside of the innermost circle. Each one felt her heart swell within herself at the responsibility of a state secret of such vast importance. And the souls of the good ladies grew big with a righteous determination to be worthy of the Judge's confidence.

The Ladies' Aid meeting that week was one to be remembered! There had been nothing like it since the last meeting of its kind!

Each sister who had spoken with the Judge was determined that every other sister should understand that *she* was on the innermost side, that *she* was the Judge's trusted ear, and that *she* knew more of the talk that was truly worth knowing than any other woman in Memorial Church. And of course every other sister who had talked with the Judge was equally fired with the same purpose. And even those who had not talked quietly with the Judge were extraordinarily active in creating the impression that they knew just as much as those who had. It was a convocation of gossiping rumor-mongers to rival any henhouse on any farm in America. So that all taken together, things were hinted at, half-revealed, and fully told about Dan and Miss Farwell that would have astonished even Judge Strong himself, had he not known just what the results would be.

The following Sunday it almost seemed as if Dan wished to help the Judge in his campaign against him. For while there was much in his sermon about widows and orphans, there was not a word of the old New Testament Gospel.

Monday evening Judge Strong and his wife called upon Elder Jordan and his family. The two church fathers held a long and important conference with the church mothers and the church daughter assisting.

The Judge said very little. Indeed, he seemed almost reluctant to discuss the grave things that were being said in the community about their pastor. But it was easy to see that he was earnestly concerned for the welfare of the church and the upbuilding of the cause of the Gospel in Corinth.

Nathan himself was led to introduce the subject. The Judge very skillfully and politely gave the women opportunities. He agreed most heartily with Elder Jordan that Dan's Christian character was above reproach, and that it was very unfortunate that there should be any criticism by the public. Such things so weakened the church's influence in the community! He regretted, however, that their pastor in his sermons did not dwell more upon first principles and the fundamental doctrines of the church. His sermons were good, but the people needed to be taught the true way of salvation. Dan was young: perhaps he would learn the foolishness of taking up these new ideas of the church's mission and work.

Because of the innate goodness of his heart and his deeply religious nature, Nathaniel Jordan had learned to love Dan, and even to a degree to believe in him. But his whole life's training forced him to question the wisdom of the young man's preaching. And while he was deeply pained by the things the sisters reported, he found, as the Judge intended, that Elder Strong's attitude was in close harmony with his own.

Thus the Ally has something for everybody. And even one like Nathaniel who would not willingly have done the Ally's bidding, yet was like putty in its hands. Those who did not doubt Dan's character questioned his preaching. And those who cared but little what he preached found much to question in his conduct.

There was one in the company that evening who contributed nothing to the discussion, except for now and then a word in defense of Dan. And everything that Charity said was instantly and warmly endorsed by the Judge.

When Judge and Mrs. Strong at last bade their friends good night and left Nathaniel and his wife to cultivate the seed the Ally had so skillfully planted, Charity retired at once to her room. But it was not to sleep. This young woman had seen and heard a great deal through the years during which she had been reared in such close touch with the inner circle of the ruling classes in Memorial Church. She was both a daughter of the Ally, and yet also a victim of it, for she knew no other world than Memorial Church. The church and its activities and its people encompassed all there was to her universe. And in such a cramped and confining world, who could not help feeling sorry for poor Charity.

In her room, she thought about Dan and about the church. If only there were some way for him to succeed where others had failed! This little conference between her parents and the Strongs was by no means the first of its kind that she had been permitted to attend. Her whole life experience enabled her to judge to a day almost the length of any minister's stay in Corinth. Few had stayed the average denominational term.

There was Rev. Swanson—but he was too old. And Rev. Wilson—it had been troubles with his daughter. Rev. Jones—troubles with his wife. Rev. George—his son. Rev. Kern did not get on with the young people. And there was Rev. Holmes—who was too young and got on with the young people too well! Charity had always thought that she and Rev. Holmes—if only he had been permitted to stay another three months! And Rev. Colby—he was eased out because he had neither wife nor sons nor daughters. In his case too, if only he had been given more time, Charity was sure she might. . . .

And now Dan!

The poor girl cried bitterly in the dark. And in her eyes she determined that desperate measures were called for.

# CHAPTER THIRTY-THREE

# HOPE AND CHARITY

The long ride alone in the buggy with Dan, the way in which he had greeted her, and his quick response to her appeal had all led Hope much nearer to a full realization of herself and her feelings for Dan than she knew. But one touch more was needed to make the possibility which she had long foreseen a reality.

That touch came early in the afternoon of the day following the Judge's call upon the Jordans. Miss Farwell was in the garden with Grace and Denny, getting the ground ready for the first planting of early seeds. Dan had suggested that they plant a much larger space this year, and everyone had been working hard. They all said it would be the best and largest garden Denny had ever grown.

With his twisted arm swinging at his side, and dragging his weak leg, Denny was marking off the beds and rows, while he kept up a chatter with the two young women who were assisting him by carrying stakes and string.

Anyone would have thought they were the happiest people in all Corinth. And perhaps they were, though from all usual standards they had little enough to be joyous about. Denny with his poor, crippled body, yearned for books and study with all his heart. Grace Conner had been marred in spirit, as Denny was in body, by the unjust treatment of those to whom she ought to have been able to look for sympathy and help. And Hope Farwell was sacrificing a successful and remunerative career in the medical profession to carry the burden of this one who had no worldly claim upon her whatsoever. What did the three have to be joyous over that sunny afternoon in the garden?

"It must be the garden that does it," said Deborah to herself, who heard their merry talk and laughter in the kitchen.

The three workers were expecting Dan, but he did not come. And when a caller finally did come, it was not someone Hope would ever have expected.

"There's someone to see you," called Deborah out to the garden. The nurse left her work and returned to the house. "I put her in your room to wait for you," said the widow.

A moment later the young woman entered her own room to find Miss Charity Jordan.

Hope Farwell was a beautiful woman—beautiful with the beauty of a womanhood unspoiled by vain idleness, empty pleasures or purposeless activity. And who could deny that the activity of the past few months, in spite of her trials, had added much to that sweet atmosphere of womanliness that had always enveloped her. The deep, gray eyes seemed deeper still, and a light shone in their depths that had not been there before. In her voice too, there was a new note—a richer, fuller tone, and she moved and laughed as one whose soul was filled with the best joys of living.

Charity rose to her feet when Miss Farwell entered. The nurse greeted her, but the poor girl who had spent an almost sleepless night stood looking at the woman before her with a kind of envying wonder. What right did she have to be so happy while she, a Christian, was so miserable?

To Charity there were only two kinds of people—those who belonged to the church and those who did not. In her tightly bordered world the latter were of the world. Those of the world were strangers—aliens. The life they lived, their pleasures, their ambitions, their loves, their spiritual values even were all matters of conjecture to this daughter of the church. They were to her people to "save"—never people to know, talk to, or be intimate with. Nor were they to be trusted or listened to, or regarded without grave suspicion until they were "saved." She wondered sometimes what they were like—if one were to really know them. As she had thought about it the night before in the dark, it was a monstrous thing that a woman of this other world should have ensnared their minister—*her* minister.

Charity was a judge of preachers. As she had grown into the most eligible young woman in Memorial Church, an obvious "catch" for a religious churchman, she had made it her business to know and scrutinize the men approved by her father and the Judge to lead the flock. All her life she had been groomed to one day take her stand beside the right such man, ultimately to become not the mere daughter of the church but its very matriarch.

In Dan she saw the ability to go far. She felt that no position in the church was too high for him to reach, no honor too great for him to attain, if only he might be steadied and inspired and assisted by a competent helper—one thoroughly familiar with every detail of the denominational machinery, and acquainted with every denominational engineer.

Thus it was maddening for Charity to be thus robbed of the high place in life for which she had fitted herself, and to which she had aspired for years, by an alien to the church. What right had this creature who never entered a church—what right had she even to the friendship of the minister? And to ruin his reputation at the same time! To cause him to be sent away from Corinth—Charity had seen it too many times not to recognize the signs! To deprive him of a companion so fitly qualified to help him realize to the full his splendid ambition! Small wonder that the daughter of the church had taken upon herself such a desperate attempt.

In the moments after Deborah had left her, Charity had examined the nurse's room with interest and surprise. The apartment had none of the signs of an unholy life. Except that it was a poorer place than any room in the Jordan house, it might have been Charity's own. There was even a Bible, and well-worn from obvious use, on a table by which a chair was drawn, as if the reader had but just laid the book aside.

And now this woman stood before her. This woman with the deep, kind eyes, the soft, calm voice, her cheeks glowing with healthful outdoor exercise, and her air of sweet womanly maturity.

The nurse spoke first. "I am Miss Farwell. You are Miss Jordan, I believe. I see you pass the house frequently. Won't you be seated, please, you seem to be in some kind of trouble."

Poor Charity! Dropping weakly into a chair, she fought back the bitter tears. But she came immediately to the point. "I came to see you about our minister, Reverend Matthews."

The color in the nurse's cheeks deepened imperceptibly. "But why should you come to me about Mr. Matthews?" she said. "I know nothing of your church's affairs, Miss Jordan."

"I know you do not," the other returned, with a coldness in her voice. "You have never been to hear him preach. You know nothing—nothing of what it means to him—to me—to all of us, I mean. How could you know anything about it?"

Her outburst was passionate, and her face had grown crimson.

Now the color disappeared from the nurse's cheeks, and she said coolly, "There is clearly a great deal on your mind, Miss Jordan. Perhaps it would be good for you to explain clearly just what you mean and why you come to me?"

In the effort to explain which followed, Charity's words came tumbling recklessly, impetuously, in all sorts of disorder. She charged the nurse with ruining the minister's work, with alienating him from his people, with injuring the Memorial Church and the cause of Christ in Corinth, and with making him the talk of the town.

"What is he to you?" the Elder's daughter finished. "What could he ever be to you? You would not dare to think of marrying a minister of the Gospel—you, you a woman of the world."

"I am not a Christian, then, in your opinion?" said Hope.

"How could you be? You have never been to church since you came to Corinth."

"And that is what makes one a Christian?"

"What else is there? How else is one to tell but whether one goes to church or not?"

Hope was silent.

But Charity was not to be deterred. "Rev. Matthews belongs to us," she went on. "He does not belong to you, and you have no right to take him from us." Then she pleaded with her to—as she put it—let their pastor alone, to permit him to stay in Corinth and go on to the great future that she was so sure awaited him in religious circles.

As the girl talked, Miss Farwell sat very still. Now and then when Charity's disordered words seemed to carry a deeper meaning than appeared on the surface, the gray eyes lifted themselves to study the speaker's face, doubtfully, questioningly.

In her painful excitement Charity was telling much more than she realized. But more than just laying her own heart bare to the nurse, by her words Charity was revealing Hope Farwell to herself.

When her visitor had talked herself out, the nurse said quietly, "Miss Jordan, it is not at all necessary that I should reply to the things you have said. But you must answer me one question. Has Mr. Matthews ever, either by word or by his manner toward you, given you reason to feel that you, personally, have a right to say these things to me—that you and he have the sort of, shall I say a 'friendship,' wherein you must take it upon yourself to act as his protector?"

The question was so frank, so direct, and yet so womanly and kind and without malice, and so completely unexpected—that Charity looked away, having no reply.

"Tell me please, Miss Jordan. After all you have said, you must."

The answer came in a whisper. "No."

"Thank you," said Hope. And there was that tone in the nurse's voice that left the other's heart hopeless, and robbed her of power to say more. She rose and moved toward the door.

The nurse accompanied her to the porch. "Miss Jordan—" she said.

Charity paused.

"I am very sorry," the nurse went on in a voice of compassion. "I am afraid you will never understand how—how completely mistaken you are—about me, and about the church. I shall not harm either your church or—your minister. Believe me, I am very, very sorry."

When she was gone, Miss Farwell could not return to the garden. Dan would probably be there by now, and she could not meet him just yet. She must have some time alone to sift through the thoughts and emotions Miss Jordan's visit had set to stirring within her heart and mind. She must go somewhere to think this thing out!

The possibility she had known of all along had suddenly become a reality, and all the pain that she had foreseen had now come upon her. Try as she had to keep hold of her heart, her grip had not proved strong enough. Now she knew she was in danger of losing it! Yet with the pain, as is always the case, there came a glad light-heartedness as well.

Miss Farwell need not have fled from meeting Dan in the garden that afternoon, however. For he did not come.

While the nurse, in her room, was greeting Miss Charity, Elder Jordan, who had stopped on his way home from the post office, was knocking at the door of the minister's study.

# CHAPTER THIRTY-FOUR

# DAN FACES HIS HEART

The Elder's visit to Dan was prompted not only by the "church situation," as he had come to look upon it in the conference with Judge Strong the evening before, but by the old man's regard for the young minister himself. Because of this he had said nothing to his brother elder of his purpose. He wished to make his visit something more than an official call on church business. Nathaniel felt that if he was alone perhaps he could talk to Dan in a way that would have been impossible in the presence of Judge Strong.

In the months of his work in Corinth, Dan had learned to love this old church father. It was true that his faithfulness to the dead past and to the obsolete doctrines of his denomination made up a large element of his religion. But he was not, therefore, without the virtues of character that come from obedience, though he would hardly have known when he was obeying Christ because for him there was no difference between that and obeying the church. But it was impossible not to recognize, that so far as the claims of his creed would permit, Elder Jordan was a true Christian man—gentle, tolerant, kind in all things.

Yet in his innocence, and perhaps even because he was such a *good* man, he had been for years an easy pawn in the Ally's hand. Thus it was impossible for the minister and his Elder to see life from the same point of view. They belonged to different ages. The younger man, recognizing this, honored his elder brother for his fidelity to the faith of his fathers, and saw in this very faith a virtue to admire. But the older man saw in Dan's broader views and neglect of the issues that belonged to the past age a weakness of Christian character—to be overcome if possible, but on no ground to be tolerated, less the very foundation of the church be weakened.

Elder Jordan's regard for Dan was wholly personal, entirely outside the things of the church. The Elder was capable of sacrificing his own daughter if, in his judgment, it was necessary for the good of the cause. But he would not have loved her the less. There was that certain something in his religion that bore the marks of the unearthly—that which has succeeded in making Christianity a thing of schools and churches and opinions, rather than a thing of farms and shops and everyday life—a thing of set days, of forms, rites, ceremonies, beliefs, activities, and meetings, rather than a thing of daily living and the commonplace, individual duties, pleasures, and drudgeries of life.

So care for him as he did, the old churchman did not spare Dan that afternoon. Because of his love, both for Dan and for the church, he felt it his duty to caution Dan in the most unmistakable of terms where he feared his course was bound if he did not moderate it. Very clearly he forced the minister to see the situation, making him understand the significance of the gossip that had been stirring about, and the growing dissatisfaction of the church leaders with his sermons.

Dan listened quietly, with no lack of respect for the man who talked so plainly. For even under the sometimes harsh words, he felt the true spirit of the speaker and his kindly regard for his younger brother.

About his preaching, Dan could make no reply. For he realized how impossible it was for the Elder to change his point of view no matter what he might say. But touching his friendship with the nurse, Dan spoke up warmly in defense of the young woman— of himself he said nothing. He told Nathaniel most plainly that Miss Farwell had come to Corinth and had proved herself a shining example of Christian love, an example the church would do well to follow. As the Elder listened, he thought he saw how Dan had been influenced in his ministry by this woman who was not of the church. Even as his daughter had pleaded with the nurse to set the minister free, Nathaniel now pleaded with Dan to free himself. Inevitably the results were the same.

"Think of your ministry, my boy," urged the old man, "of the sacred duties of your office. Your attitude toward this woman has been what the people would expect the conduct of a man to be toward the one he is seeking to make his wife. Yet no one for a moment thinks you expect to marry this woman. She is known to be an opponent of the church. What success could you hope to have as a minister if you took as your wife one who would have nothing to do with your church? Therefore, what business do you have to be so intimate with her, to be in her company so constantly? Granting all you say of her character, why does she stay in Corinth where no one will employ her, when she could so easily return to her work in the city, and take that Conner girl with her?"

Dan could find no words to answer the Elder. The Elder's words had awakened a tumult of thoughts in his brain.

At last Nathaniel took his leave, neither having arrived at a solution.

When he was gone, Dan's mind and heart resounded over and over with the words, "*No one thinks you expect to marry this woman.*"

"To marry this woman—to marry—to *marry!*"

He thought of his father and mother and their perfect companionship. "*What business do you have to be so intimate with her, to be in her company so constantly?*"

He started to walk to the window that looked down on the garden. Then he stopped himself. He was not ready to see her yet. He knew now why the garden had come to mean so much to him. He thought about how much different his life in Corinth would be without this woman who had grown to be such a part of it.

Dan Matthews was not a shallow person who could amuse

himself with a hundred imitation relationships that merely hinted
at love. In his veins ran the fierce red blood of a strong race that
had ruled by simple strength of manhood their wild mountain
wilderness. Like the tiny stream, flowing quietly through peaceful
meadows, still woodlands, and sunny pastures—growing always
broader and deeper as it runs—is unconscious of its quiet power
until checked by some barrier that dams its course, then to rise
and swell to a mighty flood as it seeks to clear its path . . . in such
a way had Dan's love grown. In the fields of friendship it had
gained depth and power. He had not even realized its increasing
speed until now, suddenly coming to the barrier, it rose in all its
strength—a flood of passion that shook every nerve in his being.
All at once it seemed that it had become a mighty force that could
not be stopped.

Going to the other window, Dan looked out upon the cast-
iron monument. As he looked at the figure so immovable, so
hideously rigid and fixed in the act of proclaiming an issue that
belonged to a dead age, he felt as if his heart would burst with
wild rage at the whole rigid-bound narrow community—people
and church together.

What business had he to the companionship of this woman?

Even before he could reflect upon the answer, Dan shrank
hopeless within himself as he thought of his position, and of her
attitude toward the church and its leaders.

*The Elder and his people need not be uneasy,* he thought. *The
barrier is too well-built to be so easily swept aside. She would never
have me anyway.*

He saw that now, once such thoughts of love had invaded his
heart, even the old friendship between himself and Hope Farwell
would be impossible. Such things could not be approached, and
then ignored and mere friendship regained. He wondered if his
removing himself from her life would make any ripple in its calm,
even current. Would she even care?

Then came the Elder's words back to him: "*Why does she stay
in Corinth?*"

"Could it be that she cared—?"

No! Dan stopped himself from even completing the thought. It was not possible. It was her interest in Grace Conner alone that held her here!

Around his room Big Dan Matthews paced, facing this thing against which the very strength of his manhood was his greatest weakness. Facing it, he too was afraid to go down to the garden. He could not meet her—not now, not with such thoughts swirling through him. He must gain a little self-control first. He must grow better acquainted with this thing that had come upon him so quickly.

Following the instinct of his ancestors to face trouble in the open, he went downstairs and out the back door of the house, turned down the street in the opposite direction from the Doctor's and the garden, and set out, bound for a long walk in the country. Perhaps he would go as far as John Gardner's and spend the night there. He went up the street for a block or two before turning north, lest his friends in the garden see him and hail him.

Then walking quickly he pushed on toward the outskirts of town, up the old Academy Hill road.

# CHAPTER THIRTY-FIVE

# THE MEETING OF HEARTS

When Hope Farwell looked up from under the oak tree in the Academy yard to see Dan Matthews coming through the gap in the tumbled down fence, it was as if he had appeared in answer to her very thoughts.

The intensity of her emotions at the moment frightened her, and her first impulse was to jump up, flee before he saw her, and escape. But she remained where she was, sitting still, watching him approach as one fascinated, while her trembling fingers picked unconsciously at the young shoots of grass by her side.

With his face turned toward the valley below, Dan came slowly across the weed-grown yard, unaware of the young woman on the knoll. Finally he looked in her direction. With her face turned quickly half-aside, she saw him stop suddenly as if halted by the same feeling that had so moved her.

For a full minute he stood, as if questioning his senses. The girl sat absolutely still. Once she thought he would turn back. But then he came forward, almost eagerly, as he had come that day from the water when he had looked up to see her on the river bank. And then he stood before her as he had stood that other day weeks ago, with the sunlight shining on his red-brown hair.

There was no word of formal greeting. None was needed.

Each seemed to instinctively know the travail of soul of the other.

Dan dropped down on the grass by her side, as if it were unnecessary that he should speak at all.

"I thought you were working in the garden this afternoon," she said.

"I had a visitor. After that I could not go to work."

"I had a caller too," she replied. "I—I could not go afterward either." The words were spoken almost in a whisper. Her trembling fingers were picking again at the short young grass, while her eyes were looking far away beyond the sweeping line of blue. One foot had slipped a little from under its protecting shelter of the blue skirt.

With a flush of anger, Dan saw that the shoe was shabby. The skirt, too, showed unmistakable signs of wear. He controlled himself with difficulty. At this moment her inability to find more work was hardly at issue.

"Your caller was—?" he asked.

"Charity Jordan. And yours?"

"Her father." Dan looked away. "Then I suppose you know what they are saying about us," he added, then slowly looked back at her.

She turned her face quickly to his, permitting him for the first time to search her eyes.

"Yes," she said softly. "Yes, I know."

Something in her confident reply caused Dan to forget all his half-formed resolutions. His work, his life, the possible outcome, the world itself—suddenly it was all loose in the overpowering rush of the flood that swept his being.

"Then you know—" His voice trembled. "—you know that—that I love you." He said the words in the simplicity of one who was laying his whole self at her feet.

In the very wonder at the fullness of the offering, the nurse sat as one transfixed. She could find no words to express her acceptance of the gift.

Dan doubted her silence, and turned away. "I'm sorry—I should not have—"

"No, Dan, please," she interrupted. "Don't mistake my silence, it's only that . . ." Still she did not know what to say.

"*Have* I not mistaken—do you—"

"You cannot doubt that I care for you," she replied. "But—"

"I do not understand," he faltered.

"Don't you see, that while you may tell me what you have, and that I may tell you how proud—how glad your words have made me, and how with all my heart I—I love you too—" her voice broke, "don't you see that this must be all—that we must not go on?"

"All?"

"Yes. Everything I said to you the first day we met here is still true. Don't you see that I can never be more to you than I am now? We stand on the opposite sides of a fence that is too high."

As one who hears himself sentenced to life exile, Dan dropped his head and buried his face in his hands.

Hope's gray eyes filled with tears that were not yet permitted to fall. In his presence she would have to be strong, for his sake—afterwards, in the privacy of her own room, her heart should have its way and her tears be loosed.

Once her hand went out slowly, but then was silently withdrawn, and the trembling white fingers again set about plucking the young blades of grass.

"Tell me," he said at last, raising his head but not looking her in the face, "if I were anything else, if I were engaged in any other work, would you be my wife?"

"Why do you ask that?"

"Because I must know," he answered almost harshly.

"If you were a common laborer, or a business or professional man, if your work was anything honorable and right—then yes, gladly, oh how gladly I would!"

"Then I will give up the pastorate!" he burst forth. "I will be something else!"

"You would give up your ministry for me?" she questioned, "your chosen lifework?"

"Yes, if need be. If there is one thing you have helped me see,

it is that other work can be just as holy, just as sacred as the work
of the preacher and the church. You do not know how in the past
months I have been teaching that very truth from my pulpit. Perhaps it is time for me to heed my own teaching. Why should I not
give my life to ministry in some other form?"

"Because it is not some other work that calls you now. Other
ministries are not yours," she answered gently. "I have learned to
love you because you are so true to yourself. You must not disappoint me now. And," she continued confidently, "I know that
you will not."

Dan argued and pled for the other side of the case. At last,
when she felt so beset by both his love and her own that she felt
her strength slipping, she said, "Don't, please! I cannot listen to
more of this now. It is not fair to either of us. You must have time
to think alone. I believe at this moment I know you even better
than you know yourself. You must leave me now. You must promise that you will not try to see me again until tomorrow at this
same hour. I will be in the garden with the others until four o'clock,
when I will go into the house alone. If then you have decided that
you can, with all truthfulness to yourself and me, give up your
ministry, come to me and I will be your wife. But whether you
come or not you must always believe that I love you, that I shall
always love you, as my other self, my friend, and that I shall never
doubt your love for me."

So she sent him away to fight his battle alone, knowing it was
the only way such a battle could be rightly fought, and because
she wanted him, for his own sake, to have the certainty of a self-
won victory. In her own heart she never doubted what that victory
would be, or what it would mean to her.

# CHAPTER THIRTY-SIX

# IN HIS ROOM

Alone in his little study, the door locked, Dan Matthews battled with himself.

Everywhere in the room were things that cried aloud to him of his ministry—his library of books of peculiar interest to ministers; papers and pamphlets filled with matters of the church, written for churchmen; his sermons, one lying half-finished on the study table; the very pictures on the walls, and the unanswered letters on his desk. Standing in the midst of these things that were all so much a part of his chosen life that they seemed a vital part of himself, he heard the voices down in the garden. He knew she was there.

Since the beginning of time men like Dan Matthews have fought for women like Hope Farwell. For such women have men committed every crime, endured every hardship, braved every danger, made every sacrifice, accomplished every great thing. Few of the race of mortals today feel such passion. It is primitive—but it was more. For there had been bred into this man something stronger than his giant physical strength—a spirit, a purpose fitting such a body.

The little clock on the mantel struck the hour. Softly, slowly, the notes rang out—one, two, three, four.

With face white and drawn Dan went to the window. All that afternoon, knowing that she was there, he had denied himself even the sight of her. Now he would look upon the object of his agony.

He watched as, without a glance toward his window, the young woman left her friends and walked slowly into the house. Five—ten—fifteen—twenty minutes went by.

The ticking of the little clock seemed to beat on Dan's brain with sledgehammer blows!

Then he saw her come out onto the front porch of the cottage. Slowly she walked out into the yard until she was screened from the street by the big lilac bush.

Turning, she faced his window. She waved a greeting. She even beckoned him to come. The man swayed and put out his hand to grip the window casing. Again she beckoned him—come. When he did not leave his place and only waved a hand in return, she went slowly back into the house.

Then Dan Matthews—minister and man—staggered back from the window to fall on his knees in prayer.

It was perhaps two hours before sunrise when Dr. Harry's horse stopped suddenly in a dark stretch of woodland some six miles from town. Dimly from his buggy the doctor saw a figure coming toward him.

"Hello!" he said sharply. "What do you want?"

The man in the road laughed a strange, hoarse laugh as he continued to advance. "I thought it must be you," came a voice from the dark. "You nearly ran me down." Dan climbed in by the physician's side.

The minister made no explanation, nor did his friend press him after the first few surprised questions. But when they were turning in toward Dan's gate, the big fellow burst out, "Keep going, Harry! I can't go home right now. Let me stay at your house for a little while!"

# CHAPTER THIRTY-SEVEN

# DAN'S STRUGGLE

Dan slept till well into the afternoon, and remained at Dr. Harry's the rest of the day, returning to his own rooms in the evening.

Early the following morning he was scheduled to take the train for the annual gathering of the denomination that was to be held in a distant city. He would be away from Corinth at least three days.

When he had lighted the lamp that night, the minister's little study seemed filled with a spirit that had never been there before. It was as if during his absence some unseen presence had moved in to share the apartment with him. The very books and papers impressed him as intimate companions, as if, in thus witnessing and taking part in the soul struggle of the man, they had entered into a closer relation to him, a relation sacred and holy. He was conscious too of an atmosphere of privacy there that he had never sensed before, and for the first time since coming to Corinth, he drew down the window shades.

In the battle that Hope Farwell had set for him to fight, Dan had sought to be frankly honest with himself, and to judge himself coldly, without regard to the demands of his heart. If he had erred at all it was in an over-sensitivity to conscience. For conscience has

ever been a tricky master, often betraying its too-willing slaves to
their own self-injury. It is a large question whether one has a greater
right to injure himself than to harm another.

Dan could not feel that he had in any way neglected the church,
or fallen short of his duties as a hired shepherd. But after all, was
he not to some degree in error in his judgment of his people? Had
he now, perhaps, misunderstood the spirit that moved them? He
had come to Corinth from his school with the thought fixed in
his mind that the church was *all* right. Had he not, by the unexpected and brutal directness of his experience, been swung to the
other extreme, conceiving conditions as all wrong? And surely
that was an equally great error to fall into.

Groping in the dark of his ministry he had come to feel more
and more keenly his inexperience. After all, was he not right in
taking the hard, seldom-traveled path? Or was the safe way of the
church fathers the true way? He had come to doubt those leaders
whom he had been taught to follow; but even more he had come
to doubt his own ability to lead, or even to find the way for
himself. It was this doubt that had led him to decide as Hope
Farwell knew he would.

Big Dan Matthews could not turn from the church and his
chosen work without the same certainty that had led him to it.

Least of all could he, after what Hope had made clear, go to
her with a shadow of doubt in his mind.

His convictions were not as yet convincing. His new love for
Hope was too large in his thinking just now for him to trust his
own motives. So in the end he made his choice—making the
greatest possible sacrifice to one of his nature—and determined to
give himself wholly to that which he still felt to be his ministry.

He looked forward now with eagerness to the gathering of
church men to which he was going in the morning. There he
would meet the great leaders of his church, those with lifelong
experience in the work to which he had given himself, those whose
names were household names in the homes of his people. There
he would come into touch with the spirit of the church as a whole,
not merely the spirit of his own local congregation. And in the

affairs of the convention, in their reports of work accomplished, of conditions throughout the country, and in the plans for things to be done, he would find—he hoped—the key that would put him in full harmony with those who were his fellow-workers.

Dan's thoughts were interrupted by a familiar knock at the door. The old Doctor entered.

The Doctor knew all about the increased talk of the community regarding Dan and Hope, and of the growing sentiment of Memorial Church. But he knew this much, even more than Dan: from long observation he understood, as Dan did not, the part that Judge Strong had played in the inspiration of this revival of activities by the Ally. Concerning Dan and Hope, he could only conjecture, but the Doctor's conjectures amounted almost to certainties. He knew that the lad so dear to him was passing through some tremendous crisis, for he had talked with Dr. Harry that afternoon. Seeing by the light in the window that Dan had returned, he had run across the street to see if all was well with the boy. It was characteristic of the Doctor, that while he did not make known the object of his visit in words, he made the minister feel his sympathy and interest, and his readiness to stand by him.

Grasping his young friend's hand in greeting, and placing his other hand on Dan's shoulder, he studied his face as he would have studied a patient. "Come on, Dan," he said at length, "don't you think it's time we went fishing?"

The minister smiled back at him. "I wish I could, Doctor. I need it, all right. But I must leave for the convention tomorrow."

"Heard who's going?" grunted the Doctor as he seated himself.

Dan named a few of his church people. The Doctor grunted again. They were nearly all of the inner circle, the Judge's confidantes in matters of the church.

"Judge Strong is going too," said the Doctor. Dan said nothing.

"Told me this evening." Then the old man chuckled. "I rather thought I might go myself."

"You!" Dan said in surprise.

The Doctor's eyes twinkled. "Yes me! And why not? I've never been to one of these affairs, but for that matter, neither have you.

I don't suppose they would throw me out. Anyway, I have some business in the city and I thought it would be almost as good as a fishing trip for us to go up together. Martha's pleased to death! She thinks I'll get it sure if I can only hear some of the really *big*-name preachers."

Dan laughed, well-pleased. He could not know of the real motive that prompted the Doctor's strange interest in this great convocation of churchmen.

The next morning at an early hour they were off: Dan, the old Doctor, some six or eight of the active men and women leaders of the congregation, Charity, and Judge Strong. The Ally went also.

There was no little surprise expressed, in a half-jesting manner, by the company, at the presence of Dr. Oldham. And there was much putting together of heads in whispered consultation as to what it might mean. The Judge and his competent associates, with the Ally, kept very much together and left Dan and his friend equally as much to themselves.

Whenever the young minister, prompted by his thoughts of the last twenty-four hours to seek more diligently to do the work of the church as he ought, approached the group, a significant hush followed. His pleasantries were met by formal and evidently forced monosyllables, which very soon sent him back to his seat with a face that made the old Doctor say things under his breath.

"Look here, Dan," said the old physician, as they neared the city of their destination, "I understand that at these meetings the visiting delegates are always entertained at the homes of the local church people. Since I'm not a delegate I will go to a hotel. You come with me, as my guest. Tell them you have already accepted an invitation to stay with a friend. Don't worry, they'll be glad enough to have one less to care for, and I want you."

The young man eagerly accepted.

# CHAPTER THIRTY-EIGHT

# THE CONVENTION

At the meeting was the usual gathering of the usual types.

There were the leaders, regularly appointed by the denomination, who were determined to keep that which had been committed to them at any cost. To this end they glorified, in the Lord's service, the common, political methods of distributing the places of conspicuous honor and power, upon program and committee, among those friends and favorites who could be depended upon to respond most emphatically.

Equally active, with methods as familiar but not equally in evidence, were the would-be leaders, who—"for the glory of Christ"—sought these same seats of the mighty, and who were assisted by those who aspired to become their friends and favorites—joint-heirs in their success should they succeed.

Then there were the self-constituted leaders who pushed and pulled and scrambled to the front. If they could be thought, only for the moment, by the multitude to be something more than they were, then would their hearts be content. It was these who were on their feet instantly to speak upon every question with ponderous weight of words, and were most happy if they could fill some vacant chair on the platform.

There were the heresy hunters who sniffed with hound-like

eagerness for the scent of doctrinal weakness in the speeches of their brothers. And upon every proposed movement of the body, they guarded with bulldog fidelity the faith of their fathers.

There were also the young preachers who came to look with awe on the doings of the great ones, to learn how it was done and to watch for a possible opening whereby they might snatch their bit of glory here on earth.

There were many indeed of this latter class who, from the highest religious motives, had answered the call to the ministry as to something sacred and holy, even as had Dan. These young men, though they knew it not, were there to learn how their leaders—while theoretically depending upon God for their strength and guidance in managing the affairs of the church—depended actually upon the very methods which, when used by the world in its affairs, they stamped ungodly.

The Ally was there in power. The day of the rack, the thumbs-crew, and the stake was long past. In place of these instruments of religious discipline, in these latter days we have instead—the Ally.

Mostly those on the firing line were ministers, though here and there a prominent woman leader pushed to the front. The rest were brothers and sisters, mainly sisters, who, like other mortals, always backed their favorites in the race that was set before them all. These prayed sincerely and devoutly that somehow, in ways beyond their bewildered ken, the good God would bless the efforts that were being made for righteousness and truth, hoping thus for heavenly results from very worldly methods.

Judge Strong was an old campaigner. A heavy contributor to the general work and missionary funds to which the leaders looked for the practical solution of their modest bread and butter prob-lems, he had the ears of them all. Nor was the Elder slow to use his advantage. He could speak his mind with frankness here, for these great men of the church lived far from Corinth and, while knowing much of the Elder—the church man—they knew noth-ing of the Judge—the citizen and neighbor. The Elder knew, how-ever, that such reports as he had to make must, in the very nature of things, for the good of the cause, be strictly private.

While the Judge was holding his little confidential chats with the leaders, and the leaders were holding equally confidential chats with their friends and favorites, and these in turn were doing as they had been done by, the Elder's assistants, assigned to various church homes in the city, were confidentially exchanging confidences with their hostesses. And thus the Ally, as he is always doing, continued that most loved of all its works: the moving into positions of power those who play its cruel game, while denying a voice to those who will not.

In the case at hand, the effect was as follows:

Dan was introduced to the Secretary. "Ah—yes, Brother Matthews of Corinth! Glad to meet you . . . Ah, excuse me. I see— ah, a brother over there with whom I must speak."

Dan was presented to the Treasurer. "Oh yes, I have heard of you—at Corinth. Why hello, Brother Simpkins,"—catching a passing preacher by the arm—"glad to see you! How are you and how is the work?"

Dan introduced himself to one or two of those whom he had hungered to see, those who were noted in the church papers for their broad wisdom and saintly character. Yet somehow he felt rebuked for his forwardness when each looked down from his pedestal at him and said, "Oh yes, Brother Matthews! I have heard of you, Brother Matthews!"

During the morning session of the second day, the order of business called for reports from the churches. In response to roll call, one after the other of the representatives of the various congregations would tell what they had done and what they were going to do. Dr. Oldham remarked later, "No one told what they had failed to do, or what they ought to have done, or what they were not going to do."

As a rule the ministers reported for their own churches, except when some delegate whom the pastor knew to be particularly qualified was present and asked him to speak instead. But in such a case the minister always must see that the report is properly prepared.

When Memorial Church of Corinth was called, as Dan started

to rise from his chair, suddenly there was Judge Strong on his feet. There was a distinct hush, and heads went forward in interest. Dan felt the red rise to the back of his neck, and he lowered his massive bulk down into his seat as inconspicuously as possible.

The Elder regretted to report that, while they had held their regular services every Sabbath, and their preacher was the most popular preacher in Corinth, the conversions for some reason had not been as numerous as in some previous years. But Memorial Church could be depended upon to remedy that very soon, for they were contemplating a great revival meeting to begin as soon as a competent evangelist could be secured.

Loud applause followed from the professional evangelists present. They felt that a series of good old New Testament Gospel sermons would put them again to the front in the matter of additions to the membership role, the Judge continued.—Loud applause from the defenders of the faith.

Dan listened in silent amazement. This was the first he had heard of such a meeting in Corinth. The Doctor saw the boy's face grow burning red.

The Elder continued his report, touching every department of the church in like vein, and finishing by "regretting exceedingly that their offering for the missionary, and for the general work for the present year had fallen short of previous years." The Judge did not explain that he had subtracted from his part in the church offering an amount exceeding the shortage, which amount he had then added to his usual personal donation to the denomination at large. As for the regular expenses of the congregation, he went on, they had been cared for.

"And," remarked the State Secretary in a loud voice, rising instantly as the Judge sat down, "I want you all to know that Judge Strong's personal contribution to our convention funds is larger this year than ever before. We who know Judge Strong's splendid Christian generosity will understand how the regular expenses of Memorial Church have been paid." Whereupon the leaders-who-were and the leaders-who-would-like-to-be joined with one accord in loud applause.

Not a preacher there could have misunderstood exactly what the Elder's report signified.

Following the reports of the churches came the introductions of the new pastors. Skillfully the preachers were marshalled upon the platform, Big Dan towering at the foot of the line. Stunned and embarrassed as he was by the Judge's report, the boy would not have gone forward at all, had not the Doctor fairly pushed him into the aisle. The old philosopher told himself that the lad might as well get everything that was coming to him. And in the ceremony that followed, Dan got it indeed.

One after another of the ministers were introduced to the Secretary, who had a glowing word for each:

"Brother Williams who has done such marvelous work at Baxter." Loud applause for Brother Williams.

"Brother Hardy who is going to do a wonderful work at Wheeler." Louder applause for Brother Hardy.

And so on down the line. Not one was excluded—from big church or small, from city pulpit or country district, all secured the boosting comment and the applause. For this was Christian enthusiasm.

Dan's turn came last. His face was now white.

"And this," shouted the Secretary, "is Brother Matthews, the present pastor of our church at Corinth." A hush, still and significant, followed. For this was church policy.

After a moment's silence the Secretary continued, "Please join me in singing hymn three-hundred and one:

Blest be the tie that binds
    Our hearts in Christian love.

Now everyone please sing!"

And the denominational papers reporting the event agreed that they made a joyful noise unto the Lord.

Were the high officials and their mates on this ship of salvation to be blamed?

Not a bit! The Elder's report made Dan "unsafe"—and indeed

he was. They were right. More than this, the Lord needed the Judge's influence—and money.

When the young minister came back to his seat, his old friend thought his face the saddest he had ever seen.

At lunch the Doctor told Dan that he was going to call upon several friends that afternoon. Among them he mentioned the superintendent of a famous steel plant in the city. Agreeing to meet at dinner in the evening, they parted, Dan going alone to the convention building. At the door he paused.

Several ministers, chatting gaily with friends passing in for the opening of the afternoon session, looked curiously at the husky, irresolute figure standing there alone. All were sorry for him. For every one understood fully the meaning of the events of the morning.

An hour later the superintendent of the great steelworks greeted the big, clean-looking fellow with admiring eyes, and wondered what had caused the look of sadness on his face.

"I am in the city with my friend, Dr. Oldham," explained Dan. "I expected to find him here. He told me at lunch he was coming to visit you. We parted for the afternoon, but then I decided to see if I could track him down."

"Oldham in town? Good!" exclaimed the man. "Of course he would look me up, but he hasn't been here yet. I'm glad to meet any friend of the Doctor's. Sit down, Mr. Matthews. He'll be here presently, no doubt. Perhaps while you're waiting you would care to have a look about the plant."

Dan replied eagerly that nothing could please him more.

With the answer, the man touched a bell, then spoke to the man who appeared, "Jack, show Mr. Matthews around. He's a friend of my friend, Dr. Oldham."

And so when the Doctor found the boy, he was standing in the very heart of the great plant, where the brawny workmen, naked to the waist—their bodies shining with sweat and streaked with grime—wrestled with the hard realities of making a living by the sweat of their brows.

The Doctor watched him for a while. Then, tapping him on

the shoulder, he shouted in his ear above the roar of the furnace, the hissing of steam, and the crash and clank of iron and steel, "Almost as good as a fishing trip, eh, Dan?"

Dan swung around with a smile on his face, the first it had experienced in a good many days.

Back in the office again, the superintendent introduced them to a gray-haired, smooth-faced, portly gentleman—the president of the steel company, a well-known wealthy capitalist. The great man repeated Dan's name, looking him over all the while.

"Matthews . . . by your name and build, you must be related to the Grant Matthews who owns Dewey Bald."

"He is my father, sir," returned Dan with a smile.

"Ah, yes. Through my interests in the lead and zinc industry, I am familiar with your part of the country. I have met your father several times. It is not easy to forget such a man."

Dan now remembered the president's name, and that he had heard it in connection with the mines on Jake creek, near his home.

The owner of the factory continued, "I have tried several times to persuade your father to open up that hill of his. He is sitting on a fortune in that mountain—a fortune! Are you interested in mining, Mr. Matthews?"

"Not directly, sir."

"Well, if your people should ever decide to develop that property, come to me. I know what it is. We would be glad to talk it over with you. Goodbye, young Matthews. I'm glad to have met you. Good day, Doctor."

Then he was gone.

The Doctor and Dan had dinner with the genial superintendent and his family that evening, and the next morning set out for Corinth.

# CHAPTER THIRTY-NINE

# THE SACRIFICE OF VICTORY

When Hope Farwell dismissed Dan that afternoon in the old Academy yard, her fears were both for him and for herself. And she could not for a moment question what Dan's decision would be.

With all the gladness that their love had brought, her heart held no hope. For she exacted of herself the same faithfulness to her spiritual convictions that she demanded of Dan. It would be as wrong for her to accept the organized church as for him to reject it.

So she had gone to the limit of her strength for his sake. But when she reached again the privacy of her room, her woman nature had its way and many tears flowed. With the morning strength returned again—strength and calmness. Quietly she went about her daily work, for while she had left the whole burden of decision upon Dan, her heart was with the man she loved in his fight.

At the appointed hour she left her friends in the garden and went into the house as she had planned. She did not expect him, but she had said that she would wait his coming. Her heart beat painfully as the slow minutes passed, bringing by his absence proof that she had not misjudged him. Then she went outside and saw him standing at his window. Smiling, she even beckoned to him. She wished to make his victory certain, final and complete. She could allow him to have no remaining doubts as to his course.

Very quietly she returned to her room. She did not again enter the garden. And now the young woman was conscious that she also had a part to play in the fight the two were waging—together and yet so alone—for the truth both believed in. She knew she could not remain in Corinth, for both their sakes.

She explained her plans to Grace, for she could not leave the girl, and the two began making their simple preparations for the journey to the city. Feeling that her strength was not equal to the strain which another meeting with Dan would cause, there was no one left to bid goodbye except for Deborah and Denny and Dr. Abbott.

The doctor argued and pled his case one final time, but to no avail. "Grace will go with me," the nurse explained. "I am sure Dr. Miles will find her a place in the hospital. So you see, in the end I will even be able to take a little of your country work back to the city with me."

"I understand," he said finally. "I regret your decision . . . but I understand."

Miss Farwell's plans for the girl, whose life she had reclaimed, did not fail. Dr. Miles, when he heard her story, gladly helped Grace to a place in the school where she might equip herself for her chosen ministry. "The best nurses," said the famous physician, "are those who have themselves suffered. No amount of professional skill can make up for a lack of human sympathy and love."

———

Home from the convention, Dan was turning wearily in at his gate. From the garden Deborah called to him. By her manner as she came slowly to the fence, Dan knew the good soul was troubled.

"It's a heavy heart I have, Mr. Matthews," she said, "for she's clean gone, an' Denny an' me's just so lonesome we don't know what to do."

Dan's big hand gripped the fence. His face went white. "Gone," he repeated blankly. He did not need to ask who she meant.

"Yes, sir—gone. Yesterday evenin' by the northbound train, leavin' her kindest regards and best wishes to you."

# CHAPTER FORTY

# THE REVIVAL AND ITS RESULTS

Dan could not fully understand his experience at the church convention.

Sadly puzzled and surprised by the spirit and atmosphere of that meeting he had approached with such confident expectation, and sorely hurt by his reception, he had no idea of the real reason for it all. He had no conception as yet how widespread and close to home was the effort to discredit him. He only blamed himself the more for being so out of harmony—for failing so grievously to find the key that would put him in tune.

In the great steelworks among the sweating, toiling men, with the superintendent of the plant under whose hand men and machinery were made to serve a great world's need, and with the president whose brain and genius was such a power in the financial and industrial world—with all of these Dan had felt a spirit of kinship. Amid these surroundings he had been as much at home as if he were again in his native Ozark hills, and for those hours had forgotten his fellow churchmen and what they called their ministries.

But as their train drew nearer and nearer Corinth, the Doctor saw by his companion's face, and by his fits of brooding silence, that the minister was feeling again the weight of his troublesome burden.

By this and by what he had seen at the convention, the old physician knew that the hour in Dan's life for which he had watched with such careful, anxious interest, was drawing near. The greatest struggle of his young life, when Dan would have to determine his true call, was at hand.

With Hope now gone out of his life, Dan turned to his work with grim, desperate, determination.

What, indeed, did he now have to turn to but his work? He realized that now he must find in this work for which he had sacrificed so much, the only thing that would justify his choice— the choice that had cost both him and the woman he loved so much suffering. He *had* to find reality in his work, or their sacrifice would be in vain. His ministry, his chosen call had now become something more to him than a so-called career, a lifework. To the high motives that had led him to the service of the church, he now added the price he had paid in giving up the woman who had grown to mean so much to him. He *must* find in his ministry that which would fulfill the great price paid!

So, with all the strength of his great nature, he threw himself with feverish energy into what had, in spite of himself, come to be an empty ministry. Crushing every feeling of being misunderstood and unjustly criticized, permitting himself no thought that there were under the surface treacherous currents working to overthrow him, blaming himself always and never others when he felt a lack of warmth or sympathy in his people, yielding for a time even his own convictions about his teaching and striving to shape his sermons more along the established lines of the Elders, he fought to put himself into his work.

And always, at the beck and call of Dan's real masters, that other servant of the church—that spirit that lives in Corinth— wrought the will of those whose ally it is.

That last meeting between Dan and Hope in the Academy yard, as if by appointment, the sudden departure of the nurse so soon after, and Dan's too-evident state of mind, were all skillfully used to give color to the ugly whispered reasons for the nurse's leaving town so hurriedly.

The old Doctor knowing, watching, waited for the hour he knew would come. He understood both Dan and the Ally as he had always understood them both. But he wisely recognized the uselessness of doing a thing by his own hand, and let his young friend go into the battle alone, in his own strong, hard, truthful way. And Dr. Harry also, knowing the malignant, cancerous power that was forcing the end, watched silently, hopelessly, helplessly, as many a time he had watched the grim drawing near of that one whose certain coming his professional knowledge enabled him to recognize, while giving him no power to stay.

Meanwhile, Memorial Church was all astir, and on the tiptoe of expectancy, preparing—they said—for the greatest revival ever held in Corinth. The professional evangelist selected by the Elder, whose choice was, as a matter of course, approved by his fellow officials and congregation, had sent full instructions, photographs, and suitably boastful—yet with an air of religious humility because "it is God who ordains such mighty works"—statements as to his "qualifications," for the proper advertising of himself, and—as his instructions stated—"the working up of expectation for the meeting."

Ignoring the slight to himself in the matter of calling the evangelist, Dan did everything in his power to carry out his pastoral duties and role in the preparations.

The evangelist arrived. Royally received as if the scripture had been mistranslated by some inept scribe and was supposed to read, "the first shall be first and the last last," he was escorted in triumph by the Elders and the inner circle to the Strong mansion, which was to be his home during the meetings. With the very hour he began his professional duty of "setting the church in order, and gathering a mighty harvest of souls."

This evangelist was a good one, of his kind.

His kind is that type of professional soul-winner evolved by the system whereby the church pays for the increase of its flock at so much per head, inasmuch as the number of his calls, and the amount of his hire depend upon the number of additions per meeting to the evangelist's credit. The record of his accomplishments is kept as a business ledger tallies dollars—the bottom line can be seen in the numbers. A soul-winner with small meetings to his credit receives a very modest compensation for his services, and short notices in the church papers. But the big fellows—those who have hundreds of souls per meeting, come higher, much higher. Also they have more space given to them in the papers, which helps them to come higher still. The success of those few who are at the very peak of their profession can be seen in the cut of their suits—custom-made by the finest tailors in St. Louis or Chicago—the shine on their shoes, the grooming of their person, occasionally by the carats in the rings on their fingers, and always by the size and looks of self-importance on the faces of those making up their "entourage in ministry."

Souls may have depreciated in value since Calvary, but one thing is sure—the price of soul-winners has gone way up since the days of Paul and his fellow ministers who walked the shores of the Mediterranean.

The evangelist imported for the occasion by Judge Strong was not yet at the pinnacle of statewide acclaim, therefore he sojourned to Corinth alone. However, he did manage to arrive in the first-class compartment of the train with several pieces of luggage, the contents of which would certainly stand him in good stead when his hour for national notoriety arrived—an hour he awaited hungrily.

Preaching every night for a week and conducting afternoon meetings, calling at the homes of the people, directing the efforts of the members of the inner circle, sometimes with Dan—oftener without him—fully informed and instructed by the Judge, whose guest he was and to whom he looked for a larger part of his generous salary, the evangelist made himself no small power in the church of Corinth. Assisted always by the skill and strength of the Ally, the effectiveness of his work from the standpoint of Elder Strong and the inner circle was assured.

Those were meetings to be remembered! With every hair in

place, the light glinting off his pearl-white teeth, holding a large open Bible in his left hand—the standard prop for those of his calling, and waving his right hand in the air—from the ring finger of which a flash of light could now and then be seen, the evangelist called the already-saved of Corinth who had packed Memorial Church to come forward down the aisle and "get their souls right with God." Scarce an unbeliever could have been found among the company, as is the case with most city-wide "revivals." But no one seemed to mind, for the invisible heavenly turnstiles at the end of the aisle counted only the bodies that passed, and repeat visitors to the altar and rocky-ground one-night conversions were given equal weight in the night's tally-sheet with the rare decision which promised any depth and staying power.

Special music, as it always does, came in for its share in the show. The more professional the performance, the more "anointed" its so-called *ministry*. And such entertainment it was! Had it not been for the particular words of several of the numbers, the audience may well have thought themselves attending tryouts for a Broadway theatrical show!

It was indeed a mighty revival—far-reaching in its influence and results! So the magazines and papers had it from Judge Strong's report, written while the services were still in progress, and edited by the evangelist. And the papers published a greater truth than they knew. There were influences of which they were ignorant, and the results reached ends they never dreamed of, though whether for the expansion or the dishonoring of the Kingdom is a question which might be examined.

Night after night Dan heard the evangelist, with harsh words and startling roughness of expression, declare the disasters that would befall every soul that did not accept and that very night declare the peculiar brand of salvation which he happened then to be offering. He listened to the long arguments and emotional appeals planned to prove the rightness, and therefore righteousness, of the evangelist himself and the pathway down which he had been called to lead the throng, and the equal wrongness, and therefore unrighteousness, of every other false door unto salvation.

Gradually as he heard these utterances and the narrow doctrines most emphatically and enthusiastically endorsed by his Elders and people as what constituted true New Testament Gospel, the conviction grew upon Dan that his own preaching would never be acceptable to the Memorial Church of Corinth. His perspective was now so much broader than this. He felt as if the blinders had been removed from his eyes to see the expansiveness of God's work among men. The call upon his life he now saw as something so much larger, so much deeper, than the mere propagation of a particular church's religious viewpoints.

And what place is there in the scheme of things as they are for the unacceptable preaching of any denomination's version of the gospel? What gospel can a preacher deliver in order to be acceptable to his peculiar church, except that church's peculiar gospel? Dan was not one to ask the oft-repeated question of the ministry, "What must I preach in order that my reputation and standing may be saved?"

In the semi-secret workers' meetings, in the still more private planning of the committees, in the jubilant reports of the uneasiness of the other churches in town, in the satisfying accounts of the answering sermons of other preachers, in the evidence of the general stirring up of the community, in the meticulous charting of the numbers—the count both in the turnstiles and offering places, and in the schemes for further advertising and boosting the evangelist and the cause, Dan felt himself growing ever more and more out of harmony—felt himself more and more alone.

In those days the sadness of his face grew fixed. His color lost its healthy freshness. Strange lines that did not belong to his young manhood appeared. And the brown eyes that had always been able to look at you so openly, hopefully, expectantly, with laughter half-hidden in their depths, were now doubting, questioning, fearful, full of pain.

The Doctor saw, and silently stood by his friend, praying for him after his own fashion. Dr. Harry saw too, and wished it could all be over.

A sense of failure haunted Dan, while he was unable to fix

upon the reason for it. He condemned himself for committing unknown offenses. What should he do? Could he honestly ever go to *another* church?

The meetings drew to their triumphant close. After one last mighty farewell effort, the evangelist departed to some other grand harvest of souls, to some other church that needed "setting in order." His work in Corinth had been well done! So well done that he was justified, perhaps, in making another substantial increase in his stated weekly "terms."

That night, when the farewell meeting was over and its final "Amens" and "Hallelujahs" died away, and the last "Goodbye" and "God bless you" had been said to the evangelist, Dan stood alone in his study, by the window that looked out upon Denny's garden.

He was very tired. Never before in his life had he known such weariness. He felt that in the past few weeks he had neglected the garden. For Denny and his mother he had planned that the little plot of ground should be more profitable that year than it had ever been before. He would neglect it no longer. *There* at least were visible, actual returns for his labor. Tomorrow he would spend in the garden.

But tonight—

He sat down at his little writing table. And then in that small room where for his ministry he had made the supreme sacrifice of his life, surrounded by the silent witnesses of his struggle and victory, he took pen in hand and wrote out his resignation as the pastor of the Memorial Church of Corinth.

For the rest of his life, Dan Matthews never outlived the suffering of that hour. He had lost the woman he loved with all the might of his strong passionate manhood. When she had waited for him to come, he had chosen his ministry. And now—God help him!—now he had lost that for which he had sacrificed both himself and the woman he loved.

When he had finished his letter, he bowed his face in his hands and wept.

# CHAPTER FORTY-ONE

# THE TRAIL OF THE GOLD

Rising early the next morning, Dan looked from his window to see a stranger already at work in the garden. He was a tall, raw-boned man who had the figure and dress of a laborer.

A few minutes later Dan found himself being introduced by the delighted Deborah to her brother Mike McGowan, who had arrived unexpectedly the afternoon before from somewhere in the West. All morning the two men worked side by side with Denny.

Returning to his self-appointed task in the afternoon, Dan was met by the brawny Irishman just leaving the house. McGowan was clearly in a towering rage.

"Parson," he roared, "it's a good man you are, even if you are only a protestant preacher—a right good man! But you've got a danged poor kind of boss, though he'll be looking more like he ought to when I get through with him!"

The man spoke as he was storming his way from the house toward the street.

"What's the matter?" asked Dan, stopping with his back to the gate and blocking his way, for he could see that the stranger was bent on violence to someone. "Who do you mean by my boss?"

"Who do I mean! Who could I possibly mean but him that runs the thing yonder they call a church, begging your pardon.

It's the Elder, as you call him—Judge Strong! I'll judge him all right, if I can coax him within reach of my two hands!" He shook his huge, hairy fists in the air. "It's not strong but weak he'll be when I get through with him! Let me pass, sir."

Dan remained where he was. "Come, come, McGowan," he said, "let's go into the house and you tell me about this."

Deborah was by now standing in the doorway. "That's right, Mr. Matthews," she called out to them. "Come on in, Mike, and talk it over quiet like. Let the minister tell you what to do. It's him that'll save us a sight o' trouble that nobody wants. Come on, Mike, come in with the minister."

The angry Irishman hesitated. Dan laid a hand on his arm, and together they walked back to the cottage.

"It was this way," McGowan said when they were all sitting down. "I was sayin' to Debby and Denny here when we ate just a while ago, what a danged fine man I took you for after workin' with you all mornin' in the garden, and then she up and tells me about you fixin' up the mortgage for them and how they never could find out how you done it with the Judge. 'The mortgage,' I said, 'what mortgage is that, Debby?' 'The mortgage on the place, of course,' she says. 'Don't you remember I was tellin' you about it when you was here before?' 'Do I remember,' I said, 'I should think I did,' and with that it all come out, and this is the way of it.

"When I come from Colorado back when Jack was killed, I found Debby here without even money enough to pay for a mass, to say nothin' of the buryin', bein' as they had put everything they had into the little place here, you see? Well I had had a run of luck the week before, which is neither here nor there, but I had a good bit of money right then. I knowed from experience that it wouldn't stay with me long anyway, and so I thought I'd kinda fix things up for Debby and the kid here, while I could, you see.

"Well, when it was all over, I paid the undertaker's bills and everythin' like that, and then the very day I left I went to that lowdown thief, beggin' your pardon, and paid off that mortgage in good, hard cash. Explainin' to him, you see, that I wanted the papers all fixed up straight and clear and turned over to Debby here as a kind of surprise, do you see, after I was gone and she would be feelin' down-hearted bein' left without her man and me besides. The Judge was, far as I knew, the main guy in the big church. I never thought but that it'd be all right. Well sir, I went away that very day as tickled as a boy over the thing, and never thought nothin' about not gettin' a letter about it from her, 'cause you see with me on the move so much, most of the letters I get from Debby never find me at all. And now here today she's tellin' me that she's never heard nothin' about it from the Judge and that she's been payin' the interest right along, and would have been turned out by him if he hadn't been for you, sir. And me with no writin' nor nothin' to show for the good money I paid him. Now ain't that a devil of a thing, sir—beggin' your pardon again! What can I do except hit the face off him unless he fixes it up right and gives back every cent he's had off her besides?"

As he listened to the story, the new, drawn lines in Dan's face deepened. He sat with bowed head as though he himself were being charged with theft. When the tale was finished there was silence in the little room for several minutes. Then Dan raised his head and the others saw in his eyes that which looked as if he had received a mortal blow.

"Tell me, Mr. McGowan," he said. "Are you absolutely sure there is not a mistake somewhere? It is very hard for me to believe that an Elder of the church—would—" His voice broke.

The rough tones of Deborah's brother now softened as he answered, "And how could there be any mistake, sir, with me givin' him the hard cash out of my own pocket after his tellin' me how much it was, and his promise to fix it up all right for Debby when I'd explained the surprise I'd meant for her?"

"You paid him the money, you say?"

"That I did—in gold coin. You see I happened to have a check—an even thousand, and I turned it in here at the bank. I remember how the feller at the window tried to make me take them dirty paper bills and I wouldn't, as neither would you if you lived as long in the West as I have, and had got used to the feel of good clean, solid coin. 'It's the gold or nothin',' I says to him, 'clean money to pay a clean debt.' An even eight–hundred and fifty I gave the Judge, one hundred and forty I paid the undertaker and the other ten I gave to Denny here as I was leavin'. The priest I paid out of some I had in my belt."

"Come," said Dan, "we must go to the bank."

They went immediately. In the rear room of the little country bank, Dan introduced the Irishman to the manager, Colonel Dunwood, who had been cashier at the time.

"I think I have met Mr. McGowan before," said the Colonel with a smile. "Mrs. Mulhall's brother, are you not? You were here after Jack was killed."

"I was, sir. Glad to meet you again."

"Do you remember cashing a draft for Mr. McGowan, Colonel?" asked Dan. The banker laughed heartily. "I should say I did—a thousand dollars in gold. I tried unsuccessfully to persuade him to take paper, and I was glad the counter was between us!"

Dan explained briefly the situation.

When he had finished the Colonel sprang to his feet with an oath.

"That explains something that puzzled us here in the bank for a long time. Wait just a minute."

He left the room, returning a few moments later with a slip of paper. "Can you tell me the exact date you cashed the draft?" he said to McGowan.

"It was the day after the funeral. I don't remember the date, but it would be easy to find."

The banker nodded. "Our books show that I paid you the money the sixteenth. And here," he laid the slip of paper before them, "is a deposit slip made out and signed by Judge Strong dated the seventeenth, showing that on that date he deposited eight hundred and fifty dollars in gold. That is what puzzled us, Mr. Matthews—that the Judge should deposit that amount of gold, there being, you see, so little gold handled around here. It makes it very easy to trace. I'll show you."

He turned to Mike. "Did you spend any more of the gold in

Corinth?" McGowan told him about paying the undertaker. After a moment the banker triumphantly laid before them a deposit slip made out by the undertaker dated a day later, showing an item of one hundred and forty dollars in gold.

"You see how easy the trail is to follow?" he said.

"Colonel Dunwood," said Dan, "would this be sufficient evidence before a jury too—" He hesitated.

The Colonel let fly another oath. "Yes, sir, and before any jury you could get together in this county it wouldn't take half this to send that long-faced, sniveling hypocrite where he belongs. He is one of our best customers too, but I reckon this bank can get along without his dirty money. I beg your pardon, sir, I forgot he is an Elder in your church."

Dan smiled sadly. "I fear it is more his church than mine, sir." And they left the banker to puzzle over the minister's remark.

That evening Dan called again at the home of Judge Strong. He had persuaded McGowan to let him act in the matter, for he feared that the Irishman's temper would complicate things and make it more difficult to secure Deborah's rights.

Dan found the Judge in his library.

Very quietly, sadly indeed, he told the story. The Elder, righteously indignant, stormed at the minister, denying everything, accusing Dan of being an impudent meddler, threatening him with dismissal from the church and the denomination, accusing him even with unlawful interest in the affairs of the widow, and taunting him with the common reports as to his relations with Miss Farwell and her companion.

With a look of sadness growing deeper on his face with every word, Dan listened without reply until the final insinuation. Then he interrupted the other sharply, and his voice had the ring of metal in it as he said slowly, "Judge Strong, you shall answer to me later for this insult to these good women. Just now you will not mention them again. I am here in the interests of Mr. McGowan. Confine your remarks to that subject."

Then he laid before the Judge the exact nature of the evidence he had obtained at the bank and pointed out its damaging strength.

The man was frightened now, though he was too proud to show it. Obstinately he continued to deny having received any money in payment of the mortgage. Dan pleaded with him, even urging him to consider the cause of the church, telling him also how McGowan had agreed to press no further charges if the Judge would simply make restitution.

The Judge answered arrogantly that he had been a faithful member and Elder in the Memorial Church too long to be harmed by the charges of a stranger, a wandering ruffian, who had nothing but his word to show that he had paid him a sum of money.

"And as for you, young man," he added derisively, "I may as well tell you now that your time is about up in Corinth, and I'll take mighty good care that you don't get another church in our brotherhood either. I'll show you that preachers get along better when they attend to their own affairs."

Dan saw that further expostulation was hopeless, and he turned to go. His final words as he stood by the door were, "I cannot believe, Judge Strong, that you will force my friends to take this matter into the courts. But we will certainly do so if I do not receive from you by tomorrow noon the proper papers verifying that the mortgage on the cottage has been paid in full, along with a check for every cent you have received from Mrs. Mulhall in interest since the date of Mr. McGowan's visit to you."

Alone in his library the Judge cursed this foul development. When he had received that money from McGowan he had been full of regret at losing the property he coveted. The cottage wasn't much, but the garden plot was substantial, and the location prime. With Deborah and Denny left alone in the world, he knew that in time the place would be sure to come to him. He only had to wait. But then had come this wild Irish bricklayer to block the Elder's plans with his handful of gold!

The gold! How well the Judge remembered that day, and how when Mike was gone he had sat contemplating the shining pieces!

What a fool the man was to carry such stuff on his person! The careful Judge never dreamed that the money had come from his own bank. The Irishman was going away the next day. Planning gleefully to surprise his sister, he had told no one his intention. He would wander far across the country. It would be years before he would return, if he ever came back at all. By that time the property would be his!

It had all been seemingly too easy. But the Judge's character was not one to resist such a golden opportunity, as it were. To have the gold *and* the place he had planned on and felt so certain of owning—that was too much to have dreamed for. And it had fallen in his very lap!

But now this big sad-faced preacher, the Irishman again, and the bank! The more the Judge thought over Dan's quiet words, the more he saw the danger. He would have no choice but to comply.

So it came about that the next morning, while in his study, Dan received a visitor—the good old Elder, Nathaniel Jordan.

# CHAPTER FORTY-TWO

# THE VICTORY OF THE ALLY

Nathaniel was greatly agitated as he faced the minister in the doorway. He moved unsteadily across the room, stumbling toward the chair Dan offered. His hand was shaking so that his cane rattled against the window ledge where he attempted to lay it—rattled and fell to the floor. Dan picked up the cane and placed it on the table.

At last the Elder found his voice—thin and trembling. "I have come about—about Brother Strong, you know," he said.

"Yes," said Dan, a great pity for this good old man in his heart. "Did Judge Strong send anything?"

The Elder fumbled in his pocket and drew out an envelope. With shaking fingers he extended it toward Dan, who opened it and examined the contents. He found the papers in order, slowly replaced them in the envelope, then looked at his visitor and waited.

Again the Elder found his voice and said with a little more self-control, "A bad business, Brother Matthews, too bad. Poor Brother Strong!" He shook his head sadly. Dan looked at him curiously, but made no reply.

"Poor Brother Strong," the Elder repeated. "Brother Matthews, I want to ask you to use your influence with these people to keep this sad affair from getting out. Do you think they will insist on—ah, on bringing action against Brother Strong now—now that he has—ah, complied with your request?"

"And why," asked Dan, "should you wish the matter kept secret?"

The Elder gazed at him blankly. "Why? Why, on account of the church, of course. Judge Strong is one of our leading members—an Elder. He has been for years. It would ruin our reputation!"

"But he is a thief," said Dan coolly. "You must know that he stole this money. Here—" he stretched out his hand, still holding the envelope, "here is his confession of guilt."

The Elder's voice trembled again. "Brother Matthews! Brother Matthews! I must protest—such language applied to an Elder!—why, it's unchristian. You know the scripture."

"Isn't what I have said true?" persisted Dan.

"Ahem! Brother Strong may have made a mistake, may—ah, have done wrong, but the church—the church! We must think of the good name of the cause. And coming so soon after the revival."

"Am I to understand, then, that the church will keep this man in his place as an Elder, that you will protect him when you know his true character, that he will continue to serve as a leader and example to the flock, and that the truth will be kept from the main body of the congregation?"

At the question the other stared blankly. "But—why—why how could we get along without him?"

"How can you get along *with* him?" asked Dan. "You know what the Word says about foundations and sand."

"But there isn't a man in Corinth who has done so much for us and for the missionary cause! No, no, we must be careful, Brother Matthews."

"So for the sake of his contributions and his position in the community, the church will shield him from the results of his crime?"

The Elder squirmed uneasily in his chair.

"Is that what you mean?" insisted Dan.

"Why—I—I don't think—Brother Matthews, for the good of our cause in Corinth, that it would be—ah, good policy to make this matter public and so create a great stir. And we certainly would not want to stumble the babes among us who look to their leaders as examples. Think of them, Brother Matthews—think of how word of this would disrupt the smooth flow of the work. Brother Strong has made restitution. We must be charitable, brother, and forgiving. You must not think too hard of him. But tell me, are these people determined to push this matter?"

"Oh no," said Dan, "not at all. They only want that which belongs to them. You may rest easy. As I told the Judge last night, this will end the matter legally. It was under that promise that he made restitution, as you call it. I was simply asking to know how the church would look upon such a thing when it touches an Elder. We as leaders are commanded to follow a higher course of integrity and purity, you know, even than the rest of the body of God's people, and I was curious to know Memorial Church's stand on that particular doctrine. I think you have explained it most clearly—defend the good Elder, gloss over the evil he has done, and go on hoping as few people find out as possible!"

The Elder stiffened. It was remarkable how quickly he revived under Dan's assurance that the danger of legal and public scandal was past!

Very dignified now, as became one in his sacred position, he moved on to other matters. "Ahem, ahem! I fear, Brother Matthews, that you are not—ah—not entirely in harmony with our brotherhood in many things."

Dan was silent.

"Ahem! The tone of your sermons has been, I may say—ah, questioned by a good many of us, and your attitude toward the board has not been quite as cordial as we feel we have a right to expect."

"Do you speak from personal experience, Mr. Jordan?"

"Oh, no—no indeed, Brother Matthews. But—ah, Brother Strong has felt for some time past that you have treated him rather coldly."

Dan waited.

"A lack of harmony between a pastor and his elder is very bad—ah, very bad. Ahem! Ahem! And so, considering everything we—Brother Str—that is, the *board* have thought it best that your relations with the Memorial Church be discontinued."

"And when was this action taken?" asked Dan quietly.

"The day before the meetings closed. We wished to have the benefit of Brother Sigman's advice before he left. He met with us and we considered the whole matter quite carefully and prayerfully. I was appointed to tell you. I should add that there is no doubt but that the people will concur in the board's decision. Many of the members, I may say, were seen before we took action."

Dan glanced toward his desk where lay the envelope containing his resignation. In the excitement of McGowan's trouble he had neglected to mail it.

"Of course," he questioned, quietly curious now, "the board will give me a letter of recommendation that I might apply elsewhere?"

"Ahem! We—ah, discussed that also," said the Elder. "Brother Strong and the Evangelist—and, I may say, the entire board—feel that we cannot consistently and with integrity do so."

"May I ask why?"

"Ahem! Your teaching, Brother Matthews, does not seem to be in harmony with the brotherhood. We cannot endorse it, and the talk in the community about your conduct has been very damaging."

"Is it charged that my teaching has been false to the principles of Christianity as taught by Jesus Christ?"

"I cannot discuss that part, Brother Matthews. It is not such teaching as churches such as ours desire to have taught."

"Does the church, sir, believe that my character is bad?"

"No, no, sir! No one really believes that, but you have been—ah, injudicious. There has been so much talk, you know—"

"Who has talked?" interrupted Dan.

The Elder continued on without answering. "These things follow a minister all his life. We cannot recommend a man of bad repute to our sister churches. It would reflect upon us."

"For the same reason that you keep in a high office in the church a man who is an unrepentant thief?" said Dan.

The Elder rose.

"Really, Brother Matthews, I cannot listen to such words about our Elder."

"I beg your pardon, sir," said Dan. "I was thinking aloud. Forgive me."

Dan rose too, and extended his hand.

"I am sorry, Brother Matthews," said Nathaniel.

"I believe you are," said Dan slowly. "Thank you."

When the Elder was gone Dan turned sadly back to his little study, the study that had come to stand for everything to which he had devoted his life with such lofty purpose, for which he had sacrificed so much.

Slowly he went to his desk and looked upon the work scattered over it. With a pang of remorse that he would not even be allowed the final dignity of delivering his resignation with head high and pride intact, he took up the envelope and tore it into fragments, dropping them into the wastebasket.

Then he slowly turned to his books, touching many of the familiar volumes with a caressing hand. He went to the table where lay his church papers and the missionary pamphlets and reports. The envelope from Judge Strong caught his eye.

Mechanically he took his hat and went to carry the message to his friends on the other side of the garden. From across the street the old Doctor hailed him, but Dan did not hear.

Delivering the envelope with a few brief words, the minister left his friends and wandered down the street in a bewildered, dazed fashion, scarcely knowing where he went, or why, until he turned in through the gap in the tumbledown fence to the old Academy yard.

But he could not stay there. The place was haunted; he could not stay! He turned his face toward the open country, but the fields and woodlands had no call for him that day. It was his little study that called—his books, his work.

As one goes to sit beside the body of a dear friend at death, conscious that the friend he loved is not there, yet unable to leave the form wherein the spirit had lived, so Dan went back to his room, his desk, his books, his papers—that which had been his work.

Deep, quiet passions stirred themselves within him. His whole sense of justice was outraged. This was not Christianity, this evil thing that had caught him in its foul snare! What was the church then, if it did not represent the Christ who was supposed to be its head? Was it nothing but a hollow mockery?

So the Doctor found him late in the afternoon—his great strength shaken by anger and doubt and injustice and pain. And the Doctor saw that the time he had been waiting for had arrived.

# CHAPTER FORTY-THREE

# THROUGH THE DOCTOR'S GLASSES

When Dan had been forced into something of his habitual self-control and calmness by the presence of his old friend, he began telling the Doctor of the action of the church. But the other checked him almost before he had begun. "I know all about that, lad," he said.

"You know!"

"Certainly. Isn't Martha one of the elect? I imagine everyone in the whole town but you knew it before noon of the day after the meeting."

"I can hardly believe what a blind fool I am," muttered Dan.

"Humph! The fools are they who see too much," the old Doctor answered. "Such blindness as yours is a gift from God. For heaven's sake don't let any of those spiritual quacks fit you out with glasses! Your vision is just fine."

Dan threw himself wearily into a chair. "But how is a blind man like me to recognize a quack?" he asked recklessly. "I would to God I had your glasses!"

"Perhaps," said the Doctor deliberately, "I might lend them to you, just for once, you know."

"Well then," said Dan, sitting up, "let me have them! Tell me how you see this thing. What have I done or not done? For what shall I blame myself? What fatal error have I made that, with the best of motives, with the—"

He hesitated, then went on, "Well, I suppose I can say it to you, Doctor, and I will—with the sacrifice of the dearest thing in the world to me, I am cast out in this fashion? If I can just find a reason for it, I can bear it."

"It is your blindness, boy. You could not help it. You were born blind. You have been blind ever since I knew you. That's why I have always known this day would come. This day comes to every man, every woman, who tries to stand against the tide and live in obedience to the truth instead of to please their fellows."

"You have really always known this would come?" repeated Dan in disbelief.

"Yes, I have always known. Because for half a century I have observed the spirit of this institution. Mind, I do not say the spirit of the people in the institution. Strong people, Dan, sometimes manage to live in mighty sickly climates. The best people in the world are sometimes held by evil circumstances which their own best intentions have created. The people in the church are the salt of the earth. If it were not for their goodness the system would have rotted long ago. The church, for all its talk, doesn't save the people, the people save the church. And let me tell you, Dan, the very ones in the church who have done the things you have seen and felt, at heart many of them respect and believe in you. It's just that they are trapped by the system. And when they see someone like you who is not enslaved by it and in fact tries to change it, they are torn—torn and powerless."

Dan broke forth in a laugh, such a laugh as the Doctor had never heard from his lips. "Believe . . . respect! Then why do they allow it to go on?"

"Because," said the old man, "it is their religion to worship an institution, not a God, to serve a system, not the race of men. They do not know they are doing it, of course. They *think* all their religious affairs and their church programs are signs of true faith. They have no idea they are just worshiping an institution, a club, a social organization. That's what makes it so lethal, because they see none of it. It is history, my boy. Every reformation begins with the persecution of the reformer and ends with the followers of that reformer persecuting those who would lead them another step toward freedom. It happens in great movements, it happens in small church settings, but it is always the same. When someone tries to implement change against the grain of the status quo—what our Lord called the 'traditions of the elders'—they will be chewed up and spit out. Misguided religious people have always crucified their saviors, and always will!"

Dan was silent. He had never seen this side of the Doctor, so perceptive about spiritual things. He found himself awed by the revelation of his old friend's mind.

Presently the Doctor continued. "There is no hatred, lad, so bitter as that hatred born of a religious love. There is no falsehood so vile as the lie spoken in defense of truth. There is no wrong so harmful as the wrong committed in the name of righteousness, no injustice so terrible as the injustice of those who condemn in the name of the Savior of the world."

"What then, as you see it—what can I do?" asked Dan.

The Doctor changed his tone. His reply was more a question than an answer. "There are other churches?"

Dan laughed with forlorn bitterness. "They have taken care of that too. They refuse to give me a letter of recommendation."

"You are not the only preacher who has been talked about by his church and branded by his official board with the mark of the devil in the name of the Lord. Nor are preachers like you the only ones who suffer. In many places the preachers themselves are the Judge Strongs, working in alliance with a ruling elite to keep out any and all who would speak truth in a different fashion than what they ordain. If such people would have a hand in the Lord's work, eventually they have to find other churches, other ministries. You must do as they do. Go farther away, get a little obscure congregation somewhere, stay long enough to establish an effective ministry, perhaps get a letter of recommendation. Lay low, keep quiet, stay away from conventions."

"But, Doctor," exclaimed Dan, jumping to his feet, "I have

done nothing wrong. Why should I skulk and hide and scheme to conceal something I never did, for the privilege of serving a church that doesn't even want me? Is this the ministry? Is this *serving* the Lord? Is this what is meant by a man's 'call?' "

"What is meant by 'a call,' I don't know that I can say," answered the Doctor slowly. "Especially would I not say what is Dan Matthews' call. There is only One who can tell you that. But insofar as the ministry itself is concerned—the organized ministry, pastoring a denominational church—I'm afraid the maneuvering does seem to be a large part of it. My boy, it's the things that preachers have not done that they try hardest to hide. As to why, I must confess that I am a little nearsighted myself sometimes."

"I can't do it, Doctor!"

"I didn't suppose you could," the old man answered softly. "I would have been more disappointed than I can tell you if you could have."

Dan did not heed but went on in a hopeless tone to tell the Doctor how he had written his resignation.

"Don't you see," he said, "that I couldn't take a church even if one were offered to me now? Don't you understand what this has done to me? It's not the false charges. It's—it's the thing, whatever it is, that has made this kind of action of the church possible. That men and women—seemingly good people—could be party to such slander and wrongful judgments, all in the name of Christianity and truth, and could so blind themselves to wrong within their own circle, their own system, their own leaders— how can it be! I am forced to doubt, not alone these people and this particular church, but everything—myself, Christians everywhere, God, the very meaning of faith itself! How can I go on with a work that for the first time in my life I don't know if I believe in?" His voice ended in a groan.

The old man who knew the lad so well felt as though he were gazing into the big naked soul within his friend's heart. Then, indeed, the Doctor knew that the hour had come.

There are many who are capable of giving but little to life, and they demand little of life in return. To such weak natures, doubt does not mean much. Because they do not probe life's meaning, they rarely question, and the doubts that are raised within them are shallow and passing. Thus their roots never extend deep. For it is only through honest questioning that truth is honed in the mind to a sharp edge. When something is true, you can look at it hard, from any and every angle—you can challenge it, assail it, beat against it with every weapon of doubt, and yet it will stand. Because it is true. Doubt never hurts truth, it only strengthens it.

Souls like that of Dan Matthews, capable of giving themselves to the last atom of their strength, demand no small return from the causes they serve. To such, doubt is both the destruction and the cement of their being. To men with large, open natures, doubt shakes the very foundations, even as it is building an unseen strength of faith and character. It was because Dan had believed so wholly in the ministry of the church that he had failed. Had his acceptance of it not been so unreserved, he would have been able to adjust himself to the actual conditions once they presented themselves. Because he did not doubt before coming to Corinth, his doubt now went much deeper.

Theoretically, the strength of the church rests in its faithfulness to the things it professes to believe. In practical and actual fact, however, the strength of the church of today lies in its tacit acceptance of its unbeliefs. It is because the church operates so much like the world, contrary to what its Founder taught, that the church stands so powerful today. Strange things indeed would befall us if we should ever get in the habit of insisting that our practice square with our preaching! If churches should make this the test of fellowship—that men must live their doctrines rather than teach them, that they must live their beliefs rather than confess them, that they must live their faiths rather than profess them—imagine the results! Our churches doors would be swung wide open—whether to empty our buildings or fill them would undoubtedly be a subject of fierce debate! We need not worry, however, for since the beginning the churches of Jesus Christ have *not* made such test of faith, and we have little reason to think they will adopt such a radical new policy anytime in the near future.

Dan's was not a nature that could preach things in which he only half-believed. He had to know! He had to find where the church, where ministry, and where the training of his youth fit into the totality of what he would call his faith. He had to discover what his *call* truly was.

It was with these things in mind that the Doctor had waited for this moment in Dan's life. For the old man realized, as the young man could not, what such moments mean.

Rising and going to the window overlooking the garden, the Doctor called to Dan. "Come over here, I want you to see something."

Together they stood looking down on the little plot of ground with its growing vegetables, where Denny, with his helpless, swinging arm, and twisted, dragging foot, was digging away, his cheery whistle floating up to them. The physician spoke with a depth of feeling he had never betrayed before, while Dan, troubled as he was, listened in wonder to his friend, who had always been so reticent in matters such as these.

"Dan," he said, "you wished for my glasses. 'Tis always a mighty dangerous thing to try to see through another man's eyes, but here are mine." He pointed below.

"Down there I see the essence of religion—of God's way with this world He has made. There it is—living, growing, ever-changing, through age after age of seasons. Sometimes it lies dormant, but the life-giving power of the ground is always there. It yields to each season the things that belong to that season, depending for its strength and power upon the God of all strength and power that put life within it. Yet at the same time it depends just as truly upon man's efforts. For that ground down there—full of the life of God!—to reach its potential and produce that life for which God made it, requires man's cultivation and care too.

"There is variety, harmony, law, freedom, growth, faith—it's all part of Denny's garden! Because there is God! He has filled that ground and those plants and that water and that sunlight with himself—with life! Something for everybody—potatoes, peas, turnips, cabbage. If you don't care for lettuce, perhaps radishes will satisfy. And there, in the midst of his church, ministering to the needs of his congregation, and thus ministering to men—is my minister. Crippled, patient Denny gives his frail strength and pours out his life to keep the garden growing. And grow it does, providing food for people all over this town! For that's the way with the things where God's life is—they grow, they reach out, they spread life!

"But look at that great rock in the very center of the field! How often has Denny wished it out of his way! I caught the poor lad digging one time, to find out if he could how deep it was in the earth, and how big it truly was. For three days I watched him. Then he gave it up. It is beyond his strength and he wisely turned to devote his energies to the productive soil around it.

"There is a rock in every garden, Dan. The truths of the Christian faith always grow about the unknowable. There are hindrances. There are things we do not understand. There are doubts—like that rock there—that we will never get to the bottom of. But Denny's ministry has nothing to do with the rock, it has to do with the growing things about it. Denny's *call*, if you want to use that word, is to minister to this town by cultivating the soil, not to dig up that rock. His is a ministry of soil, of roots, of growth, of water, of doing his part to allow the life of God within the earth to come up and out and into the lives of his friends and neighbors. He does not have to mind the rock. The rock is God's business. So Christianity is in the knowable things too, not in the unknowable. Such men as you must find it there—in what you can know and do, in the soil where dwells the life of God. The rock after all—both Denny's and your's—was not put in the garden by men. It is part of the earth itself."

The whole time the Doctor was speaking his eyes had been fixed on the crippled boy in the garden. He turned now for the first time to face the young man by his side. Dan's eyes held that wide, questioning look. The old physician moved slowly to the other window.

"Now, come and see what men have done." He pointed to the cast-iron monument. "These people around here will tell you that was erected to commemorate the life of my friend. His was a warm, tender, loving spirit—a great, growing, enlarging soul. What can that hard, cold, immovable mass tell of him? How can that thing—perpetuating a passing political issue of a past age that has nothing to do with the life of today—how can that thing speak of the great heart that loved and gave itself to men?

"Through my glasses that is the church. How can an institution, or a system of theological beliefs—with cast-iron prejudices, cast-iron fidelity to issues long past and forgotten, cast-iron unconcern for vital issues of the life of today, cast-iron viewpoints and doctrines, and cast-iron lack of sympathy with the living who toil and fight and die on every side—how can such speak the great, loving, sympathetic, helpful spirit of Him whose name only it bears, as that monument down there bears the name of my friend?

"But would the people of this town, out of love for my dead friend, tear down that monument if Denny should leave his garden to argue with them about it? Why, they would tell him that it is because of their love for the Statesman that they keep it there, and they believe it. They believe it because they do not realize that true love involves the living of life not the building of monuments.

"Well, then, let them keep their monument and let Denny work in his garden! And don't you see the irony, Dan, that the very ones who fight to preserve the cast-iron monument must depend for their lives and strength upon the food that Denny grows in his garden? Yet they look down on his work as unimportant, while they see their programs and services and conventions—their monument building—as of the greatest eternal significance. Their blindness is enough to make an old man like me laugh, if it weren't for all the pain they unknowingly inflict."

He stopped, drew in a deep breath, looked over at Dan and said, "Now there! That's the first and only sermon I ever preached!"

# CHAPTER FORTY-FOUR

# A HIGHER CALL

The day came for Dan's farewell sermon. It was to be given in the evening.

John Gardner—who, true to his word, had become a regular attendant—was present in the morning service. That afternoon he called on Dan in his study.

"Look here, Dan," he said, "I think you are making a mistake. You have done a lot of good in this town."

"So have you, John."

"You have helped me more than you know," said the farmer.

"And I could say the same of you."

"You know what I mean. I've been listening pretty close to your sermons and so have a lot of others. I have talked with a good many church people since it was known that you were going, just common plugs in the congregation, like me, you know."

Dan smiled.

"We all know what you have been driving at in your preaching, and we know pretty well what the bosses think about it and why they have pushed you out. No one takes any stock in that foul gossip, not even Strong himself. Now what I came to say is this: a lot of us want you to stay. Why couldn't we have another church for our people right here in Corinth? There's enough of us to back you, and we mean business."

Dan shook his head sadly.

"Thank you, John," he said simply. "I cannot begin to tell you what your words mean to me, and how much good they do me. But I cannot do such a thing. You do not need another church in Corinth. You have more than you need now. Starting new churches is never the way to bring about change or to take the Gospel into a town or a community. It's people that make that happen, John, not a new church. No, you and the others stay in the churches that are already here and *live* the Gospel. If enough people do that, they will one day make the church what it is supposed to be."

Gardner saw that no further argument could move him.

"Well," said the farmer, when at last he gave it up and rose to say goodbye, "I suppose I'll keep right on being a church member. But I reckon I'll have to find most of my religion in my work."

"And that," said Dan as he gripped his friend's hand, "is the best place I know of to look for it. If you cannot find God in your everyday work, John, you'll not find Him on Sunday at the church."

That farewell sermon is still talked about in Corinth. Or rather—it should be said—it is still remembered, for it was one of those sermons of which, while little could be said, much could never be forgotten.

And the picture of the big lad—whose strong, clean-looking body drooped so as if in great weariness, whose frank open countenance was marked with drawn lines, in whose clear brown eyes were shadows of trouble and pain, and whose voice betrayed the sadness of a mighty soul—will also remain long in the memories of those who were there that evening.

The place was crowded. The triumphant Judge and his friends of the inner circle were present in force, striving in vain to hide, with pious expression of countenance, the satisfaction and pride they felt in their power. The other members of the church were there too, the rank and file, curious to hear what Dan would say, wondering how much he knew of the methods that had brought about his dismissal; a little sorry for him, a little angry, but with a feeling of impotence through it all that made their sorriness and anger of no worth whatever. With identically the same emotions, except that they felt free to express them more freely, many members of the community at large were in attendance also. To a portion of the congregation Dan stood in the peculiar position of a friend whom, as an individual, they loved and trusted, but whom, as a preacher, they were forced to regard as unsafe and dangerous.

It would not do to report all he said, for much of his sermon was not fashioned for the printed page. But his final words were as follows:

"It is not the spirit of wealth, of learning, or of culture that can make the church of God a thing of value, or a power for good and righteousness in the world, but the Spirit of Christ only. It is not in fidelity to the past but in fidelity to the present that the church can be Christian. It is not the opinions of man, but the eternal truths of God that can make it a sacred, holy thing.

"It is holy to the degree that God is in it. God is as truly in the fields of grain, in the forests, in the mines, and in the laws of nature by which men convert the product of field and forest and mine into the necessities of life. Therefore these are as truly holy as this institution. Therefore, again, the ministry of farm and mine and factory and shop, of mill and railroad and store and office, and wherever men and women toil with strength of body or strength of mind for that which makes for the best life of their kind—that ministry is sacred and holy. The call of God upon men's lives is not a call to preach or attend church or to be religious in any of a thousand ways in which our church traditions have come to define religious. The call of God upon our lives—yours and mine—is a call to *live* the things Jesus Christ taught. That is the only call worthy of the name.

"Because I believe these things I will be, from this hour, no longer a professional preacher, hired by and working under the direction of any denomination or church leaders. This closes my ministry as you understand it. It by no means closes my ministry as I have come to understand it. I sincerely hope and pray that today marks the *beginning* rather than the end of my call—a call to serve God by ministering to my fellows, which is, I believe, the highest call of all."

When he had finished they crowded around him to express regret at his going—sorry that he was leaving the ministry, for the church needed men of his great ability—prayed God to bless him wherever he would go—all this and much more, with hand-shaking and many tears from the very people who had made it impossible for him to stay.

As quickly as he could, Dan left the church, and with the Doctor walked toward home. The two made no exchange of words, until they reached the monument, where they paused to stand silently contemplating the cast-iron figure.

At last Dan turned with a smile. "It is very good cast iron, I suppose, Doctor."

Then, as if dismissing the whole matter, he took his old friend's arm and, with a note of joy in his voice that had been missing for many months, said, "You'll do me one favor before I leave, won't you?"

"What?" asked the Doctor.

"Go fishing with me tomorrow."

# CHAPTER FORTY-FIVE

# LAST ENCOUNTER

Early the next morning Dan and the old Doctor set out for Wheeler's Ford. It was the nearest point, and while the fishing was not so good as at other places, they knew the spot was just what they wanted. This was one of the days when they would go fishing—but not for fish.

Leaving their rig by the roadside near the fence, the two friends wandered away up the stream, casting their hooks now and then at the likely places, catching a few fish, pausing often to enjoy the views of silver water, overhanging trees, wooded bluffs, rocky bank or grassy slope, that changed always with the winding of the creek.

They returned to the rig for their lunch and to give the old horse his allowance. In the afternoon they went downstream, this time leaving their rods behind.

"Really, you know," said the Doctor, "the tackle is such a bother on this kind of fishing trip."

Dan's laugh rang out so freely at the sage remark that the woods on the other side of the little valley echoed back the merry sound.

Dan felt strangely light-hearted and free. In the Doctor's eyes the lad was more like himself than he had been for months. The truth is that Dan's gladness was akin to the gladness of homecoming. He felt as one who, having been for long years in a foreign land, returns to his own country and his own people. He was again a man among his fellowmen, with no barrier between him and his kind. Once more he was in the world to which he belonged, and it was a good world.

There was, too, a strange, delightful feeling of nearness to her—the woman he loved. He had had no word since she left Corinth, nor did he know where she was. He would never find her again, perhaps, but he no longer belonged to a world separate and apart from her world. He felt nearer to her even than when they were together that last time in the old Academy yard.

Dan was conscious of a sense of freedom—of a broader, fuller life than he had ever known. Through the old Doctor's timely words, setting his thoughts in new channels, he had come out of his painful experience with a certain largeness of vision that made him stronger.

He had found . . . *himself.* He did not yet know what he would do. There were dimly formed possibilities in his mind, but nothing fixed.

What did it matter? Somewhere he felt his garden was waiting for him—he would find his work. He was free from the deadening influence of the cast-iron monument, and that, for the moment, was enough. So far as his Corinthian ministry was concerned, only one shadow remained out of all the dark cloud of his troubled experience. When that was lifted he would turn his back upon Corinth forever. But until then he did not feel free to go.

They were lying on the grassy bank of a woodland pasture, where a herd of cattle grazed or lay contentedly in the shade of the scattered trees.

"I believe I will go with you," said the Doctor after a long silence. It was almost as though the old man had spoken to his companion's very thoughts.

"Go where?" asked Dan, turning over on his side and half-raising himself on his elbow.

"Why home to Mutton Hollow, of course. You'll be leaving pretty soon now, I reckon."

"I suppose so," mused Dan vaguely. "But I'm not going home."

The old Doctor sat up. "Not going home!"

Dan smiled. "Not just yet," he answered. "I want to run about a little first."

"Want to get your hair dry and your shirt on right-side-out before you face the folks."

Dan laughed. "Perhaps I want to look for my garden," he said.

"Good!" exclaimed the other, now very much in earnest. "Let me help you. You know what I have always hoped for you. My profession needs—"

Dan interrupted gently. "No, Doctor, not that. I have a notion—but there—it's all too vague yet even to discuss. When I am ready to go home I'll write you and you can meet me there. Will you?"

The old man hid his disappointment, answering heartily, "Sure I will. I'll be there when you arrive, to help kill the fatted calf." He did not tell Dan of a letter from his mother urging him, for certain reasons, to visit them, or that he had already promised her to be with them when Dan should return.

The shadows were beginning to stretch toward the river, and the cattle were moving slowly in the direction of the farmyard, hidden somewhere beyond the fringe of timber, when the two friends began walking leisurely back to the road to find their rig and start for home.

Climbing the fence they paused, watching a team and buggy just coming down the opposite bank of the stream to cross the ford. Midway through the horses stopped to drink.

"What do you know," muttered the Doctor, "it's our friend the Judge!"

The same instant, Dan recognized the man in the buggy. All the brightness went out of his face, and a cloud of sadness returned.

"Doctor," he said, slipping down from the fence as he spoke, "excuse me a minute. I must speak to that man."

The Doctor sat on the top rail of the fence, while Dan stepped into the road. When they had left the ford, the team came toward them, then stopped when they reached Dan.

"How do you do, Doctor?" called the man in the buggy in a loud voice. Then to Dan he said, "Well, sir, what do you want now?"

Dan stood near the horses' heads, his eyes fixed on their driver. Seeing the sorrow in his face, the Judge, as always, misunderstood.

"Judge Strong," said Dan. "You are the only man in the world with whom I am not at peace. I cannot be content to leave Corinth, sir, with anything between us."

The crafty Judge thought he understood. He took Dan's words as an acknowledgment of defeat, an act of submission. The Elder had not believed that the young man had really wished to leave the ministry. He was quite sure now that the preacher, recognizing at last the power that had thrust him from his position and place in the church, wished to sue him for peace, so that he might help him gain another position. *So this big upstart was tamed at last, was he*, thought the Judge.

"Well?" said the Elder haughtily.

Dan hesitated. "I wish to ask a favor, sir," he said finally, "one I feel sure a Christian could not refuse."

Now the Judge was confident of his position and power. He grew still more dignified and looked at Dan with the eye of a master.

"Well, out with it! It is growing late and I must be going."

"You will remember, sir, that the last time I called on you in your home, you made certain grave charges against three women who are my friends."

"I repeated only the common—"

"Wait, please," interrupted Dan. "This is a matter between you and me. I understand that you were angry and spoke hastily. So what I would like to ask you now is this—won't you please retract those words now?"

Dan's voice was almost pleading in its slow sadness. His eyes were fixed on the Judge with a look of appeal.

Disappointed at the request, which was so different from that which he had expected, the Judge answered angrily, "Get out of my way. I have no time for this!"

But quietly, carelessly it seemed, Dan laid one hand on the back of the nearest horse, almost touching the rein, and moved a step or two closer to the buggy.

"Sir, I am sure you do not understand. Miss Farwell and I— that is, I had hoped to make her my wife. We parted because of the church."

The Doctor on the fence felt a lump in his throat at the pain in the boy's voice. Dan continued, "I am telling you, sir, so that you will understand. Surely you cannot refuse to take back your words under the circumstances, now that you see that there was nothing amiss in my relationship with Miss Farwell."

"Oh, I see," sneered the Judge. "You lost the girl because of the church, and then you lost the church! A fine mess you have made of your pious interference with other people's business, wasn't it?"

Then the Judge looked straight into Dan's sad, pleading eyes, and laughed.

"The old fool," muttered the Doctor on the fence.

"Am I to understand that you refuse to retract your words even after my explanation?" Dan's tone was one of quiet disbelief.

The Judge could not have been more pleased at what he had heard. "I have absolutely nothing to take back, sir." He laughed again. "Now if that is all, stand aside!"

His whip cracked, just missing Dan's hand. The horses sprang into a gallop and Dan leapt back, falling at the side of the road, just in time to keep from being hit by the passing wheel of the Judge's rig. As he watched the cloud of dust recede in the distance, he could hear the sound of the Judge's voice still laughing as he urged his horses on.

Dan looked over toward the fence.

"Well, lad, you made a mighty fine try of it at least."

Dan considered his words for another moment, then a smile broke across his face. He threw his head back and answered the Judge's laugh with one of his own.

"Well," he said, "if I cannot leave Corinth having made peace with my enemy, perhaps it is time I go anyway!"

So they went home in the dusk of the evening.

Two days later, Dan spent his last evening in Corinth with Dr. Harry, and the next morning he left.

# CHAPTER FORTY-SIX

# AND CORINTH?

Corinth still talks of the great days that are gone, and the greater days that are to come. In between—the days that *are*—are dead days, shadowed by the cast-iron monument which yet holds its place in the heart of the town, and makes of the community a fit home for the Ally.

Judge Strong has gathered to himself additional glory and honor by his continued activity and prominence in Memorial Church and in his denomination, together with his contributions to the various funds for state and national work.

Elder Jordan has been gathered to his fathers. But Nathaniel came to feel first the supreme joy of seeing his daughter proudly installed as the wife and assistant pastor to the last of Dan's successors. They live at the old Jordan home and it is said he is the most successful preacher that the Memorial Church has ever employed. The prospects are that he will serve for many years to come.

Dr. Harry is still a member, though still not of the inner circle. He still works too hard and hopes someday for a capable nurse to assist him.

John Gardner still plants and harvests wheat. He has never again seen the like of Dan Matthews, he declares, in either the pulpit *or*

the harvest field. To his companions, John has come to be recognized as something of a workingman's philosopher, for he is
always talking about God in the fields and dirt and all growing
things.

Denny, through his minister friend, has received his education,
and—surrounded now by the books he craved—cultivates another
garden, wherein he bids fair to grow food for men and women
quite as necessary as cabbages or potatoes. Deborah is proud and
happy with her boy, who, though he remains crippled in body,
has a heart and mind stronger than given to many.

The Doctor seldom goes fishing now, though he still cultivates
his roses, and, as he says, meddles in the affairs of his neighbors.
And still he sits in his chair on the porch and watches the world
go by. Martha says that more and more the world, to the Doctor,
means the doings of that minister who got his start in life in their
town, Dan Matthews.

It was more than a month after Dan left Corinth when he
wrote his old friend that he was going home. The Doctor carefully
packed his fishing tackle and started immediately for Mutton Hollow.

# CHAPTER FORTY-SEVEN

# THE HOMECOMING

And now this story goes back again to the mountains to end where it began, back to where the tree-clad ridges roll like mighty green billows into the far distant sky, where vast forests lie quivering in the breeze, shimmering in the sun, and the soft blue haze of the late summer lies lazily over the land.

Beyond Wolf Ridge, all up and down Jake and Indian Creeks, and even as near as Fall Creek, are the great lead and zinc mines. Over in Garber the heavily loaded trains, with engines puffing and panting on the heavy grades, and waking the echoes with wild shrieks, follow their iron way.

But in the Mutton Hollow neighborhood, there are as yet no mines, with their ugly piles of refuse, smoke-grimed buildings, and clustered shanties to mar the landscape. Dewey Bald still lifts its head in proud loneliness above the white sea of mist that still, at times, rolls over the valley below. The paths are the same as always. From the Matthews' house on the ridge you may see the same landmarks. The pines show black against the sunset sky. And from the Matthews' place—past the deerlick in the big, low gap—past Sammy's Lookout and around the shoulder of Dewey—looking away into the great world beyond, still lies the trail that is nobody knows how old.

So is life.

With all the changes that time inevitably brings, with all our civilization, our inventions and improvements, some things must remain unchanged. Some things—the great landmarks in life and religion, the hills, the valleys, the mists—must ever remain the same. Some things, thank God, are beyond the damning power of our improvements.

In minor things that can be seen around the place, the Matthews' home itself is altered here and there. But Dan's father and mother are still—in spite of the years that have come—Young Matt and Sammy.

It was that best of all seasons in the Ozarks—October—the month of gold, when they were sitting on the front porch in the evening with the old Doctor, who had arrived during the afternoon.

"Now, Doctor," said the mother, "tell us all about it."

There was no uneasiness in her calm voice, no shadow of worry in her quiet eyes. And the boy's father by her side reflected the same serene confidence. They knew from Dan's letters something of the trials through which he had passed, and they had often assured him of their sympathy and prayers.

"Yes, Doctor," came the deep voice of the father. "We have had Dan's letters, of course, but the lad's not one to put all of his inner fight on paper. Let's have it as you saw it."

So the Doctor told them—told them of the causes that had combined to put Dan on the rack, that had driven him in spite of himself to change his views of the church and ministry and what a call from God truly might entail. He told of the forces that had been arrayed against him, how the lad had met these forces, and how he had battled with himself—all that the Doctor had seen in the months of watching he opened to the loving father and mother.

Several times the narrator was interrupted by the deep-voiced, hearty laugh of the father, or with exclamations of satisfaction. At other times the Doctor was interrupted by a quick eager question from the mother that helped to make the story clear. Many times they uttered half-whispered exclamations of wonder, distress, or indignation.

"When he left Corinth," said the Doctor in conclusion, "he told me that he had no clearly defined plans, though he hinted at something he had in mind."

"But, Doctor," asked the mother, "haven't you forgotten a very important part of your story?"

"What have I forgotten?" he said.

"Why the girl, of course. What happened to the girl?"

"I reckon Dan will tell you about that himself," the Doctor answered, "though I have heard nothing more of her."

The next day Dan arrived and after a brief time of joyful family reunion, he took up the story were the Doctor had left off.

From Corinth Dan had gone to the president of the big steelworks whom he had met at the time of the convention. With his assistance and advice, he had been visiting some of the big mines and smelters and studying zinc and lead. He had worked out his plan and had found some interested investors, and now had come home to consult with his parents concerning the opening and development of the mine on Dewey Bald.

Then he talked to them of the power of wealth for good, of the sacredness of such a trust—talked as they had never heard him talk before of the Grace Conners and the crippled Dennys, who needed elder brothers willing to acknowledge the kinship. He told them of new developments in the industry which could reduce the damage to the countryside, and that he hoped they could keep the old landscape much like it had always been.

When he had finished, his mother kissed him and his father said, "It is for this, son, that your mother and I have held the old hill yonder. It is part of our belief that God put the wealth in the mountains, not for us alone, but for all men. So it has been to us a sacred trust, which we have never felt that we were fit to administer. We have always hoped that our firstborn would accept it as his lifework—his ministry."

Thus Dan found his garden—and entered the higher call that has made his life such a ministry and blessing to men.

The next morning his mother was up early saddling her horse. At breakfast she announced that she was going over to the Jones ranch on the other side of Dewey.

"And what are you planning to do today?" she said to Dan as he followed her out of the house.

"I was going over to old Dewey myself," he answered. "I thought I would like to look the ground over." He smiled down at her. "But now I can go with you. Just wait a minute until I saddle a horse."

She laughed. "Oh no, I'm going over to the Jones' place by myself."

"But, mother, I want to talk to you. I have something to tell you about."

"Yes, I know," she nodded. "You have already told me about her."

"Did the Doctor—" he burst forth.

"No, indeed! You know Dr. Oldham better than that. It was in your letters for anyone with eyes to see. And—"

She stopped herself. "But I thought you could tell me the rest this evening. Go with your father and the Doctor to look at the stock this morning and write your business letters while I attend to *my* affairs. Then, the first thing after midday dinner, you slip away alone over to Dewey and do your planning. Perhaps I'll meet you on the old trail as you come back. You see, I have it all worked out."

"Yes," he said slowly, "you always have things fixed, don't you. What a mother you are! There's only one other woman in all the world like you." His voice held a sadness he could not hide.

"Yes, I know, dear," she said. "I have always known it could come, and I am glad, glad my boy. But—I—I think you'd better kiss me now."

So she left him standing at the fence and rode away alone down the old family path, while Dan wondered about her strange words.

He spent the morning with his father and Dr. Oldham, then after dinner Dan set out.

# CHAPTER FORTY-EIGHT

# THE OLD TRAIL

Leaving the ridge just below the low gap, Dan made his way down the mountainside into the deep ravine, below Sammy's Lookout, that opens into the hollow.

For an hour he roamed about, his mind on his plans for the development of the wealth that lay in the heart of the mountain, what he would do with the income generated. After a time, still intent upon his work, he scrambled up the end of the little canyon, regained the ridge near the mouth of the cave, then climbed up on the steep slope of Dewey to the top. From here he could follow with his eye a possible route for the spur that should leave the railroad in Garber to the east, round the base of the mountain and reach the mine through the little ravine on the west.

From the top he made his way slowly toward the Lookout, thinking there to gain still another view of the scene of his proposed operations and to watch the trail for the coming of his mother.

Drawing near the great ledge of rock that hangs so like a cornice on the mountainside, he caught a glimpse—through the screen of trees and bushes—of a figure seated on the old familiar spot. His mother must have come sooner than she intended, he thought, or else he had been longer than he realized.

He looked at his watch. It was early yet. How had she got back here so soon?

He went on a little further, and was about to open his mouth to hail her, when suddenly he stopped.

It was not his mother!

He took several more steps nearer and pushed aside a bush for a better view.

His heart leapt. There was the familiar blue dress with its white trimming! The figure turned slightly as if to look up the trail. The big fellow on the mountain shook with disbelieving emotion.

Softly, as if fearing to dispel a welcome illusion that his brain had imagined, he walked slowly nearer—nearer. Suddenly a dry twig on the ground snapped under his foot. She turned her face quickly toward him.

She sprang to her feet and stood waiting with joy-lighted face, as Dan now came stumbling and running in wondering haste down the hill.

"I thought you were never coming," said Hope. "I have been waiting so long."

Dan took her in his arms, and she returned his embrace with her face and its tears against his huge trembling chest. For a little while there was nothing more said that we have any right to hear.

When, after a few minutes, he insisted upon an explanation of the miracle, she laughed merrily.

"It's like most miracles, I suppose, if only one knew about them—the most natural thing that could happen after all. Dr. Miles came to me some time ago and said that he had a patient whom he was sending into the mountains with a nurse, and asked me if I would take the case. He didn't tell me at the time that he had been in touch with Dr. Oldham. He said he thought that I would like to see the Mutton Hollow country, and that he thought I needed the trip. You can imagine how quickly I said that I would go! I am living down at the Jones' place."

"Where my mother went this morning," Dan broke in eagerly.

She nodded. "Yes," she said demurely. "Your mother and I have become—very good friends."

"Does she know?"

Hope blushed. "I couldn't help telling her. She had your letters and she already knew a great deal. She—"

"I suppose she told you all about it—my finish at Corinth, I mean, and my plans?" interrupted Dan.

"Yes," replied Hope.

"Then there's nothing more to do but—but—" He paused. "How is your patient?" he asked abruptly. "How long must you stay with the case?"

She turned her head away. "My patient went home to the city three days ago."

When the sun was touching the fringe of trees on the distant ridge, and the varying tints of brown and gold, under the softening tone of the gray-blue haze that lies always over hollow and hill, were most clearly revealed in the evening light—Dan and Hope followed the same path that Young Matt and Sammy walked years before.

At the edge of the timber beyond the deerlick, the two young lovers found those older lovers, and were welcomed by them with the welcome that can only be given or received by those whose hearts and souls are big enough to follow the trail that is nobody knows how old.

# AFTERWORD

It will be easy for some to read this book and mistake Wright's point, and thus dismiss him as the prophetic voice I believe he is for our time. This incorrect reading of Harold Bell Wright can take several forms.

*One*, his stinging critique of the organized, denominational structure of the church will cause many to consider Wright (as some have mistaken George MacDonald) anti-church. Nothing, however, could be farther from the truth. Harold Bell Wright pastored churches in five cities and three states. The ministry and organized church was dear to his heart. He agonized over it, wept for it, and yearned to see the church enter into the fulfillment of God's purpose for it as His body to minister to the world.

As I have commented about George MacDonald, I would also say of Harold Bell Wright. He "had a right to comment on the church, its function, and the state of those who lead it, because he spoke from within. He was no external finger-waving faultfinder, but a sore-hearted member of its ranks. He himself was a clergyman. He merely burned with the desire to see God's true church emerge glorious and triumphant."

*Secondly*, don't make the error of considering this old-fashioned, outmoded church to be purely a thing of the past. We may not have quilting bees too much anymore. The denominational influences of the past are—at least in some cases—lessening their grip. But Phariseeism is an ever-recurring disease of the church, rearing its head in every age in different ways and in more subtle disguises, and it infects the most lively, the most growing, the most Spirit-led congregations just as invisibly as it does dull, old-fashioned places like Memorial Church. The religious spirit which is the Ally is at work everywhere it finds the tiniest foothold.

When a writer is trying to make a point, often he must, in a sense, *overdo* it a bit in order to make clear what he wants to say. If I want to describe a character, for instance, whose eyes are so pale blue that you feel you are looking right through them, I'm naturally going to *overdo* my description of that person's eyes. If you only went by what I specifically said, you might think there was nothing to him but the eyes! I probably won't tell you much about the ears, whether the hair is straight or wavy, the nose, the neck, the wrist, etc. I'm trying to make a point about the eyes, so I focus my attention there. Because if I went on and on for page after page, trying to describe every detail and every subtlety of that person's look, you wouldn't get the point I wanted you to get about the eyes.

That's probably not a very good example. But the idea is that Wright in a sense had to overdraw the situation at Memorial Church in order to enable us to see his point. In reality the work of the Ally in our churches today (and yes, the Ally *is* active in your church!) is much more subtle, much more disguised.

Your elders will not be pulling guns out of drawers, foreclosing mortgages on widows, nor committing such blatant illegalities. The people in this book are caricatures. They're not supposed to be real. They're overdone to enable you to see truth. But in applying that truth you must turn the caricature into reality by recognizing the subtleties the symbols of this story point to.

The crime here is an "actual" one. Yet how many crimes are committed daily by unknowing Christians—crimes against the heart, against the emotions, against self-esteem, sins of judgment, sins of mistrust against worthy men of God, sins of exclusion, sins of hurt—all of which the Ally just as effectively makes sure we ignore and gloss over.

*Third*, it will be a mistake to take this story too literally. Do not expect the parallels always to be precise.

This is a parable. The Ally may not always seek to destroy physically as in Grace's case. Because someone close to you has not attempted suicide does not mean that one of your dear friends does not find himself at this moment filled with Grace's same feelings of rejection and aloneness. There are a multitude of instances in which persons of potential promise are subtly squeezed out of a church's inner circles in many different ways because they, like Grace, do not "fit the mold" of acceptability. Grace is a "type," a symbol, a representation of something that is constantly occurring within our groups and churches and congregations—usually in such subtle ways that most within a given church remain completely oblivious to it.

Likewise, the Judge's extreme and visible, even criminal methods and attitudes serve as but an allegorical likeness of persons and means of "judgment" that are usually far more difficult to see. I can guarantee that nearly *every* church has its Judge Strong and its Ladies' Aid Society, its clique of who's in and those who are out. Whether he is an elder, a pastor, a janitor, or a cook, every one of us knows a Judge Strong. And we've all seen this same evangelist preach. The specifics change. But the Ally is everywhere.

Should we therefore lose heart? Not at all! Because the Spirit of God is at work everywhere too. Every church also has its John Gardner, its Doctor Oldham, and its Harry Abbott. All around us are honest, hard-working pastors and ministers like Dan Matthews and Thomas Wingfold—yes, clergymen like Harold Bell Wright and George MacDonald and how many countless others!—who have made it the purpose of their ministry to combat the Ally. Most importantly, every church is blessed with many Grace Conners who desperately need our love and compassion and acceptance. The garden in which God is at work is indeed vast, and Denny needs our help! And for every Grace who is beaten down on all sides, there is *hope* and as Paul said in Romans, "we are saved by hope," and "hope does not disappoint us." The compassionate ministry of hope to the spiritually and emotionally and physically downtrodden is a ministry that has been placed within each of our hands and the specifics of which can take many forms.

I met my own personal "Hope" when I discovered an old author by the name of George MacDonald, whose books—like Hope Farwell's love to Dan Matthews—encouraged me to hang on in the midst of my troubles.

Of one thing we can be sure, whenever we are on the train approaching a time of difficulty in our lives, on the train accompanying us—though we yet know not her face—sits also a Hope who has been sent to minister to us during that trying season, who will not disappoint us, and who will be with us still when we emerge on the other side. And at the station waits a Doctor to help Hope sustain and strengthen us.

The most serious mistake, however, will be to read this parable of life within the church, and perceive its truth, and see its application, and then to allow attitudes of judgment to infect *you*. For you to judge your own personal Judge Strong will be, as Jesus said, to find yourself judged by the same measure. The only true response to Wright's message is to fall on your knees and cry out, "Oh, God, be merciful to me a sinner! Help me to see the hurts of the Grace Conners before it is too late, and let me serve and minister to them in the spirit of Hope Farwell!"

Neither you nor I will set right these wrongs by waging war against the Ally. We will only right these wrongs by keeping the Ally from infiltrating our *own* attitudes, and by doing the work the Ally hates—namely, the work that Jesus gives us to do, ministering love and compassion and kindness to those around us.

Michael Phillips